BLOODLUST CHRONICLES – FAITH

by

LISETTE ASHTON

The characters and situations in this book are entirely imaginary and bear no relation to any real person or actual happening.

CHIMERA

BloodLust Chronicles – Faith first published in 2003 by
Chimera Publishing Ltd
22b Picton House
Hussar Court
Waterlooville
Hants
PO7 7SQ

Printed and bound in Great Britain by
Cox & Wyman Ltd, Reading.

BLOODLUST CHRONICLES – FAITH

Lisette Ashton

'Bend over my knee, Faith.'

Trying to beseech her with a final, pitiful expression, Faith realised there was no hope of a reprieve. She pressed her stomach against the thrust of the choir mistress's knees and slowly bent over.

Ms Moon's slender hands touched her shoulders and hips, encouraging Faith this way and that until she was positioned with her bottom pushed in the air and her body pressed embarrassingly against the older woman's legs. It was impossible to believe she was subjecting herself to this archaic discipline, but her mind wasn't allowing her to contemplate the indignity. The nearness of the choir mistress, the floral scent of her perfume and the pressure of her feminine body, were all sparking urges that Faith was loathe to acknowledge. Her throat was viciously dry and her blushes burnt more deeply than ever. Wondering if there was a chance for a last minute reprieve she tried glancing back over her shoulder as she whispered, 'I'm sorry, Ms Moon.'

The First Prophecy

Dank squalor hung on the air like the fetid breath of a gargoyle. A ring of blazing torches filled the sconces on the lair's wall and their spluttering flames licked orange tongues against the soot-encrusted masonry. A pair of ecstatic neophytes, still high from an early evening blood-rush and giggling hysterically, danced together in the black and amber light. The remainder of the clan lurked in the lair's furthest shadows and watched the naked gypsy kneeling at the foot of the dark one's throne.

Her hands, small and dirty, trembled as they touched the final rune. She frowned at its position in the earth, shook her head unhappily, and then dared to glance up at him. 'Death,' she whispered softly. 'It's the same message again. It doesn't matter how many times I read them for you. The stones say you're going to die.'

The dark one seemed unperturbed by her sombre warning. He studied his fingernails thoughtfully, buffing them with an emery board before glancing up and fixing his crimson gaze on her terrified expression. 'Tell me a better fortune,' he said slowly. 'Prophecies of doom bore me. I want to hear about my love life.'

'But the runes say…'

'Fuck the runes.' A glimmer of impatience was beginning to show through his mask of equanimity. 'Fuck the runes, the tarot cards and reading my bloody tealeaves. I asked for my fortune telling and I expect it to be a good one.' His hand had curled into a fist and he slammed it against the chair arm. The sonorous echo shook the walls of the lair and made the giggling neophytes fall silent.

Everyone stared at him, none of the clan daring to breathe, and after the silence had scraped on for an age it was the frail, vulnerable gypsy girl who found the courage to speak. 'I can't tell the runes what to…'

The dark one was out of his chair and holding her before she could finish the sentence. He dragged her from the floor, one hand circling her waist, the other cupping her bare breast. The small orb was lost beneath his large palm and the pliant flesh dimpled as his long nails pressed against her. Her naked body moulded against his formidable figure; one leg snaked behind him; she tried to fend him off with her arms and only managed to embrace him wantonly.

Effortlessly lifting the girl from her feet, moving his mouth close to her shoulder, he opened his lips to expose elongated canines. The flawless length of her neck was open to him and a thread of pulsing blue vein throbbed beneath her sun-bronzed skin. The perfume of honest sweat and cheap cologne were a whisper away and he knew he could take her with a single, swift bite.

'Sire!'

The warning came from the shadows on the walls. He guessed it was his sister, Lilah, and so he was happy to ignore the cry. Toying with the breast in his palm, he was amused by the way the nipple stiffened to his touch in spite of the gypsy's obvious terror and revulsion. It crossed his mind that she was his for the taking; he could have plunged two fingers between her legs and her sex would have been sodden, warm and welcoming. Yet still, he only wanted to watch the undulating pulse of her jugular. The sight inspired a stiffness in his pants, made his throat sandpaper dry, and had him desperate to quench his thirst. And when he saw the glint of raw terror in the girl's eyes it was enough to make him inch his mouth closer.

'Sire, there are rules that we all must abide by. We can't go out in sunlight. We can't tread on hallowed ground, and we must never feed on nuns or gypsies.'

Unhappily he glanced up and glared into the shadows. As he knew, it was Lilah warning him and he balked at her didactic tone. 'I've been leader of this clan for the last two hundred years or more,' he breathed softly. 'And I was walking in shadows two hundred years before that. What makes you think you can talk to me as though this is my first victim?'

She stepped out of the darkness and each sultry sashay of her hips was like an exercise in catwalk deportment. Lilah was an elegant figure with porcelain skin and hair like polished jet. Dressed entirely in black leather, from the contour hugging curves of her jeans to the zippered cuffs of her biker jacket, he thought she looked disquietingly attractive for a sibling. The only colour in her otherwise monotone appearance was the characteristic flecks of red in her eyes and the full, scarlet pout of her lips.

'I don't just command this clan,' the dark one bellowed. 'I command you as well, little sister. What makes you think you can talk to me as if I were a lowly neophyte at his first tasting?'

'With all due respect, sire, perhaps it's because you're acting like one.'

A handful of the clan gasped at Lilah's audacity, but she continued boldly in the face of her brother's potential wrath. She nodded at the girl, still held in the dark one's clutches, and said, 'She's a gypsy. She's a gypsy and our laws expressly forbid—'

'I know what our laws forbid,' he snapped.

'And yet you're staring at her neck as though you're

7

ready to feast,' Lilah said simply. 'Wouldn't you say that was behaviour you'd expect from a neophyte?'

'She wouldn't tell me a good fortune,' he complained. His anger had lessened to a petulant whine. 'She wouldn't tell me a good fortune and I'm bored with hearing that the time of my death is approaching. I've been listening to that same depressing shit since the American civil war.'

'Sire,' Lilah said quietly. Carefully, she moved her brother's hands from the gypsy and escorted him back to his throne. Turning back to the girl, caressing her cheek with a talon-like fingernail, Lilah slyly appraised her nudity. It was easy to understand why her brother had come so close to feeding, because she looked truly arousing with her hourglass figure, full breasts and the delectable tuft of dark curls that covered the secrets of her sex. The sight was enough to make Lilah lick her lips hungrily as an eager appetite stirred in the pit of her belly.

The gypsy blushed and lowered her gaze. The buds of her nipples stood solid with arousal and, although she looked to be in a state of absolute terror, she squirmed from one foot to the other as though trying to contain a greedy itch that growled in her loins.

'Read my brother his fortune,' Lilah commanded. 'Tell him that the future holds a thousand pleasures each day, and that he will be blessed with a never-ending supply of virgins to satiate his most depraved appetites. Tell him everything he wants to hear.'

'I only read the runes,' the gypsy girl whispered. 'I don't write them.'

Lilah was as quick as her brother and just as commanding. She pushed the girl against the wall, ingratiating a knee between her thighs and placing her mouth inches from the gypsy's face. The swell of their breasts rubbed together, the contact made maddeningly exciting by the layer of leather coating Lilah's lean frame. 'Our laws forbid us from feeding off your kind,' she whispered darkly. 'But that doesn't mean we won't use you for other pleasures.' She raised her knee, teasing her thigh against warm, slick pussy lips. The friction was only subtle but enough to have them both drawing ragged breath. 'How many of us could you satisfy before you were used and spent?' Lilah breathed. 'We have a good supply of hungry young men like my brother. And there are plenty of demanding women, like myself, who'd want to experience whatever pleasures you could bestow. Which do you want to do, gypsy girl? Do you want to spend the night as the plaything of horny vampires? Or do you want to read my brother his fortune?'

With a bitter grunt the gypsy tore herself from Lilah's embrace, and unmindful of her nudity she stepped back to the circle she had drawn in the earth. She glared defiantly at the dark one as she cast a fistful of runes to the floor.

It didn't seem to trouble her that she was naked, her bare bottom hanging inches from the filth, her dirty legs, arms and belly exposed for all the clan to see. Calmly brushing her fingers over the stones in the same ritual way her mother had taught her, she muttered the incantation that always accompanied every true reading. The sconces fluttered in unison, as though brushed by an unseen presence entering the room. In the flame-lit squalor of her surroundings, there was something nearly mystical about the figure the gypsy girl presented. 'I think this casting will be different,' she said eventually.

Lilah stepped closer.

The dark one shifted position in his chair, his eyes narrowing to curious slits.

'The stones are showing me an innocent. They're

showing me a virtuous girl.'

As one, Lilah and her brother both licked their lips.

'Who is she?'

'Where is she?'

'What does she have to do with my future?'

The gypsy ignored the questions, drawing her fingertips over one stone before turning it and placing it next to the first. 'She has a strength about her. She has a formidable power.' She lifted her gaze to meet the dark one's and added, 'And she's going to come looking for you.'

'An admirer?' Lilah mused. Her seductive tone sounded as though it was trying to add levity to the unsettling gloom of their surroundings. 'I didn't know you had a fan club, darling brother. Have you been hiding your light under a bushel?'

'I have hoards of adoring minions,' he boasted idly, then glaring down at the gypsy he said, 'Tell me something more about this virtuous girl. What can she do for me that makes her stand out from the rest?'

The gypsy turned two more stones, and nodded as though she had expected the result. 'The virtuous girl will be something out of the ordinary,' she told him. 'You'll know when you meet her because of her special ability.'

Lilah winked lewdly at her brother. 'A virtuous girl with a special ability. Isn't that something you've always fancied?'

He waved for his sister to be silent, staring intently at the gypsy. 'What special ability does she have? Who is she? And how will I know her?'

'You'll know her by her special ability,' the girl repeated. She raised her gaze defiantly to his. 'The virtuous girl is the one who will have the power to rip your cold, black heart from your chest and send your corpse to the grave where it should have rotted centuries ago.'

The outburst left a stunned silence in the lair.

Lilah glanced from the gypsy to her brother, wishing she could control his inevitable reaction and knowing she would be powerless to intervene.

Furiously he launched himself from his throne. He grabbed the girl from the centre of the circle and dragged her all the way to the wall of the lair. Pinning her against the crumbling masonry, clutching her breast with one huge hand and tugging her head to the side with his other, he exposed her neck and pressed his mouth over the frantic beat of her pulse.

'Sire!' Lilah called. 'Our laws!'

'Fuck the laws,' he growled, placing his teeth over the girl's neck. The pounding of her veins trembled against his lips. He glanced down and noticed her nipples now stood more rigid than ever. The tops of her thighs glistened wetly and he knew she was as close to the point of orgasm as he was. Her breathing came in short gasps and he could hear her heartbeat pounding madly. The knowledge that they would briefly share the same surge of pleasure was disturbingly warming.

'You can't feast on her, darling brother,' Lilah gasped. 'You know you can't.'

The dark one pressed his mouth to the gypsy's neck and drank. The fading sounds of her heartbeat intermingled with his greedy slurping as he swallowed. She beat her fists against him but she was overpowered to begin with and, as her life ebbed away, her protests weakened to an ineffectual caress before fading to nothing. As soon as she was drained the dark one allowed her to fall to the floor. He wiped his mouth dry with the back of a hand and his smile dripped tears of scarlet. Turning to his sister he said, 'Were you telling me I couldn't drink from this one? Were you telling me our laws forbid me feeding from gypsies?' His cheeks were flushed from the feasting and his lips glistened with a succulent red glaze. 'I've got a question for you, little sister: who's going to stop me?'

Lilah glared at him. 'Didn't you hear the gypsy, you fool? Didn't you hear her say that a virtuous girl will come and tear the cold, black heart from your chest? Maybe she's the one who's going to stop you. Or didn't that thought cross your mind?'

The dark one considered this for a moment before a grin etched its way over his bloody lips. 'What if we find this virtuous girl first? What if we find her and strip her of her virtue? From what the gypsy was saying, it doesn't seem like I'll be in any danger if she isn't virtuous.'

Thinking back, remembering the way the gypsy had phrased her warning, Lilah decided her brother might just be right.

Faith

Act I, Scene I

It was the curse, Faith thought bitterly. It was the Harker family curse, and once again it had chosen her as its victim. Standing alone in the cemetery, lost and scared and struggling not to panic, she clutched her bare shoulders and trembled. She was chilled by the icy fingers of the night, but shivering more at the knowledge of how greatly she was exposed and in jeopardy.

Half an hour earlier her world had been perfect. There had been a reception after the choir's performance at Castel Sant' Angelo and she had been feted for her interpretation of Tosca. The appearance had been rewarding; the applause had lifted her; and afterward everyone showered her with praise. Ms Moon, the austere choir mistress and official in charge of their tour, clutched Faith's hand while telling her she had been brilliant. Todd Chalmers, director of the production and the man responsible for negotiating their use of Castel Sant' Angelo, said he had never seen a better rendition of the tragic heroine. Her friends and fellow choristers lavished her with compliments and even Marcia, the nastiest bitch in the whole of the choir, had grudgingly congratulated Faith on her triumph. It had been a grudging 'I doubt I could have done much better', but Faith knew it was meant as praise.

And yet it was a set rule of the Harker family curse that, as soon as life seemed to be going well, everything had to change. And it was a codicil to the curse that everything had to change immediately, and always for the worse.

Her first impulse had been to talk to her sisters and tell them about her spectacular night. With Charity already being a successful singer, Faith felt sure she would be most impressed, but she knew Hope would be just as pleased to hear that everything had gone so well. However, because Ms Moon had forbidden the choir from bringing mobiles to the performance ('I will not have my Vissi d'arte defiled by a ring tone,' she had warned), and because Faith wasn't carrying enough loose Euro cents to attempt an international call from a payphone, she decided to return to the chalet and use the telephone there.

Her best friend in the choir, Claire, had tried cajoling her to stay but Faith was anxious to contact her sisters. Claire offered to accompany her back to the chalet, reiterating Ms Moon's instructions about how none of them should travel alone in the city, but Faith didn't want to spoil the reception for anyone, especially not her best friend. So assuring Claire she would be safe, insisting that she had to go and call Hope and Charity straight away, Faith discreetly left the Castel Sant' Angelo and started looking for the first convenient taxi.

After about a hundred yards of fruitlessly trying to hail passing cabs, and still buoyant from her success in the role of Tosca, she decided she didn't need to take a taxi. Between rehearsals over the previous three days she had spent some time sightseeing and familiarising herself with the layout of the eternal city, and felt confident she could make her way back to the chalet without paying for one of the most expensive taxis in the whole of Europe.

And, she supposed, that was when everything started to go wrong. Thinking back over events, she realised that was when the Harker family curse had started to take affect.

Trusting her sense of direction, assuring herself that sights only looked different because it was night and she had been used to seeing them during the daylight, she headed along Via della Conciliazione and crossed St Peter's Square. But convinced that the chalet complex lay on the other side of the Tiber, she had soon left the bustle of the brightly lit streets and found herself in eerily unfamiliar territory. The streets seemed narrower and almost medieval. The buildings had an aged look that quickly convinced her she was exploring areas she had never visited before. And, although she tried to retrace her steps, it didn't take long to realise she was no longer so certain of her route. Her reservations had grown as the darkness encroached and her doubts increased as the busy pavements became emptier. When she realised she was lost and alone she knew panic wasn't far away. After stepping through an open gateway, hoping she had miraculously found her way back to the complex of chalets, she was horrified to find herself in an unlit cemetery.

'The Harker family curse,' she sobbed miserably. Charity had summed up their collective misfortunes best when she said, 'A Harker's happiness is the moment just before the shit happens.' Glumly, Faith realised the truth in that pessimistic statement and, if she hadn't been cold, scared, and in a cemetery of all places, she would have sat down and cried with bitter frustration.

She hugged herself tighter, surprised by the night's relentless chill and wishing she had worn something warmer. The combination of a strappy top and high-split pencil skirt had been ideal for the reception, but it was woefully inadequate for the inclement graveyard. Night's cold hand clasped her shoulders and its frigid fingers delved through her skirt's split and caressed her upper thighs. Thinking about her inappropriate clothes, Faith decided she must look like the heroine from one of those trashy American horror movies where a prom queen ends up stumbling into the lair of a demon, or a monster, or a...

'Bite me!'

Faith's thoughts remained unfinished as she struggled not to cry out in surprise. The words had come from a woman, close by, and speaking in clear, comprehensible English. She had almost forgotten that Rome was a cosmopolitan city, its voice rich with a hundred different languages from tourists and the international business community. But the sound of an English speaking woman didn't surprise her and she began to believe her nightmare might soon be ended. She was touched by the hope that she might be able to speak to someone who could either give her directions or help her get safely back to the chalet. Peering cautiously around the graveyard, Faith tried to find the source of the voice.

'Bite me,' the woman insisted. Her plaintive tone was roughened with need and her cry resounded like a desperate sob. 'Please bite me, Nick. Don't make me beg.'

Uneasily, Faith placed a hand over her throat and touched the familiar weight of the small, silver crucifix. The jewellery had been a gift from Hope earlier in the year, to mark the occasion of Faith's eighteenth birthday. Caressing the smooth silver usually gave her a surge of comfort and confidence, but this time she was worried the delicate cross might be seen as a target for rogues or thieves. She glanced warily over the head of a prominent gravestone and bit her tongue to stop herself from exclaiming.

If the graveyard hadn't been populated by so many monoliths, and perhaps if the moonlight hadn't been gliding in and out from behind mackerel clouds, she might have seen the couple sooner. He was tall and swarthy; she was dark-haired, fair-skinned and voluptuous. As Faith had half-expected, the pair were intimately embracing. Their mouths devoured each other as their hands roved, explored and caressed. The man held the woman's raven tresses with one hand while his other massaged the thrust of her breast. Clearly revelling beneath his attention, the woman pressed herself against him and ground her pelvis obscenely against his groin.

Faith clasped a hand over her mouth and told herself she had to leave before she was discovered. She supposed it would have been helpful if the English-speaking woman could have given her directions, but Faith didn't think the couple would want to be disturbed during this act of intimacy. She also doubted if it would be safe to ask for help from a couple who seemed so happy to give in to their carnal urges in a cemetery.

But, as sensible as it seemed to discreetly creep away, the instinct was impossible to obey. The way the couple touched was a spectacle Faith had never seen or experienced and she found herself caught in a thrall of voyeuristic excitement. The sight of their kisses, and the intimate touching, stirred an empathy in her loins that she knew was unwholesome. But she also knew it couldn't be denied.

'Don't make me beg, you bastard,' the woman moaned. She dragged her hair from his grip and pulled the shoulder of her blouse to one side. 'Make me,' she gasped, tilting her head and exposing her neck for him. 'Make me, Nick. Change me.'

His hand slipped from her breast to the waistband of her skirt. Deftly unfastening a button, pulling the zipper easily down, he pushed the garment to the ground so that it puddled around her ankles.

Faith could see the woman was wearing dark stockings and pants – she had a chance to notice that the black fabric contrasted starkly with her pallid flesh – and then she was amazed to see the man stroking the woman's cleft. He touched lightly against the gusset of her underwear, his long fingers stroking back and forth until she moaned. Taking his time, seeming to enjoy her pleasure, or at least some malicious level of torment that came from teasing, he slowly pulled the crotch to one side.

Faith slapped a second hand across her mouth, her eyes growing wider.

The woman's sex lips were exposed to the night and the man was gliding his wet fingertips over the flushed pink flesh. Every caress inspired another sigh and instigated furious bouts of shivering. She raked her nails against his arm, cursing in a mixture of Italian and English, before grabbing his head and pulling his mouth over her face. Their previous kisses seemed almost chaste compared to the greedy way they now consumed each other and Faith couldn't decide if she was feeling green with disgust or envy.

'What do you want me to do, Nick?' the woman gasped. She bucked her cleft toward his intrusive fingers and writhed against his touch. 'Just say it and you know I'll do it,' she insisted. The urgency in her voice sounded painfully close to panic. 'Whatever you want me to do, I'll do it. But you have to tell me first. What is it you want?'

Nick chuckled darkly and pulled his fingers away from her sex. The tips glistened with dewy wetness and shone like silver beneath the moonlight. Almost thoughtfully, he pushed them towards his lover's mouth. As she worked her tongue against his wet skin he continued to laugh and mused, 'What do I want from you?' Barely giving himself the chance to consider his reply he asked, 'You have a sister, don't you?'

Without taking his fingers from her mouth the woman nodded. 'You know I have,' she said, speaking around his hand. 'You've seen the photographs on the wall of the trattoria and I—'

'Bring her here,' Nick broke in abruptly. 'Bring her here tomorrow night.' He pulled his hand away and stroked the exposed flesh of the woman's neck. It was a feather-light caress but it shocked his lover into orgasmic convulsions. She studied him with fresh desire and her seductive smile gleamed brightly. Nick resumed his hold on her hair and pushed his mouth over hers. This time the kiss lasted longer and the couple's intimacy became more profound. Nick tugged her blouse open, exposing one breast, and he squeezed and kneaded the plump balloon of pale flesh. His thumb stroked back and forth over the rigid bud of her nipple until she was sobbing with frustrated delight. Breaking the kiss he grinned cruelly into her needy expression, pushed her down to her knees, and unzipped himself.

For Faith, her own predicament was all but forgotten. The invasive coldness of the night was no longer an issue and she couldn't be bothered to think about the fact that she was lost and alone. Watching Nick and his girlfriend was all that mattered and she peered at them intensely for fear of missing one shocking, revelatory moment.

Nick pulled his hardness from his pants and pushed it toward the brunette's face. His shaft was long, and more slender than Faith had expected a man's erection to be, but it was tipped with a large round end that looked purple and swollen. Faith couldn't decide if she thought the sight was repulsive or arousing, and before she had the chance to make up her mind, Nick was moving it out of her sight. He tugged on the brunette's hair, guiding her mouth to his glans, and forced her to accept the length. As soon as her ripe lips closed around his shaft, in the moment when she first stared meekly up at him, Nick sighed contentedly.

The woman sucked on him with an enthusiasm that left Faith shocked and curious. She had heard other girls in the choir talking about this sort of thing, there were even rumours that Marcia was something of an expert, but Faith had never seen a couple doing something so personal or so passionate and she was amazed by the excitement the scene generated. Pressing her thighs tight together, squeezing one arm against the heaving swell of her breasts, she leaned avariciously over the gravestone.

The woman allowed Nick's length to fall from her mouth. He frowned when he saw she had briefly stopped sucking, but as she began to work her tongue along his rigid flesh, he nodded grudging approval. Her grin was sly and her gaze was fixed on his face as if she was watching for any praise he might care to bestow. Nick seemed content to endure her brief tease for a few moments before pulling roughly at her hair and pulling her mouth back over the end. Obediently, the brunette closed her lips around him and resumed her previous chore. Her cheeks dimpled with exertion, her eyes grew rounder and more open until Nick cried out in a stark, guttural exclamation.

The cry sounded hollowly around the desolate cemetery.

Faith allowed her hands to fall away from her mouth and gaped incredulously. She no longer needed to contain her own cries because she now felt so shocked and surprised she didn't think she would ever speak again. She knew what she had been watching, there had been no doubt about what the woman was doing for Nick, but it was only with the release of his climax that Faith realised it had all been genuinely happening. Transfixed by her own disbelief, she remained mesmerised and silent.

'Make me tonight,' the woman begged. Her lips dripped traces of Nick's semen as she stared helplessly up at him. 'Please,' she gasped, clutching his leg. 'Please, Nick. Make me tonight. Change me.'

'What about tomorrow night?' he suggested. 'What about our arrangement for your sister?'

Closing her eyes against the threat of bitter tears, the woman dragged herself from the ground and shook her head. 'I'll bring my sister tomorrow night,' she promised. 'And you can do whatever you want with her. But you have to make me tonight. You have to.'

He stroked her neck again and laughed. His mirth had a nasty edge that reminded Faith of the night's dangerous chill. 'What if I don't change you?' he whispered.

Faith had to strain to hear his lowered tone.

'What if I decided to feast on you, then claim your sister by myself?'

'Either,' the brunette sobbed. 'Make me. Take me. Change me or feed on me. The choice is yours but please, do one or the other.'

With lightning speed he swept her into his embrace and placed his mouth against her neck. The movement was so swift Faith wondered if she had blinked and missed something. She caught a brief glimpse of Nick's smile, was shocked to think his canines looked long and wickedly sharp, and then he was pressing his lips over the brunette's neck.

She moaned and writhed against him. One stocking clad leg rubbed against his hip as she rocked her pelvis hungrily back and forth. The crotch of her panties still remained askew and Faith caught a disquieting glimpse of the woman's sex lips sliding against the leg of Nick's pants.

He growled as he continued to treat her with his kiss, his embrace tightening and his own hips moving in a rhythm that matched the brunette's. His mouth remained pressed against her neck but, rather than simply kissing, Faith thought it looked like he was trying to bite her. She didn't fully understand what was happening between the pair but felt certain it was something dark and powerful.

The brunette groaned. Her cries sounded like a protest that contradicted her gasps for him to carry on. She clutched at his back and tried to pull him into her embrace as she squirmed and writhed with passionate abandon. Her hips began to move with a mechanical urgency as she rocked more vigorously and encouraged him with a string of Italian words that Faith had never heard before.

Faith wasn't entirely certain but she thought the exclamations might be vulgarities. There was something wicked about each hissed sibilant and she doubted she would find translations in any of her approved guidebooks. The roar of expletives built to a euphoric scream and then the brunette held herself absolutely still.

A bloody red line trickled from between the union of Nick's mouth and her throat. She remained rigid, her mouth gaping wide as she screamed triumphantly into the night.

Mesmerised, Faith watched the woman's eyes flare red as she stared gratefully up at Nick. She wondered if she had really seen the phenomena, unable to think anyone's eyes could ever have such an unnerving pigmentation, and eventually decided it had been a trick of the faltering moonlight.

The brunette pulled herself from Nick's embrace and stared wondrously around the graveyard. Watching attentively, Faith thought she seemed suddenly anxious to experience every sight that the night had to offer. The brunette inhaled deeply, her gaze shifting this way and that, and then she stared directly at Faith.

Nick wiped his lips dry on his sleeve and grinned broadly. 'I'm holding you to your promise,' he told the brunette. 'Your sister has a nice pair of tits on her, and tomorrow night—'

'We were being watched,' the brunette hissed. She pointed and said, 'We still are being watched.

Faith tried to stumble back behind the gravestone but she knew it was already too late. She didn't want to think about the end of the scene she had just witnessed, not sure how the climactic kiss fitted with the secretive tales she had heard about what went on when a man and woman were being intimate. She felt sure she had just seen something that went beyond the unusual, but that was as much as she would allow herself to think about the biting and the screaming and the blood.

'Watched?' Nick sounded scornful at first, then wary. Taking his direction from the brunette's piercing gaze, he glanced towards Faith and his tainted smile resurfaced. 'Bloody hell,' he said cheerfully, 'the graveyard's full of life tonight.' Confidently, he started walking towards her.

Faith took a quick step back, her mounting panic briefly eased when the brunette placed a steadying hand on Nick's arm.

'She's scared.'

Nick laughed. 'Of course she is. And with good reason.' Faith blanched.

'She'll run,' the brunette told him.

He nodded. 'And I'll catch her. I haven't lost one yet,' he confided. Stroking the brunette's arm, smiling at her eagerness, he said, 'I didn't let you escape when you first saw me, did I?'

'Perhaps I didn't want to escape?'

Unable to stop herself, Faith continued to watch. She knew she should be trying to run away, hurrying to make a head start while she had the opportunity, but the interaction between the couple was too compelling. It was only when she reminded herself of the danger she was facing that she made up her mind to turn and flee.

Before she had taken two steps she discovered the pair were virtually on top of her. She couldn't understand how they were able to move so quickly, or how they were able to race with such stealth and lack of effort. All she knew was that Nick blocked her way forward and his girlfriend barred her retreat. Her heart began to pound frantically.

'She's very pretty,' the brunette enthused. She reached out and trailed a finger against Faith's cheek, who couldn't decide if the woman was trying to reassure or excite her, but she wanted none of their perversity. She flinched from the caress and tried to step away.

'I don't know who either of you are,' Faith said meekly. 'And I don't want to know. I just want you to leave me alone and let me go back to my chalet.'

The brunette giggled and turned to glance at Nick. 'Are you going to let me feed on this one?' she asked eagerly. 'I'm hungry and I want to savour every new experience.'

Nick took hold of Faith's chin and tilted her face from side to side as he critically appraised her. His fingers were ice cold and his grip inescapable. 'This one looks quite tasty,' he conceded. 'She might be a little too rich for your first feed.'

Faith didn't understand what they were talking about and didn't want to hear any explanation. She tried pulling herself out of Nick's grip and pushed angrily at his arm, but her blows fell ineffectually against him and he continued to hold her without any show of effort or exertion.

'I don't think we want you wearing this,' he said firmly, and before she realised what he was doing, Nick was pulling at the silver necklace that held her crucifix. Faith began to complain as she felt the delicate chain tugging against her neck, then she heard the hateful sound of links separating as the cross fell away. She tried to catch the jewellery before it was lost on the ground but Nick didn't allow her the opportunity.

Resuming his grip on her jaw he fixed her with a ferocious frown and said, 'I didn't want you wearing that.'

The brunette drew hungry breath. 'Let me taste her,' she pleaded.

'We could share her,' Nick compromised.

The brunette sighed. It was a sound of such unbridled desire Faith was chilled. She stared from one tormentor to the other, disturbed by their hungry appreciation.

'You'll let me have a taste?' the brunette whispered.

Nick chuckled indulgently and pulled Faith into his embrace. His body pressed against hers and she was nuzzled by the stiffness that lurked in his pants. One hand cupped the swell of her breast and she was appalled to find herself excited.

Nick seemed oblivious to her arousal, and speaking to the brunette he said, 'You may have a taste. But you'd better make sure you honour your promise and bring me your sister tomorrow night.'

He relaxed his hold around Faith but she felt just as powerless to resist him. His flesh exuded a scent that wasn't particularly pleasant, but the musky fragrance still managed to stir a dark longing in the pit of her stomach. When he smiled down at her, his eyes glowing red and his wicked canines glistening brightly, she didn't feel terror or even apprehension. The only emotion Faith was consciously aware of was anticipation.

Gradually, Nick lowered his mouth towards Faith's throat.

Unable to resist, she tilted her head to one side. She held her breath, not sure what to expect, only knowing it would be immensely satisfying.

'You can't feast on her!' a woman shrieked. The shrill voice, surprisingly familiar, echoed across the cemetery. Faith felt Nick stiffen against her and saw the brunette shift posture, as though she was preparing to attack. With a flood of sickening guilt, Faith realised how close she had come to succumbing to those dark urges the pair aroused. Repulsed by what she had been about to do, she pulled herself from Nick's embrace and staggered towards the approaching figure.

Ms Moon – illuminated by moonlight, and with a frown accentuating her severe features – looked more formidable than ever as she bore down on them. 'You can't feast on her because she is truly virtuous,' she declared. 'The lore of the undead forbids you from feasting on nuns and gypsies, but the laws of nature make it impossible for you to feed on the virtuous. Stop wasting her time; stop wasting my time; and be gone.'

Faith stared at Ms Moon incredulously. She wondered where the prim woman had come from and how she dared speak so boldly to the couple. Glancing back to see how the pair would respond, she was amazed to discover they had disappeared into the night. Overwhelmed by a thousand questions she turned to the choir mistress with a mixture of relief and gratitude.

But before she got the chance to speak, Ms Moon slapped her hard across the face.

Bewildered and hurt, Faith placed a hand against her

blazing cheek and stared at the choir mistress. 'The Harker family curse,' she mumbled, the last words she spoke before the flood of miserable tears began.

Faith

Act I, Scene II

The taxi journey was conducted in crushing silence.

Floodlit monuments and magnificent architecture flashed past, but miserably studying her ankles, Faith saw none of the passing history. She had been looking forward to seeing the Coliseum by night, already having explored its decaying grandeur on one of the choir's organised excursions. She had half-expected the timeworn yellow stone to glow like gold at night, but even though they travelled right past it once they had crossed the Tiber, Faith couldn't be bothered raising her head to admire the spectacle. Her cheeks burnt with dull shame and she found herself struggling against the constant threat of tears. Occasionally she cast a wary glance in Ms Moon's direction, hoping for some indication of the woman's mood, but the choir mistress remained inscrutable.

Staring fixedly through her own window, watching the night and the bustle of traffic hurtle by, Ms Moon gave away nothing about what she might be contemplating. She was attractive and almost classically elegant with her long-sleeved blouses, high-button collars and full-length skirts. But Faith considered the woman to be an unknown commodity. New to the choir, employed specifically for this engagement at Castel Sant'Angelo, she was regarded as something of a mystery to Faith and her friends. None of the singers knew where she came from, how old she was, whether she had a man in her life, or even her first name. After the success of their performance her competence as a choir mistress remained undisputed, but still Faith was disturbed to reflect on how little was known about the woman.

Ms Moon directed the driver along Via del Cerchi and towards Parco del Celio, back to their accommodation. Once they were safely in the haven of the familiar complex, she ignored Faith's attempts to pinpoint the choir's communal dormitory and told the driver to drop them at her own private chalet. Eager to avoid the embarrassment of Ms Moon's inevitable reprimand, Faith thought of insisting she be allowed to return to the dorm she was sharing with the other singers. It only took one quick glance at the choir mistress's austere features for her to realise the request would be flatly refused. As she stood outside the darkened chalet, waiting for Ms Moon to finish paying their fare and dismiss the taxi, Faith clutched herself tightly and fretted.

The choir mistress said nothing as she stepped past Faith and opened the door. Summoning her to follow she started turning on lights to illuminate the simple living room of the chalet. It was sparsely furnished with magnolia walls and polished floorboards underfoot. Faith thought it was more antiseptic and unremarkable than the communal dorm, with only a large settee and a single high-backed chair beside the unused fireplace. She guessed that all Ms Moon's personal belongings were neatly tidied in her bedroom because, aside from a bottle of sherry on a table in the corner, the room gave no indication that the chalet was occupied.

After placing herself in the high-backed chair the choir mistress finally turned to Faith, her disparaging mood briefly dismissed as she smiled lightly and asked, 'Did you enjoy performing as Tosca this evening?'

Surprised by the question, and anxious to take advantage of this unexpected shift in the woman's demeanour, Faith nodded. The performance seemed to have happened an age earlier and she wondered if she had misjudged the choir mistress's intentions for bringing her back to the chalet. The simple enquiry sounded nothing like the censure she had expected. 'I loved every moment,' she said enthusiastically. 'It's the most wonderful opera, Mr Chalmers made for a seriously menacing Scarpia, the orchestra were magnificent and, although I know it probably sounds big-headed, I don't think I've ever sung better.'

'It sounds a little big-headed,' Ms Moon allowed. 'But I also think it's true. I don't think you've ever given so much to a performance.' Relaxing a little in her chair, smiling curiously up at Faith, she asked, 'Do you recall what happened to Tosca at the end of the third act?'

Faith answered quickly. 'She dies.'

'More specifically.'

'She throws herself off the battlements of Castel Sant' Angelo. She kills herself.'

'Ah!' Ms Moon made the exclamation as though she had suffered a blinding revelation. 'Perhaps that's why you acted the way you did this evening? Perhaps playing the role of the tragic heroine, Tosca, filled you with the same suicidal tendencies?'

Faith felt her cheeks burn crimson. The conversation about the opera had lulled her into a false sense of security and she hadn't expected the choir mistress to suddenly turn on her with such scathing sarcasm. Blushing furiously she lowered her gaze to the floor. 'It wasn't like that,' she began.

'It's the only explanation I can think of,' Ms Moon continued as though Faith hadn't spoken. 'Aside from leaping off the battlements of Castel Sant'Angelo, I can't think of behaviour that's much more suicidal than walking alone, at night, through the Trastevere region, and taking a midnight stroll across a graveyard.'

'I wasn't trying to—'

'Be quiet,' Ms Moon said crisply. 'I'm speaking now and this time you're going to listen. Do you understand?'

'Yes, Ms Moon.'

'You didn't listen when I told you not to travel alone in the city. You didn't listen when I told you never to go to the Trastevere region at night. But this time you are going to listen to me and you'll heed every word. Do you understand?'

'Yes, Ms Moon.' The back of her neck was burning as her blushes settled deeper. Ms Moon's condescending tone made Faith feel as if she was ten years younger and suffering the displeasure of a primary school teacher. Falling easily into the role of a truculent pupil she shuffled unhappily from one foot to the other. 'Yes, Ms Moon,' she repeated. 'I understand.'

The choir mistress nodded subtly. 'I can't let this incident go unpunished.' There was a note of regret in her voice, but Faith was disquieted to hear it was only a small note. 'You're over eighteen, and I should be able to treat you like a full grown woman, but your behaviour this evening was downright dangerous.'

Faith started to speak in her own defence but Ms Moon raised a warning finger and continued. 'You jeopardised your own life, and that alone would be bad enough, but you also risked so much else. You jeopardised the run of our current production. You jeopardised the opportunity for future productions. And, if something had happened to you, I suspect it would have been the last time I would be put in charge of a choir on a trip like this.' Her piercing

31

gaze fixed on Faith as she finally said, 'I can't see that I have any alternative. You will have to suffer a suitable punishment.'

Faith swallowed thickly. She didn't like the way the words had been spoken and wondered what sort of reprimand the woman would consider a 'suitable punishment'. It crossed her mind that she could be stripped of her title role in the opera and that, as a further punishment, the part could be given to Marcia. Or, to atone for her lack of judgement, she might be expected to do some sort of demeaning chore like the choir's washing, or cleaning the chalets. But something in Ms Moon's voice told Faith that the woman had other ideas about what would be deemed suitable and Faith couldn't work out why she was suddenly unnerved.

'You agree that I'm right, don't you?'

Faith didn't want to agree to anything and she answered guardedly. 'What suitable punishment?'

Ms Moon considered her with a cold, unblinking stare. 'I think you need spanking,' she decided eventually. 'I think you need spanking until you realise how foolish your behaviour was.'

Faith stared at her in disbelief. She contemplated asking the woman to repeat what she had said but she knew there would be no point. She had heard the words clearly enough and repeating them wouldn't change anything. 'You want to spank me?' she gasped.

'I never said *I want* to spank you,' Ms Moon corrected. 'But I think that's the punishment you deserve for your transgression.'

Faith was struggling to find a coherent argument to avoid the punishment, but the concept had been presented so suddenly it was difficult to focus her thoughts. 'Don't you think I'm a little too old to be spanked?' she tried.

Ms Moon shrugged. Like every movement she made it was a small, contained, almost imperceptible gesture. 'Perhaps you are a little too old,' she conceded. 'But then, I also thought you were a little too old to disobey my direct instruction about travelling alone, or to do something as foolhardy as go creeping around graveyards in the Trastevere region. So it seems my judgement was somewhat flawed in that regard.'

They studied one another for a moment in stiff silence. Faith was determined that she wasn't going to submit to the woman's ridiculous suggestion, but she could see Ms Moon was equally adamant that she would win the battle of wills. Eventually the choir mistress broke the tension of the moment and raised her hands.

'The choice is yours, Faith. We're both agreed that you need punishing for your irresponsible behaviour this evening. But it's up to you how that punishment is meted. If you want, I can send you home tonight – there are regular flights leaving Fiumicino for Gatwick or Heathrow – or you can defer to my authority and let me spank you.'

Faith felt suddenly sick. The air in the chalet had turned too thick to breath and her stomach twisted with a shameful thrill of mortification. She hadn't expected to be faced with such a wicked choice and knew she wasn't really being given an option. Having to pick between the alternatives of leaving her cherished role in the performance, and then returning home under a cloud of shame, or simply suffering the indignity of Ms Moon's chastisement, she realised there was no choice. She had enjoyed the performance immensely and was prepared to do anything to avoid being banished in disgrace. Resigning herself to her fate, curtailing the look of venom she wanted to fix on the choir mistress, Faith asked, 'How are you going to do it?'

Ms Moon snapped her fingers and pointed to her lap, then smoothing the fabric of her skirt across her slender thighs she said, 'Come here, Faith. Bend over my knee. We can get this unpleasantness over and done with now.'

Faith's hesitation only lasted for a moment. She didn't want to surrender to this indignity but she knew she no longer had a choice. Reluctantly, making her unease obvious with every sullen step, she walked slowly to the choir mistress's chair. Studying the woman's face, searching for some trace of compassion that would tell her the woman was joking, or prepared to consider some alternative arrangement, she was disappointed to see Ms Moon remained adamant.

'Bend over my knee, Faith.'

Trying to beseech her with a final, pitiful expression, Faith realised there was no hope of a reprieve. She pressed her stomach against the thrust of the choir mistress's knees and slowly bent over.

Ms Moon's slender hands touched her shoulders and hips, encouraging Faith this way and that until she was positioned with her bottom pushed in the air and her body pressed embarrassingly against the older woman's legs. It was impossible to believe she was subjecting herself to this archaic discipline, but her mind wasn't allowing her to contemplate the indignity. The nearness of the choir mistress, the floral scent of her perfume and the pressure of her feminine body, were all sparking urges that Faith was loathe to acknowledge. Her throat was viciously dry and her blushes burnt more deeply than ever. Wondering if there was a chance for a last minute reprieve she tried glancing back over her shoulder as she whispered, 'I'm sorry, Ms Moon.'

Ms Moon turned Faith's face so she was once again facing the freshly polished floorboards. 'I'll give you time to apologise when we're finished,' she said pointedly. Smoothing her hand against Faith's bottom, making the caress gentle and hatefully exciting, she delivered the first smart blow.

Faith stiffened.

It had not been a particularly strong smack to her buttocks, in truth she had hurt herself more the last time she sat down too heavily on a hard chair, but the shame of the punishment was more cutting than she would have believed. Gritting her teeth, steeling herself for the indignity of the next blow, she shivered when Ms Moon slapped her for a second time.

'This is no good,' the choir mistress grumbled.

Pressed against the woman's thighs, Faith could feel her shifting position in her chair. She wanted to glance back and see what was happening but her fears made her stay absolutely still, and it became disturbingly clear what Ms Moon was doing when Faith felt her tug on the hem of her pencil skirt.

'These clothes are getting in the way,' Ms Moon complained, pulling the skirt upward. 'They're getting in the way and stopping me from doing this properly.'

Mortified by shame, Faith could only remain rigid as the hem was inched higher. The woman's cool hands brushed the backs of her knees, then grazed the smooth flesh of her upper thighs, but Faith was struggling to ignore every disquieting sensation. She knew her skirt was being lifted, and she didn't doubt the exhibition of her bare legs and bottom would make for a humiliating spectacle, but she felt helpless to resist or complain. But when she heard the harsh growl of a seam tearing, she couldn't stop herself from crying out in complaint.

'Don't take on so.' Ms Moon's encouraging voice should have been cool and soothing. Yet all Faith could think of was the indignity of her position and the shameful view she would be presenting. It was criminally easy to picture her buttocks being displayed for the choir mistress and, even though she knew her panties would modestly cover her cheeks, she still thought the whole situation taught new realms to the meaning of the embarrassment. 'You'll know to listen to me in future,' Ms Moon reminded Faith.

As she spoke she slapped her hand heavily against Faith's rear. The crisp smack of flesh striking flesh echoed flatly from the chalet's polished floorboards. This time, because the hand had connected with the bare flesh at the top of her thighs, the force of the blow stung Faith. She caught her breath, stopping herself from complaining for fear it would encourage the choir mistress to strike harder with her next shot.

'You were wrong to disobey my orders, weren't you, Faith?'

Faith took a deep breath before replying. She was determined that she wouldn't reveal her upset and struggled to keep her voice free from emotion when she spoke. Blinking back the promise of tears that welled on her eyelids, she exhaled softly and said, 'Yes, Ms Moon. I was wrong.'

The choir mistress delivered another brisk slap. The first had scored the top of Faith's thighs, stinging fitfully against the sensitive flesh. This one struck the rounded cheek of one buttock and Faith was relieved to realise her panties had cushioned some of the impact. It still hurt, and she could feel the flesh blushing as deeply as the shame that reddened her face, but it wasn't the penetrating chastisement she had dreaded.

'You were wrong to travel alone,' Ms Moon said. 'Tell me you were wrong.'

Faith drew another breath before responding. 'Yes, Ms Moon, I was wrong and I'm sorry.'

Another slap landed, harder this time. It struck flatly against her other cheek, and again Faith was grateful for the negligible protection her panties provided. She was trying to concentrate her thoughts on the future, eagerly anticipating the moment when this humiliation would be over and she would be allowed to climb from the choir mistress's knees. It was all she could bring herself to think about because the alternative was to consider the disturbing excitement of her predicament and the slick, sly warmth that each slap generated.

'You should never have gone to the Trastevere region after dark,' Ms Moon declared, and quivered as she threw all her strength into delivering another smack to Faith's cheeks.

Faith waited until the sting had subsided before she answered. Struggling to draw another breath, uneasy with the way the punishment was making her respiration so forced and strained, she said softly, 'No, Ms Moon. I shouldn't have gone there. I really am sorry.'

'Blast these panties,' Ms Moon complained. 'I'd swear they are protecting you just as well as your skirt. I don't think you need them for the conclusion of this discipline. Let me take them off.'

Faith hadn't realised how easily she had been accepting her punishment until she heard the choir mistress's final words. She had thought the spanking was as crushing a misfortune as anyone could suffer, but the discovery that Ms Moon now intended to slap her bare bottom made her realise she was only just learning the meaning of the word shame. She racked her brains for the argument that would stop the woman reaching for her underwear and pulling the fabric away, but disbelief and terror turned her helpless and mute.

'Lift yourself slightly,' Ms Moon said briskly, reaching under Faith's skirt, her cool fingers inquisitively feeling for the elastic waistband.

Faith thought of placing a protective hand against herself, or pulling away from the choir mistress and demanding an early end to the punishment, but she didn't dare. Ms Moon had said this was the conclusion of the discipline and, now that she had surrendered to this much suffering, she didn't suppose one final indignity would matter so greatly. Her stomach churned with trepidation as she raised herself and allowed the choir mistress to draw her panties away.

'That's better,' Ms Moon enthused.

She dropped the panties on the floor and the sight inspired a fresh knot of unease to tighten in Faith's stomach. It had felt wrong to agree to being spanked, it had seemed worse to allow the woman to remove her panties, but somehow the sight of the crumpled underwear discarded on the chalet floor made her embarrassment cut deeper.

'That's much better.' Ms Moon sounded as though she was smiling with approval, but Faith could hardly hear as her shame rang like a church bell. She was eighteen years old, supposedly a grown woman, yet she was being subjected to the humiliation of having her bare bottom spanked by the choir mistress. Bent over her knee, her naked buttocks already blushing, and now with the secrets of her sex on open display, she thought it was impossible to imagine a more demeaning position.

Ms Moon stroked the palm of her hand lightly against Faith's flesh. The contact was sickeningly exciting, inspiring waves of some emotion Faith couldn't identify. Her body prickled with heightened awareness and a flood of warmth swathed her with perspiration. Inside her bra she could feel her nipples hardening as they pressed against the restrictive cotton. Between her legs the muscles inside her sex seemed to clench and convulse with unbidden need.

Swiftly, with no warning other than the subtle movement of the woman's body, Ms Moon slapped her hand hard against Faith's rear. The blow was sharp and stinging. Its after-echo resounded crisply from the chalet walls. The choir mistress grunted slightly as she delivered the smack, but it was the only sound she made to indicate any exertion.

Faith squeezed her eyes closed as the first of her tears began to fall.

'Do I have your word that you will obey my instructions in future?' Ms Moon demanded, and unable to find a voice to reply, not trusting her tone to remain even, Faith could only nod. 'Do I have your word that you won't travel alone in this city ever again?' She slapped harder this time, and in her mind's eye Faith could picture a crimson handprint blazing against the pale flesh of her bottom. Close to tears, and no longer caring if the choir mistress knew about her upset, she groaned and nodded vigorously.

'Yes, Ms Moon,' she sobbed. 'You have my word.'

'And are you going to apologise for the worry and upset you caused me this evening?'

Sensing the punishment was almost over, Faith would have happily agreed to anything. Nodding eagerly, beyond worrying about the embarrassment of her position or the shame of her tears, she said, 'I'm sorry, Ms Moon. I'm truly, truly sorry and I won't do it again. I promise I won't.'

The choir mistress's hand remained on her bare buttocks, the fingertips infuriatingly close to the lips of Faith's sex. The contact was unsettling and Faith was torn between the conflicting ideas of wanting the moment to end and needing it to continue. She couldn't understand what it was about the chastisement she was enjoying, but she couldn't ignore the rush of disappointment that came when Ms Moon slipped her hand away and said the punishment was concluded.

Easing herself from the woman's knees, only daring to look at her with sly, unsure glances, Faith pushed her skirt back down over her hips. She considered the panties that remained on the floor, briefly contemplated putting them back on, and then decided the friction might exacerbate the blazing warmth that still burnt her bottom. Deciding she could dress herself properly when she had escaped Ms Moon's company, she snatched them from the floor and asked, 'May I go back to my chalet now?'

Ms Moon shook her head. 'We've taken care of the disciplinary matter,' she said quietly. 'But there are other things we need to discuss before you go to your bed tonight.'

Faith regarded her warily, wondering if there was more punishment to come. 'What other things?'

Ms Moon's smile was almost apologetic and made her features surprisingly attractive. 'I think you might have some idea what I'm talking about. Perhaps that couple in the graveyard gave you a clue? Perhaps you heard what I said to them before they fled?'

That particular ordeal seemed to have happened so long ago Faith thought it was like being reminded of a childhood memory. She shook her head slowly, not knowing what the choir mistress was trying to imply. 'I don't remember what you said to them,' she answered honestly. 'I didn't even know the couple. I don't know anything about them.'

Ms Moon rose from her chair and walked to a table in the corner of the chalet. Taking two glasses she poured small measures of sherry and handed one to Faith. 'The couple you saw in the graveyard were vampires,' she explained, and speaking quickly, seeming to realise that Faith was going to ridicule the idea, she said, 'They were vampires, and they were going to try and feed from you.'

Faith shook her head. 'I don't believe you,' she said firmly. 'There's no such thing as vampires. Not outside films and books. I don't believe you.'

Ms Moon smiled. 'It's a lot to take onboard in one evening. But you're going to have to believe me, and you're going to have to believe me soon. It's your destiny to defeat the leader of their coven and I've come to prepare you for that task.'

Unnerved by the serious way the woman was speaking, Faith took a tentative sip from her glass of sherry.

Interlude

Part I

Slouching on his throne, the dark one ponderously studied the two women. There was a manila folder on his lap, open with the contents exposed to him, but rather than looking at the document his morose gaze was fixed on the lair's challenge for the night.

The two women were naked, young and attractive, and they writhed together with the perfect synchronisation of furious arousal. They had both started the evening fully dressed, but it hadn't taken long before each was tearing the clothes from the other's body. As was usual, someone had cast a switch between them and they struggled furiously for possession of the weapon. The blonde snatched it first, holding the flaccid leather high above her head as though it was a victor's trophy. But the mulatto had pushed her to the floor, torn the leather from her hands, and then begun to stripe her with slice after slice from the punishing strap.

The blonde tried to retaliate and the interaction had been briefly antagonistic. There was a bout of hair pulling and a flurry of nail scratching, but it hadn't taken long for the animosity to become controlled as the dark-skinned vampire exercised her natural authority. Once they were both naked, and the blonde had learnt to respect the switch, the mulatto turned the challenge into an episode of sexual combat. The blonde was a natural submissive and she succumbed to every advance and instruction the mulatto made. She bucked her hips eagerly forward, yielded to every kiss and caress, and groaned with the honesty of undisguised passion. As the mulatto towered over her – muscular legs parted, switch pointed menacingly, and fingers spreading the folds of her flushed labia – the blonde hurried to please her and pushed her tongue against the woman's coffee-coloured folds of flesh. The mulatto's sigh was drawn out with urgent excitement.

'Look at this fucking pathetic spectacle,' the dark one growled from his throne.

'I already was,' Todd Chalmers replied.

He leant against the dark one's seat, standing at the traditional right-hand side reserved for trusted advisors. The scrutiny from his pale blue eyes hadn't faltered from the scene since he entered the coven's underground lair and he was familiar enough with its inhabitants to not bother disguising his appreciation. The two women would have been attractive enough to engage his attention even if they hadn't been naked or involved in a bout of vicious wrestling. They were creatures of the night, and because they both glowed with that sultry beauty he admired in every female vampire, Todd thought the scene was nothing short of captivating.

'Don't you find this charade tiresome?' the dark one asked. 'Maybe it's because Lilah isn't here that I find this so frustrating. Why isn't there a proper challenger to take on my favourite?'

Oblivious to the praise being bestowed upon her, the mulatto held a fistful of blonde tresses in one hand. She raised the switch in an unspoken promise of retribution and directed the submissive woman to tilt her head and press her mouth closer. Greedily she curled her hips to make her pussy more accessible, then smiled as though savouring the pleasure of being properly tongued.

The blonde's nipples were a pale rose colour, the areolae a faded hue that was barely darker than the pallor of her swollen breasts. But as she suckled against the mulatto's cleft, her pale pink flesh darkened, her nipples visibly pulsed and slowly filled with colour, until they were a rich, bloody claret.

'Don't you agree?' the dark one demanded, flashing his glare in Todd's direction. 'Don't you find this tiresome?'

'Tiresome isn't the first word that sprang to mind,' Todd replied.

The blonde had one hand between her own legs and rubbed furiously at her sex. Todd didn't know if his hearing was improving, if it was a trick of the coven's acoustics, or simply a symptom of his overactive imagination, but he could have sworn he heard the squelch of pussy lips slurping wetly. She knelt with her legs apart, knees buried in the earth, and he could see two fingers sliding easily in and out. The labia glistened in the golden glow from the lair's torches as she made each thrust deeper and more frantic. Her chest heaved with a quickening pace and Todd guessed she was fairly close to reaching a climax.

'These challenges bore me,' the dark one grumbled. 'If the truth be known, I think these fucking bitches are beginning to bore me as well.'

Todd shook his head in amazement. His gaze never left the mulatto and the blonde but he was speaking to the dark one when he said, 'I don't know how you can say that. I could watch your favourite defending her title for hours and hours.'

'Do you want one of them?' The dark one glanced at him curiously, snapping his fingers for silence in the lair. Even the two writhing women held themselves rigid as they waited attentively for their master's permission to continue. 'Do you want one of them?' the dark one pressed. Speaking quickly, as though the idea had just occurred to him, he asked, 'Do you want both of them?' Turning to the blonde and the mulatto, he pointed at Todd and said, 'He wants the pair of you, you sluts. Entertain him. Satisfy him.'

Before Todd could politely decline the two vampires were on him. The blonde had her mouth over his, her breath scented with feminine musk and her lips glossed with wetness from the mulatto's sex. The other woman tossed her switch aside and clung to his arm. She caressed him through the fabric of his suit and pressed her naked body eagerly against him. One leg rubbed against his as she tried to ingratiate herself closer. The modest swell of her athletic breasts was crushed against his sleeve as she smiled adoringly into his face.

Todd noticed the glimmer of scarlet that flashed in the mulatto's eyes but he didn't let the observation spoil his appetite for the woman. He had been excited by the effortless way she dominated the blonde but there was something about her svelte frame, and possibly the added allure of her exotic complexion, that fuelled him with a ravenous need. Dragging his mouth away from the blonde's, he placed his lips firmly over the dark-skinned vampire's and kissed her.

A hand snaked inside his trousers and ice-cold fingers encircled his shaft, but rather than spoiling his arousal the characteristic chill of a vampire's touch only made his hardness stand more rigid. He didn't know which of the women was handling his length, and in truth he didn't care. They were both attractive – wickedly beautiful, he thought, with their glinting red eyes and devilishly dangerous smiles – and either would make for a perfect partner for the night. The opportunity to share them both was something he hadn't anticipated and he intended to enjoy every moment.

The dark one sat back in his chair and began to leaf blindly through the report on his lap. Occasional illustrations, photographs, maps and coloured diagrams broke the sheets of neatly typed text, but the coven's leader didn't seem to see any of the carefully prepared contents. His foreboding frown creased his brow and it remained as he flicked unenthusiastically from one page to another.

Todd barely noticed the dark one's ennui while he revelled in the attention of the two vampires. The blonde had her bottom to him and the cheeks were spread as far apart as she could force them. The pouting pink lips of her sex were flushed with gluttonous need and she wriggled ever closer to him. The dark hand holding his shaft guided the end of his glans against the blonde's pussy lips and stroked him lazily. The sultry friction of the slippery flesh was unexpectedly exciting and he regarded the dark one's favourite with fresh respect.

The mulatto smiled devilishly for him, and then pushed her mouth back over his. Her kisses were cruel and threatened to be dangerously cutting, but he was prepared to tolerate that risk and the discomfort for the sake of the pleasure she silently promised. Even the teasing – the slow way she drew his end back and forth over the other women's labia, and the perpetual promise of nearing satisfaction – was a torment he was willing to endure.

Gasping for breath, he broke their kiss and allowed the dark-skinned vampire to nuzzle against his shoulder. He was relishing the exquisite excitement of her embrace – the thrill of having her hold his erection against the other woman while she writhed her feminine nudity against him – when the dark one spoke abruptly.

'Don't fucking bite him,' he snapped. He glared at the

mulatto and fixed her with a warning finger. 'You might be my current favourite, and I might have allowed you some leniency in the past, but you won't enjoy any special dispensation if you disobey this instruction. I need this mortal to walk in the daylight for me and I won't have you upsetting that arrangement.'

Todd glanced at the mulatto and saw her teeth were bared and the tips of her canines had been ready to pierce his neck. His flesh dimpled beneath the pressure of the teeth and he realised it would only take a fraction more pressure for her to break the skin. It occurred to him that her smile looked too full – too broad to be believed – and he couldn't help but think the image was disgustingly exciting. Her lips were riper than the lushest cherries and he realised a part of him craved her penetrating kiss. A hot coal of arousal filled his stomach as he realised how close he had come to being properly bitten. But more worrying than the danger he had been facing was the discovery that, in his state of high arousal, he didn't care if she bit him: he almost longed for it.

The dark one kept his warning finger raised and switched his gaze between his favourite and the blonde. 'If either of you bite him, without my permission, I'll take you on a personal excursion of all seven layers of hell,' he promised.

Neither of them seemed overly concerned about their leader's warning, and Todd wondered if he had misjudged their servility to the master. The worry added fresh fuel to his arousal when he realised how mortally dangerous his situation could become. It crossed his mind that it might be prudent to extricate himself from the two women but the blonde chose that moment to push herself backwards, and Todd was elated to feel his shaft being ensnared by her slick, velvety depths.

The mulatto retained her hold on his erection, squeezing the base of his shaft while lightly kneading his scrotum, and Todd had to struggle to contain a cry of excitement. He savoured every glorious moment as the two women continued to work on him, one of them kissing occasionally at his face while the other rode up and down on his length.

Eager to experience every sensation that could be offered to him, Todd reached for one of the mulatto's small breasts and pressed his hand over the flesh. Her nipple was a rigid bullet against the centre of his palm, and when he squeezed and massaged the orb it pressed more firmly into his hand. Enjoying her response he caught the hard nub between finger and thumb. The mulatto glared at him, Todd watched her features tighten with displeasure, and then saw her hide her antipathy behind a mask of indifference. He wondered if he would be able to force some reaction from her, if it might be possible to see a flicker of emotion spoil her perfectly composed features, but he doubted he had the strength to break her obvious resolve. Relishing the sensation of the stiff nub of flesh, he rolled it back and forth as the dark-skinned vampire studied him coolly.

The blonde continued to ride his erection, squeezing her inner muscles and writhing her hips to add new dimensions to each entry and egress. Todd couldn't see her face, and was unable to tell if her sounds of pleasure were real or fake, but he was certain he could feel the mounting tremors of excitement that were shivering through her pussy.

With his urgency building, he snatched his hand from the mulatto's breast and grabbed the blonde's backside with both hands. Greedily, he pulled her buttocks closer and buried himself deep inside her warmth.

The mulatto kissed him briefly, her tongue plundering his mouth before she pulled her face away and turned to the dark one. With one hand holding the base of Todd's stiffness, and her other stroking his cheek, she fixed her master with a desperate plea. 'Let me bite him, sire,' she begged. She drew a tongue along her razor sharp teeth as she paused for breath. 'I can either make him or feed on him, but you have to let me bite him. I can find you another mortal that will walk in daylight.'

The dark one continued leafing through the dossier and didn't bother to look up. 'Bite him and you'll suffer my wrath,' he said gravely.

Cursing bitterly, the mulatto pushed her blonde partner aside and stepped in front of Todd. Opening her legs for him, she maintained relentless eye contact as she guided his shaft to the lips of her sex and then held him against the pulsing centre.

The blonde easily recovered from her brusque dismissal and rushed to Todd's side. Although she didn't seem willing to kiss his face, her hands slipped under his jacket, inside his shirt, and she began to stroke lovingly against his bare flesh.

Todd didn't bother to acknowledge her, his gaze fixed on the domineering fury in the mulatto's expression. He allowed the dark-skinned vampire to stroke his glans back and forth, suppressing the urge to shiver as his pleasure approached a climax. Although he had heard her being warned, he didn't fully trust the vampire not to bite him if the temptation proved too great. The combination of danger and sexual excitement added to his mounting pleasure and he bit his own lip to stave off the encroaching climax.

Slowly, she guided him inside. He didn't know if she was squeezing her inner muscles; performing some trick experience had taught her; or if she was simply a more capable lover than the blonde; but he couldn't deny that she felt better. It took every effort of his concentration to fight the need of his own release, and when she began to buck her hips mechanically to and fro he knew the eruption wouldn't be long in coming.

The blonde was tugging on his chest hairs, scratching viciously at his nipples and exciting him with crude, barbaric caresses. But his gaze remained fixed on the mulatto as she rode him to a brisk, gratuitous orgasm.

It was a bitter release, made somehow less sweet by her obvious lack of response. She continued to ride her hips back and forth, milking every last drop of his spend before his flaccid length spilt from her sex lips. Even though he had wanted to satisfy her, and had been anxious to hear her grudgingly give voice to her own pleasure, he still thought the experience had been rewarding.

'That was what you wanted?' the dark one asked curiously.

Todd nodded as he extricated himself from the blonde's embrace and continued to watch the dark-skinned vampire. She had ridden him with such mastery he longed for the chance to have her again and see if she could control him so easily when his stamina was better prepared. Grudgingly he supposed she would still triumph because, as a creature of the night, she undoubtedly had little else to do except practice her technique. Not wanting to seem too eager, but anxious not to miss an opportunity, he considered asking the dark one if he could take the mulatto back to his hotel and have use of her again. It would be dangerous to be with her away from the dark one's protection, but his need to experience her again made him ignore that consideration. 'That was more than I wanted,' he began honestly. 'And, if—'

'I wish I could be so easily satisfied,' the dark one said

morosely. He slapped the dossier closed and slouched deeper into the recesses of his throne. 'Here in the coven everything seems to be falling apart. Lilah has disappeared, and no one's seen or heard from her in weeks. We used to enjoy these tournaments; I'd take the winner as my prize for the night; my sister would amuse herself with whatever was left of the loser; but without Lilah these entertainment sluts are failing to entertain me.' Fixing his sullen frown on Todd, he added, 'And even you are no longer providing the service I expect.'

Todd dragged his thoughts away from the chance of having the mulatto again and snatched his gaze from her mesmerising stare. Forcing himself to speak with the reverence he knew the dark one enjoyed, he asked, 'How do you think I'm failing you, sire?'

The dark one glowered. 'You were employed to help me with my problems regarding the virtuous girl.'

Todd shook his head, unable to understand where he was supposed to have failed. 'I have been helping,' he said quickly. 'You've just been looking at my report. You must have read that I went through half a dozen shamans to find out that the prophesied girl is one of three sisters. I've provided you with biographical details, addresses and photographs of Faith, Hope and Charity Harker.' Growing more indignant as he realised how his efforts were being slurred, Todd's voice began to sound strident. 'I've invested a lot of money in acquiring the casino where Hope Harker works. I've established a reputation as a media agent so I have control over Charity's band, BloodLust. You'll find there's even a signed copy of her debut album with the report I gave you.'

'Was that the shiny disc?'

Todd nodded and fought to hide his frustration. He had invested two hundred and fifty grand of the dark one's money in establishing a modest production company; he had gone to the additional trouble of building a recording studio; and his efforts were dismissed as the manufacture of a shiny disc.

'A debut album,' the dark one mused. 'I thought it was a rather plain coaster.' Waving a hand he said grudgingly, 'You did some work, I'll grant you that. But you never told me you were bringing the virtuous one here to Rome.' His features turned menacing as he leaned closer to Todd and roared, 'You never told me you were bringing my nemesis to meet me this fucking week!'

Todd's brow furrowed. The rest of the coven had fallen silent and watched them intently. He realised he was facing the full lethal threat of the dark one's anger, but it wasn't in his nature to back down from any intimidation. 'If you'd bothered to read it, you might have discovered that my report says Faith will be here for a week, performing in the title role of a choral production of Tosca.' Rolling his eyes with exasperation, he went on, 'I even included tickets for tomorrow night's performance, and I'm a bit pissed that you aren't valuing the hard work I've done on engineering her arrival here. I went to the trouble of orchestrating the choral version of this damned opera; I harangued the management at Castel Sant'Angelo to host the production; I've gone to the extent of taking the role of Scarpia myself; and I even went through the rigmarole of scheduling flights and accommodation for a party of twenty-five dizzy schoolgirls. I did all that, and I included every detail in my damned report.'

It was only after he had bellowed the last word that Todd realised he had been shouting. The coven had been silent before but now he could sense a breathless anticipation coming from the shadows. He supposed that others had dared to stand up to the dark one before, but it wouldn't have surprised him to learn that none of them had ever seen another night after.

Lowering his voice to a sensible volume, he tested a conciliatory smile for the dark one and said, 'In spite of all I've done to keep tabs on Faith, I think you're misguided in believing she is the virtuous one you're looking for. I'd be more likely to think it was Charity, or Hope. I don't think it will be Faith because—'

'Two of my neophytes encountered Faith in a Trastevere cemetery this evening,' the dark one broke in. 'Doesn't that sound like she might be the one?'

Todd considered this, not bothering to disguise his frown of consternation. The news surprised him and made him wonder if he had misread the facts he'd uncovered. 'Faith was in a cemetery? What was she doing there?'

'I suspect she was looking for me,' the dark one scowled. 'I can't think of any other reason.'

Todd digested the statement uneasily. His thoughts were flowing at lightning speed but still he fretted that he wouldn't be able to think fast enough for the demands of this situation. The dark one's suggestion made sense and Todd now thanked the professional pride that had encouraged him to follow the lives and developments of all three sisters. 'At least you now know which of them it is,' he said with forced optimism.

'That sentiment doesn't offer me a great deal of comfort.'

Todd zipped up his trousers and straightened his dishevelled clothes. Then glancing uncertainly at the coven's leader, he asked, 'Now that you know which of the sisters it is, what do you propose doing with her?'

The dark one's frown proclaimed his impatience. 'She's virtuous and I'm undead, therefore I can't kill her.' Glancing slyly at Todd his smile widened and his red eyes gleamed diabolically. 'But you're only a mere mortal,' he said quietly. 'The undead might not be able to kill the virtuous, but an amoral creature such as yourself could do the…'

Deliberately, Todd shook his head. 'I can't do that. I don't have many ethics but killing virtuous young women exceeds the few standards I've set myself.'

'Are you refusing me?' the dark one breathed. 'You have the temerity to raise your voice to me, and now you have the gall to fucking refuse me?' He held his finger and thumb in front of Todd's face, and the space between them was less than a millimetre. 'You're this far from taking your last breath, Mr Chalmers. Are you sure you don't want to reconsider your response? Do you really want to refuse my order?'

'I'm not killing girls,' Todd said defiantly. 'I thought your sister had a plan.'

'I told you that Lilah hasn't been seen for days.' The dark one sounded irritable and on the verge of a typical show of his vile temper. Todd half expected the coven's leader to leap from his throne and attack, but instead he simply sank deeper into his seat.

'Lilah claimed she had a great plan: a plan to strip the girl of her virtue so she would no longer present a threat to my safety. But Lilah has base appetites and I suspect she's found another diversion and forgotten about her family here at the coven.'

'That was your sister's great plan?' Todd struggled not to laugh. 'If that's all she intended doing, I can easily manage that for you.'

The dark one studied him doubtfully. 'I thought you said you had ethics?'

'I do have ethics,' Todd assured him. 'I won't kill the girl. But I have no qualms about stripping her of her virtue.'

Smiling eagerly he considered asking for the use of the mulatto vampire as part payment for the job, then decided there would be little need for her. 'I'll start the necessary arrangements straight away,' he declared confidently. 'And by the end of the week I'll have Faith completely stripped of virtue.'

'Why will it take you so long?' the dark one asked.

Todd grinned as though expecting the question. 'It's going to take me so long for one reason, and one reason only: it's going to take me so long because I intend to savour every glorious moment.'

Faith

Act I, Scene III

It was impossible to sleep, but that didn't surprise Faith. After all that Ms Moon had told her; compelling stories about the undead; a reminder about the important role of blood worship in most religions; the nefarious histories of Erzsebet Bathory and Gilles de Rais; and some remembered testimonies from the Moldavian and Wallachian vampire epidemics of the seventeenth and eighteenth centuries; Faith was surprised she had the courage to lay in the darkness and close her eyes. The stories were gruesome and chilling: Erzsebet Bathory was a relative of the original Count Dracula and a sadistic pervert who bathed in the blood of tortured virgins. Ms Moon had detailed the woman's adventures with an unconscious smile resting on her lips. Gilles de Rais had been Joan of Arc's patron, and the choir mistress gleefully explained that he had a fetish for the blood of young boys. The histories were perverse and unsettling but, Faith thought, they seemed entirely plausible after the events she had witnessed in the Trastevere cemetery, and she didn't doubt a word of what Ms Moon told her.

But it wasn't the dark revelations that caused her to remain wide awake.

She could have blamed her sleeplessness on the noise that filled the dormitory. Three or four of the choir snored, a couple of them mumbled through their dreams, and Faith felt sure she could hear the distinctive sounds of one girl masturbating. She didn't like to think that she was listening to someone's personal intimacy but the rhythmic squeak of a bed frame, and the half-choked sighs, all painted a disturbingly clear picture. Although she wasn't letting her mind dwell on the details, Faith thought it most likely she was listening to Marcia.

Marcia made no secret of her active libido and regularly boasted about the men she slept with and how she ranked them as lovers. Because Ms Moon had forbidden them from sampling the local nightlife, Marcia had spent her evenings after rehearsals watching the outrageous pornographic channels that were shown on the Rome television network. And, now she thought about the matter, Faith realised there had been similar sounds coming from Marcia's bed each night throughout the week. She remembered the noise went on for about half an hour and knew it was always concluded by the acrid odour of Marcia smoking a cigarette.

But, even though the background noise of Marcia's self-pleasure was disconcerting, Faith conceded that the sounds weren't the reason she was still awake. As loathe as she was to admit the fact, she knew her restlessness had been caused by Ms Moon's punishment.

Every time she shifted position on her bunk she caused friction against the sore seat of her bottom. She was wearing a pair of thin cotton shorts that matched her T-shirt, but as light as they were the fabric persisted in being abrasive against her buttocks. The discomfort was a reminder of the punishment she had suffered, and on top of that shame's return came the memories of how she had secretly liked the discipline. It was impossible to understand the twisted values that allowed her to enjoy being physically chastised, but she could see no sense in pretending her responses had been different.

Turning from one side to the other, struggling to find a position that wouldn't exacerbate her burning cheeks and might allow her the chance to finally close her eyes and sleep, she sighed with exasperation.

'Faith?'

Out of the darkness a hand fell against her arm, and she would have squealed in surprise if she hadn't recognised Claire's voice.

'Are you okay, Faith?'

'I'm fine,' she whispered. 'I just can't seem to get to sleep.'

'Moonie had you in her chalet for a long time this evening,' Claire said. 'What did she want?'

Faith blushed as she remembered being bent over the choir mistress's knee. The image came with sickening clarity and she could picture Ms Moon's hand slamming heavily against the soft flesh of her blushing, bare bottom. She was thankful that the darkness concealed her embarrassment because the memory brought her close to mortified tears. Speaking in a soft whisper that matched Claire's, she said, 'Ms Moon was pissed that I'd broken the rules. She said it was dangerous for me to have attempted travelling back here on my own. She wasn't best pleased.'

'Moonie always looks like she's pissed at someone,' Claire said sympathetically. 'What did she do? Did she tell you you're a naughty girl? Did she stop your spending money privileges? Or did she threaten to stop you from having pudding at teatime?'

'No,' Faith replied, then drew a deep breath and added, 'Ms Moon spanked me.'

The still silence was only broken by the quickening grunts and squeaks that came from Marcia's bed, and blushing more furiously than ever, Faith couldn't bring herself to contemplate what Claire might be thinking as she digested this news in the darkness.

'Ms Moon did what?' Claire switched on a torch as she made her exclamation and Faith was unsettled by the outrage she could see on her friend's face, spots of scarlet anger rouging her cheeks. 'You're kidding me, aren't you? She didn't really spank you.'

Faith told Claire to lower her voice before saying it was no big deal. 'You don't know the full story,' she explained. 'It was pretty stupid of me to set off on my own, I did get lost, and I ended up in a dreadful situation. Ms Moon saved me from suffering a truly horrible fate and I guess she had every right to be pissed at my stupidity.'

Claire adjusted her grip on the torch, giving Faith a brief glimpse of her friend's pyjamas. The jersey fabric clung to the shape of her large breasts and the details of the Winnie the Pooh and Piglet appliqués contrasted against the severity of Claire's eerily illuminated face. Her sombre expression didn't shift as she said, 'Tell me all about it. Tell me everything that happened, Faith.'

Only hesitating for a moment, making up her mind that she didn't want to keep secrets from her best friend, Faith told Claire about the entire evening. She started with the ill-fated journey from Castel Sant' Angelo, her arrival in the Trastevere cemetery, the strange couple and their shameless intimacy, Ms Moon's eleventh hour rescue, and then the choir mistress's revelations about vampires. She glossed over the details of the spanking, briefly mentioning that she had been punished for disobeying the rules, and concluded by saying, because she had put herself and the choir's production in so much jeopardy, she thought it was right for Ms Moon to discipline her the way she did.

Claire remained silent and the only sounds Faith could

discern came from Marcia. With her hearing attuned to every nuance in the room she thought she could detect a low wet slurp that was synchronised to Marcia's sighs. 'Say something, Claire,' she whispered. 'Even if you just tell me I'm a doormat or a tool. Please say something.'

'Let me see,' Claire said eventually.

Faith balked at the suggestion. She had wanted her friend to speak but those weren't the words she expected to hear. 'No way,' she said firmly. 'Don't you think it was embarrassing enough having to suffer that sort of punishment? After what I've been through this evening, do you think I'm really going to show you my bottom?'

Claire tugged at the thin blanket covering Faith's bunk. Her torch wavered, flashing over the beams on the ceiling, and there was a brief struggle as the pair fought to get their own way. Sensing the determination and concern that were governing her friend's actions, Faith finally relented and allowed Claire the victory. Turning onto her face, she pushed her bottom up to show where she had been spanked.

She was surprised to be so acutely aware of every sight and sound and wondered where her supernatural responsiveness had come from. The room remained still, save for the occasional snores and the perpetual creak of Marcia's bed, but now Faith could hear Claire's slow, deep respiration. When the beam of the torch brushed against her body she felt sure she could feel the warmth from its ineffectual light. Her skin was tickled by the sensation and the experience was like a paler version of the excitement she felt when Ms Moon punished her.

Claire's fingers slipped under the elastic waistband of Faith's cotton shorts, and startled, Faith turned on the bed and placed a protective hand over her rear. 'What do you think you're doing?' she gasped.

There was enough light from the torch for Faith to see Claire's hurt confusion. 'I was going to look at your bum,' she explained defensively. 'I was going to see if Moonie had done any lasting damage. I thought that was why you turned over.'

'I thought you were just going to look at the tops of my legs,' Faith objected, but Claire rolled her eyes and pushed her back to the bed. Firmly she pulled the cotton shorts down and Faith was crippled by the embarrassment of exposing her backside for the second time in the same evening. The beam of the torch burnt more brightly than ever and Faith was aware of the smouldering light searing her flesh. When Claire stroked a tentative finger against one cheek she flinched from the touch and then tried to remain rigid and unmoved. It was almost impossible to stay still as Claire stroked and touched the aching skin.

'There are hand prints all over your arse,' Claire confided.

Faith closed her eyes and said nothing.

'They're bright red. It's no wonder you can't get to sleep.' She lowered her voice and added, 'You can see the exact shape of the woman's hand.'

Because she was whispering it was impossible to work out if Claire was offended or excited. Faith didn't doubt Ms Moon's handprints were visible on her buttocks because she could feel Claire pressing her own hand over the same spot, but rather than being the cool discipline that Ms Moon had inflicted, Claire's touch was infuriatingly warm and lubricated by a sheen of perspiration. When she moved her hand away Faith was touched by a pang of regret.

'It must hurt like hell,' Claire observed.

Faith was about to reply, and then caught her breath; Claire was using the tip of one finger to trace the outline

61

of Ms Moon's handprint. Lightly she caressed the rounded flesh, her path faltering from the blazing pain of where Faith had been slapped to the sensitive flesh that remained unpunished. Faith struggled not to be moved but the sensations were exquisite and powerful. Each time Claire's touch pressed too heavily against a patch of reddened flesh, the stinging heat of the discipline was fully rekindled. 'It does hurt like hell,' Faith agreed.

The light shifted as Claire put the torch down on the bed, and then began to work on the prone girl with both hands. Faith considered complaining, saying the contact was too intrusive and more than she could cope with, but she didn't want to upset her friend. There seemed to be little logic in the idea that she could readily submit to a stranger's punishment, yet deny a friend the chance to confirm she was unharmed, and Faith bit back her protest and allowed Claire to climb on the bed beside her.

'Does this part still sting?'

Faith didn't need to concentrate to feel Claire's knuckle rubbing back and forth over one cheek. A rush of burning excitement stole from her rear and she swallowed thickly; rather than just reminding her of the discomfort, Claire's touch was bringing back all the wicked thoughts she had entertained during Ms Moon's discipline. She shut her eyes and tried to distance herself from the swelling need between her legs, but she knew it would prove a futile struggle. 'Yes,' she said, gritting her teeth so her tone didn't reveal her arousal. 'It stings quite a lot.'

'What about here?'

There was a moment's pause, and then Faith was shocked to feel Claire stroke a finger against the split between her legs. The tip traced lightly against her labia, its gentleness inspiring a shock of excitement that made Faith dizzy. She had been trying not to notice the awakening sensations in that part of her body but she realised it was all too easy to enjoy every delicious aspect. It felt as though Claire's touch was lubricated and Faith's stomach churned as she tried to work out why. She wondered if her friend had licked the end of her finger before placing it there, or if the moisture had come from inside her sex. The wetness was warm, and made Claire's caress easier and more fluid, but that detail told Faith nothing.

'She didn't touch me there,' Faith said stiffly.

'Are you sure?' Claire asked, her fingertip brushing up and down against the split of Faith's sex.

Every casual contact struck her with another blow of need and she wondered why her friend was subjecting her to this wicked exercise in torment. She longed to glance up over her shoulder and watch while Claire touched her. A single glance would be enough to discern if her friend was performing the examination with an expression of clinical concern or the breathless excitement Faith could hear underlying her questions. But not daring to find out which emotion was dictating Claire's actions, she kept her face buried in the pillow.

'Are you certain she didn't touch you here?'

Faith recalled Ms Moon holding her after the punishment, one hand resting on her bottom, the tips of her fingers so close to her sex that they brushed against pubic curls. But although her hand had been close, she was certain the woman's touch hadn't connected. She knew there had been no contact because she remembered a part of her wanting one of the woman's cool fingers to stroke her burning need. 'I think I would know,' she said softly. 'Ms Moon didn't touch me there.'

'Okay,' Claire said, drawing her finger away. 'It doesn't look like she did you any lasting harm.'

63

Faith sighed with relief, not sure if she was grateful for the news Claire had given her, or the fact that her friend had moved her hand away. The delicious teasing had fuelled an urgent need within her loins and she knew it wouldn't have taken many more caresses before a rush of arousal overwhelmed her.

Thankful the torment was over she raised no objections when Claire lay down beside her and said, 'So, what did Moonie tell you about vampires? And why?'

Faith tried to slide back into bed, but because it was only a single cot she found herself pressed close to Claire. The swell of her friend's large breasts pushed against hers, and as they both fidgeted into comfortable positions, she felt Claire's thigh slide between her legs. Ordinarily she wouldn't have worried about such close contact, but without the security of her cotton shorts, and after the way Claire had just been touching her, she couldn't help but think the episode was still in danger of turning sexual. She tried to read Claire's expression, not sure if she had ever known her friend to be so tactile before, but all she saw was her usual good-natured smile.

'What did Moonie say about vampires?' Claire repeated.

Faith shook her head to clear her thoughts. 'Ms Moon told me lots of stuff,' she said, laughing grudgingly. 'I think she told me more than I needed to know. Sunlight kills them. Crosses burn them and ward them off. And they don't like garlic.'

'Was that all she said?'

'Not by a long way,' Faith said. 'You can destroy them by cutting off their heads or staking their heart with either iron or wood. They bite people and then drink all their blood and kill them. If they only drink some of their blood it makes the victims into vampires. There's the Bethesda Stone, a black crystal that can change a vampire back into their human form. And most covens have a mortal employee or two, to do work and run errands for them during daylight hours, but I'm a bit shaky on those last few details because I was suffering from information overload.'

Claire stroked a stray strand of hair away from Faith's face. The movement brought them closer and Faith was appalled to notice a growing stiffness between their chests. She couldn't decide if she was simply feeling the pressure of the buttons from Claire's pyjamas, or if she was becoming aware of a hardening nipple. Suspecting it to be the latter, sure she could feel a dull pulse beating behind the thrust of her breast, she tried to work out if she was feeling a symptom of Claire's arousal, or an indication of her own.

Glancing up, seeing the honest curiosity in Claire's expression, Faith realised her friend was almost crying out to be kissed. Her full lips looked wet and soft and inviting, and the urge to kiss her was a maddening impulse and, not bothering to fight that need – tired from having spent an evening resisting such urges – she reached up and their lips met.

Claire responded greedily, pulling Faith into her embrace as their mouth's joined. Her thigh pressed heavily against the lips of Faith's bare sex, and when Faith found her own leg caught between Claire's, she relished the sensation of heat that smouldered from her friend's cleft. Through the crotch of the pyjamas she could feel the yielding weight of Claire's sex lips and the intimate contact inspired her to shiver.

It no longer mattered whether the hardness against her chest had come from the stiffness that tipped Claire's breasts or the arousal that controlled her own because she knew they were both charged with the same furious need. A part of her was tempted to lower her hand and cup the shape of Claire's orb. She wanted to know how it would feel to hold the pliant flesh and yearned to stroke her thumb against the rigid bud of Claire's nipple.

But, because they shifted positions, because Claire chose that moment to press her thigh more firmly against Faith's sex and spark another burst of deep-seated longing, she didn't get the opportunity to touch her as she wanted. She savoured her friend's penetrating kiss and didn't stop until Claire finally pulled away.

They lay side by side on the bed; both of them breathing so heavily that Faith could no longer hear Marcia's bed rocking.

'And Ms Moon says you're a virtuous vampire killer?' Claire giggled.

Faith shared her mirth, wondering if the choir mistress would still consider her virtuous if she had seen her being embraced by Claire. There had been nothing chaste about the kiss, and when their tongues had explored she knew her behaviour couldn't have been much further from anyone's interpretation of virtuous.

Sensing that her intimacy with Claire was now concluded, sure it wouldn't go any further, she turned her mind back to the subject of Ms Moon. After the shock of touching and kissing, it seemed somehow easier to think about the choir mistress with proper perspective. 'I'm not entirely sure I trust Ms Moon,' she said quietly. 'But I believe everything she told me about vampires.'

Claire nodded. 'There could well be some truth in the myths,' she said philosophically. 'Maybe there are too many stories about vampires for it all to be Hollywood hype and fairytales?'

While Faith agreed, she didn't think her own belief in the undead was quite so simplistic. Her belief didn't just come from such suspect rationalisation, and not even from the stories Ms Moon had told her. Faith knew she believed because she had seen vampires in the Trastevere cemetery.

'I believe everything Ms Moon's told me,' she said again, 'so I'm going to go along with her plans. She says she's going to start training me to defeat the dark one tomorrow night, after the performance.'

'No,' Claire said firmly. She pulled herself up and shone the torch in Faith's face. 'Believe in vampires, go along with Moonie's plans, but not tomorrow night. I was going to invite you to come with me tomorrow night.'

Faith raised an eyebrow. 'Come with you? Where?'

'You know my sister lives here in Rome?' Faith nodded. 'She wants to introduce me to her new boyfriend and I thought you could come along with me.'

Faith considered this, and was suddenly amazed that she and Claire could still talk so easily after doing something as naughty as they had just done. A part of her had expected the kiss to end their friendship, but on some level she couldn't quite understand it seemed to have actually strengthened their bond.

'Your sister wants to introduce her boyfriend to you?' After all the stories she'd heard about Claire's aloof sister, she was surprised by her unexpected sense of family. Trying to think of a reason for such uncharacteristic behaviour, she said, 'He must be someone special, do you think? Has she got plans to marry him?'

Claire shrugged. Her breasts jostled against Faith's body but this time there was no sense of intimacy or excitement in the contact. 'I don't know anything about him, or why she wants to perform introductions. All she's said is that his name's Nick, and she wants me to meet him.'

The name unsettled Faith but it was too much of a struggle to work out why. The idea of Claire going to meet her sister's new boyfriend sounded a warning bell that made no sense, and she was about to voice her objections – knowing they would sound nonsensical but prepared to make them anyway – when the silence was broken by the crackle of a match being struck.

Faith and Claire stiffened until they realised the sound had only come from Marcia's bed as she lit herself a final cigarette for the day. The unpleasant smell of tobacco smoke wafted towards them and they both released sighs of relief. Claire shone the torch back in Faith's direction and then frowned with obvious upset.

'Where's your necklace?' she asked suddenly.

Faith clutched her throat, easily able to recall the way the chain and her crucifix had been snatched from it. She had tried to retrieve it from the grass but Ms Moon was leading her away and hadn't allowed her the chance. All thoughts of Claire, her sister, and her sister's boyfriend were instantaneously vanquished as she sat up in bed, determined to go back and find the jewellery. 'It's still in the cemetery,' she explained, getting up and searching for clothes in the darkness.

'That's terrible,' Claire sympathised, 'but why are you getting dressed?'

Faith rolled her eyes, surprised Claire could be so dense. 'I'm getting dressed because I can't go to the cemetery in just this T-shirt and a pair of thin cotton shorts.'

'You're going back there?' Claire gasped.

'It was a present from Hope,' Faith reminded her. 'I have to go and get it back.'

Faith

Act I, Scene IV

The crucifix glinted like a sliver of sunlight beneath the torch's beam. Smiling, pleased with herself, Faith snatched it from the ground and clutched it tight in her fist. The fine links of the necklace were snapped and would have to be replaced or repaired, but the crucifix was the important thing and she felt overjoyed to hold it in her hand. Annoyed that she hadn't thought to wear something with pockets, she quickly wrapped the silver chain around her fingers to secure her hold on the cross, and heaving a sigh of relief, she glanced at her macabre surroundings and shivered uneasily.

It was difficult to remember where she had found the courage to brave this journey, or how she had managed to dissuade Claire from coming along, but she was quietly proud of both accomplishments. She knew there would be repercussions if Ms Moon discovered she had made her way alone across Rome, and then into the heart of the Trastevere cemetery, but retrieving the crucifix made her believe the risks had been worthwhile. Congratulating herself on her achievements she took a deep breath and told herself to hastily retreat from the cemetery and return to the chalet.

It was sage council, and sorely tempting, but Faith didn't immediately head for the exit. She had first seen the pair of vampires close to this spot and puzzled over how they had been able to disappear so quickly. Ms Moon had told her that the undead were gifted with superhuman abilities, and that they could move with devastating speed, but the couple vanished so swiftly Faith suspected she and the choir mistress might be overlooking something obvious. Shining her torch into the darkness beyond the headstones, she edged closer to a decorative copse of rowans. Inching nearer, puzzled by something unusual in the way the trees were gathered, the torch's beam picked out the shape of a dark, open doorway.

It was common knowledge that the underbelly of Rome was riddled with catacombs, and that most of them were attributed to the early Christians. Faith had heard that they stretched for more than a hundred kilometres underground, but when Todd Chalmers took the choir on a sightseeing tour on their first day, he said there were also many pagan burial vaults running parallel to the orthodox sites. He had also suggested that some of the more extreme cults residing within the city might still be using them.

Staring at the gaping doorway, uneasy at the thought of entering and following its path down, Faith wondered if this was the entrance to one of those pagan catacombs. She told herself that having found this potential hiding place for the vampires she ought to investigate, but her doubts nagged incessantly.

Ms Moon had assured her she was the virtuous one, but Faith thought there was a possibility the woman might be mistaken. She didn't think anyone could ever associate virtue with her licentious response to the choir mistress's spanking, or with the easy way she had allowed Claire to touch and kiss her. Also, as she brooded on her unsuitability, she couldn't convince herself that someone virtuous would directly disobey Ms Moon's order to avoid travelling alone at night.

The internal arguments heightened her self-doubt and

she took a tentative step away from the doorway. If she wasn't virtuous, that meant she couldn't really be the virtuous one. And if she wasn't the virtuous one, she knew she would have no defence against any vampires that might be lurking inside the doorway. Not sure she dared brave an encounter, thinking it might be more prudent to tell Ms Moon about this discovery and return to the potential lair with an ally, she took a last glance at the doorway and told herself she wouldn't be going through it this night.

'And what have we got here?'

The voice came from behind her, and startled she span around and flashed the torch's beam on a diabolically handsome face. The eyes glinted crimson and the mouth overflowed with glistening white teeth. She didn't know how long he had been standing there and wondered how someone so tall and broad could move with such stealth. There was no question in her mind that he was one of the undead, and horrified she struggled to stifle her scream.

'I assume there's no need for introductions,' he grinned easily. 'I take it you're aware that I'm the dark one whom you're destined to vanquish. And I recognise you from your photograph. Your name is Faith. You're the virtuous one who I'm trying to avoid.'

His tone was mocking and derisory and she was appalled that he knew so much about her. Ms Moon had mentioned the dark one – had told her it was her duty to rip the cold black heart from his chest – but she hadn't said he would be aware of who she was or what she looked like. Unnerved by his confidence, Faith took a single step away from him.

The dark one crept closer. 'Would you care to explore my lair?' he suggested, extending his hand towards the foreboding doorway she'd been contemplating. He made the offer as though it was a genial invitation to share an espresso or sample the cuisine in a local trattoria. 'Perhaps you'd like to meet some of my coven?' he added, dropping her an amiable wink. 'I'm sure they'd want you to stay for a bite.'

She thought about running but he had a hand over her shoulder before she realised he was so close. Her struggle was brief – a handful of pathetic punches to his arm and an ineffectual swing that made her lose her hold on the torch – before she realised there was no chance of escape. Fighting her mounting panic, determined to bide her time and flee at the first opportunity, she had no choice except to go with him into the darkness.

Her heart raced madly. She tried shrugging free and squirming out of his grip but he maintained his hold without any discernible show of effort. Swiftly he urged her along a descending, unlit passage, and her eyes had only just grown used to the blackness when they turned a corner and he led her into a wide vault lit by burning torches. She didn't want to enter the cavernous room, scared of the shifting shadows and the grinning strangers, but the dark one's grip was uncompromising and she knew she would have to follow.

'Look what I've brought you, children,' the dark one roared, his rich voice echoing from the time-stained walls. 'Stop sating your depraved appetites for a moment and take a look at this little treasure.'

If she hadn't believed in vampires before entering the catacomb, the sight of the coven convinced her. Lining the walls – some lurking in the shadows of the connecting corridors, others revelling in the centre of the room – they languished as couples and trios and quartets. Engrossed with each other, none of them glanced in Faith's direction as the dark one led her through their ranks. She glimpsed bloody, hungry smiles; teeth piercing flesh, crimson ribbons trickling over bared shoulders and breasts. But none of the scarlet eyes followed her as she was led through their midst.

An unseen CD player churned out a thrash metal ballad from her sister's first album, and she wondered if the music had been chosen specifically to mark her arrival, or if it was simply one of those coincidences that came with having a successful sibling. She supposed there was a strong likelihood that the BloodLust group appealed to a cult like this one because the band's neo-gothic style was perfectly recreated by the coven's pallid flesh and dark, sunken eyes. Turning her thoughts to anything other than her invidious predicament, Faith also decided the music's harsh discordant melodies and nihilistic lyrics didn't seem out of place being played in the pagan burial vault.

'You've fed from me for the very last time; your kiss bites deep but you've got no spine; you can go to hell and I'll get along fine.'

Beneath the mounting anger of Charity's solo, coming from the members of the coven rather than the CD, Faith heard grunts, moans and mortified sobbing. They were chilling cries borne from desire, lust and pain and she didn't want to hear any of them. Nevertheless, the sounds were as inescapable as the intoxicating scent of animal arousal that pervaded the air. The dark one dragged her through the body of his coven, pushing aside those who didn't step away quickly enough, while bellowing and swearing for them all to pay heed.

Finally they began to do as he demanded, but not all his subordinates seemed so eager to obey his commands. A handful fixed him with glares of loathing and contempt and others glowered as though his arrival was an inconvenience. But despite their reluctance they all put their passion's aside and fixed their attention on the leader and his guest as he settled on an ornate throne. Someone in the shadows kicked the CD player and the music was replaced by an expectant silence.

Throughout the ordeal Faith was painfully aware of the dark one's talon-like fingers maintaining their hold on her shoulder. She was also unnerved by the realisation that rather than looking at their leader, every head was stopping and turning to stare at her. At first she tried to meet each inquisitive glance with defiance, but there were so many crimson eyes fixed on her that eventually she had to lower her gaze. She couldn't see all the vampires, there were some figures lurking in the shadowy corners of the lair, but she easily recognised Nick and his brunette lover from her encounter with them earlier.

The silence was underscored by the crackle of flames licking against the wall, but Faith could barely hear that noise over the dull thud of her heartbeat.

'Children,' the dark one cackled, 'lessers, minions and slaves. I'd expect you to be a little more welcoming to our guest. I've brought you the virtuous one and I want everyone to take a good look at her. I want you all to know the face of the most dreaded enemy we've ever faced.'

Despite his imposing speech the room echoed with coarse brays of laughter, and Faith grew more uneasy as she saw a couple of the braver vampires step closer. One of them reached out to touch her arm, and to his obvious amusement she slapped his hand away. She turned to glare at the dark one and said, 'Why have you brought me in here? Why are you doing this to me?'

He raised an eyebrow. 'You're a danger to my immortality and the safety of my coven. I feel it only right that my subordinates should get a chance to know you.'

She tried to pull away from him but there was no escaping his hold. 'I'm not a danger to anyone,' she said indignantly. 'Why don't you let me go?'

Rather than answering he pulled her onto his lap. One arm encircled her waist and she was horrified to see his mouth moving closer. Beneath her buttocks she could feel the monstrous presence of his erection. Instinctively she tried to wriggle away, but that only made her more aware of the persistent pulse that throbbed from his groin. Her attempts to silently beseech him went unheeded as he moved his mouth over hers and kissed.

It was a brutal exchange, his tongue forcing its way between her lips as he made his hold inescapable. One arm snaked behind her back, reaching around her side to clutch the shape of her breast. The other clasped her knee and began to slide slowly up her thigh. Faith watched the tips of his fingers disappear beneath the hem of her skirt and she quivered with excitement from the intrusive caress. Needing to show some sign of resistance she stiffened, then wriggled, longing to escape and fearing that her situation had already grown hopeless.

The dark one briefly broke their kiss and wiped the back of his hand over his lips. 'I'm beginning to doubt you're so virtuous,' he growled. 'Perhaps my sources were misinformed.' Not waiting for her response he kissed her again and continued to work his tongue between her lips.

She held her breath, wishing his hold wasn't exciting her and trying to pretend there was no heat smouldering in her loins. A prickle of arousal itched between her legs, and as the pulse beneath her buttocks beat more urgently she was almost won over by the idea of letting him take her.

'Give me your opinion,' the dark one snarled.

Faith blinked herself back from the dream of having the vampire's bite press against throat and tried to understand what he was saying, and searched his eyes for a clue before realising he was calling to one of his coven. She glanced towards the eager crowd and was disquieted to note they were creeping closer. Nick's familiar face loomed to the front of the throng and then he was pushing out of the hoard and stepping to the dark one's side. His crimson smile was eager and wet and his eyes glinted the scarlet colour of pure lust. While his features looked wicked and monstrous, she couldn't deny he also stirred the growing warmth between her thighs.

'Tell me if you think she's virtuous,' the dark one said, urging Faith from his lap. 'Try her,' he coaxed. 'Test her. Taste her. Tell me what you think.'

She stumbled into Nick's embrace, feeling so weak she swooned against him. He caught her easily, placing one hand in the small of her back while his other went to her breast. The subtle way he massaged and kneaded the orb went almost unnoticed as he placed his lips over hers. She was barely aware of the delicious arousal he inspired in her nipple while his tongue snaked hungrily against hers. Faith returned his kiss, tasting the coppery flavour of blood on his lips and testing the razor-sharp whiteness of his smile.

Her thoughts were a turmoil that had her helpless and confused. The dark one's words made sense when he said he doubted her virtue, because she was beginning to think that concept couldn't be further from the truth. She didn't think that someone virtuous would be so willing to submit to strangers; especially strangers as dark and sinister as the coven of vampires. And she didn't think her eager responses to the dark one and then to Nick were indicative of her alleged high calling. It took an effort of willpower to resist the urge to grind her crotch against Nick's leg and she knew she was returning his kiss with a furious passion that even exceeded his eagerness.

Nick pulled his mouth away with a guttural sigh, and glancing at his groin, Faith could see his trousers bulged with the shape of his hardness. Remembering how his erection had looked when she saw him with his brunette lover, she lifted her hand and traced the shape of the stiffness beneath the fabric, delighted to feel it pulse against her fingertips.

'I can't tell if she's virtuous, or trying to lull us into a false sense of security,' Nick told the dark one. He stepped away from her, almost leaving her to fall to the catacomb floor, then as an afterthought he pushed her in the direction of his brunette lover and she found herself being enveloped by the woman's powerful embrace.

'Try the taste test, Helen,' Nick grinned. 'Tell us if this one's virtuous, or if she's just a slut like you.'

Faith didn't see the scowl Helen flashed in Nick's direction, and dizzied with the thrill of being passed from one vampire to another, she stumbled to maintain her balance. Her body ached from the arousal that had been awoken, and rather than just passing her around, she wished one of them would satisfy her need and end the torment of her excited suffering.

Helen's kiss filled her with the same thrilling excitement she had found from Nick and the dark one. The woman's breasts pressed against hers and she was briefly reminded of the intimacy she had shared with Claire. That moment seemed to have happened so long ago and to someone else, she thought distantly, but the memory still burnt strong. Yet, unlike Claire's tentative exploration, Helen's kiss was demanding and intrusive. Her teeth nipped lightly at Faith's lips and the syrupy rich flavour of blood never seemed to be far away. Thinking back over the evening, Faith remembered seeing Helen's mouth devouring Nick's erection and she was thrilled to know she was kissing lips that had done something so shocking. The memory inspired a fresh wave of longing and she pressed herself hungrily into Helen's embrace.

'She's as virtuous as I am,' Helen scoffed, and briskly yanked at the front of Faith's blouse and tore it open. A handful of buttons flew into the orange-edged shadows but Faith didn't see them as she concentrated her efforts on trying to cover herself. The lacy edges of her bra were providing an indecorous show and she blushed furiously at the sudden embarrassment. Pushing Faith's hands aside, Helen reached for the bra and snatched at the cups. One of them was easily torn from the straps while the other only ripped and remained mostly intact. Gasping at the way she had been exposed, Faith tried to turn on Helen but the woman was already pushing her into the arms of another vampire, her cruel laughter resounding over the approving cheers of the coven.

Faith blinked back her tears. She tried to clasp a hand across her exposed chest but the attempt was futile. The next vampire held her arms behind her back while his fingers stroked her bared breast. He kissed her as passionately as the others had done and, to her shame, Faith knew she responded with the same desire.

The torment lasted forever, one vampire tasting her, touching her and exciting her, before passing her to the next so the whole torturous process could begin again. She was dizzied by the growing need for satisfaction and frustrated by the way her appetite was perpetually awoken, fuelled, and then ignored. Men and women, old and young, desirable and despicable, kissed her. Her libido responded to each with the same shameless enthusiasm and she craved the moment when one of them would take things a little further and give her the release she yearned. Dozens of different hands groped her breasts. One of the more forceful males finished the job Helen had begun and tore the remaining cup of fabric from the remnant of her bra. The most daring of her tormentors placed their lips over her nipples and she was treated to the exquisite joy of needle-sharp canines threatening to pierce the rigid buds of flesh.

Fingers stole beneath her skirt, sliding up her thighs and rubbing against her crotch. Every illicit touch sparked excitement and fired her urgent need. Faith squirmed against the hands, eagerly parting her legs for them and relishing the frisson of cool flesh against her melting sex lips. The protective gusset of her cotton panties sheathed the contact, but the fabric had grown so sodden it adhered to her labia like a film of skin. Each caress against her crotch trembled through her pussy as though it had rubbed against bare flesh. And just as Helen had made an attempt to pull the bra from her breasts, Faith secretly longed for one of the vampires to snatch the panties away from her sex.

The final vampire to kiss her – a dishevelled blonde, half-naked and with her breasts and shoulders striped with the scratches and marks from a recent fight – returned Faith to the dark one. She wiped her bloody lips and fixed the coven's leader with a reluctant smile. 'She doesn't taste virtuous,' the blonde told him earnestly.

Faith felt shamed by the words.

'She doesn't taste virtuous, but I'd be scared to risk feeding from her.'

The dark one ignored her as he pulled Faith back onto his lap. He held her in a viciously exciting embrace, stroking her exposed breast with one hand, clutching her buttock with the other. Through the fabric of her skirt she could feel his fingers teasing against her sex and she wanted to writhe against him. The idea of surrendering to his commanding presence was so tempting she didn't understand why her mind had any hesitation. Her body's greedy need for him was a pulsing, vibrant force and she craved the satisfaction she knew he could give.

'Regardless of what my coven say, you are the virtuous one,' he sneered. 'I wonder what that means? I wonder how virtuous you really are? Our laws forbid us from feeding off gypsies, nuns and the virtuous, but I've never been much of a one for obeying rules. If the truth be told, I quite like feeding from forbidden fruit because I always think it tastes so much better.'

She tilted her head, offering him her throat.

'Are you going to give yourself to me now, Faith?' he asked, the musical lilt of his voice so tempting it was almost hypnotic. 'One day soon you're going to slip,' he continued. 'One day soon you'll lose your virtue. There's a coven of eager vampires here who are all acquainted with you now. They're all eager to take advantage of that first available opportunity. Why not save us all the time and trouble and let me take you now? All you have to do is ask for it.'

The hand against her breast squeezed. One thumb rubbed her nipple and the sharpest spear of arousal stung her. She glared at him, not knowing if she wanted him to let her go or if she would beg him to fulfil the promise of his touch. When she saw the contempt glinting in his eyes, and realised he was studying her like another piece of meat he could devour, she acted instinctively. Not thinking about the danger she was facing, her arousal disappearing as if it had never been there, Faith raised her hand and slapped his face.

The dark one staggered back and howled. He had one hand clutched to his cheek and glared at her with the blackest venom.

Faith was momentarily stunned, not sure how she could have hurt someone so powerful and menacing, but glancing at her palm she saw the crucifix was still there and one quick look at the dark one showed a blazing cross burnt into his cheek.

'You fucking bitch,' he spat, but stunned by the sudden advantage Faith didn't stay around to trade insults. Sure she had come away from the encounter because of pure luck she pushed through the coven of startled vampires and finally made her escape.

Interlude

Part II

Vacuous, thought Todd Chalmers.

'...and, in the magazine, there was a feature showing all that season's...'

Absolutely and completely vacuous, he thought glumly.

Marcia sat across the table from him, oblivious to his thoughts and continuing to regale him with her insights on the splendours of Rome. Because she only seemed to have absorbed the delights of the Via Veneto boutiques – and then only those stores whose international acclaim had been featured alongside a celebrity photo shoot in some glossy celebrity magazine – Todd thought a lesser mortal might have struggled to make so much of such an insubstantial subject. But he had realised at the beginning of the meal that Marcia would never let the dullness of a topic stop her from talking about it incessantly. And as she droned on about colour swatches, complementary designs and the vagaries of credit card protocol, she was proving him infuriatingly right.

He nodded.

He ate his gnocchi.

He sipped his way through a bottle of frascati and then called room service to order a second.

And he listened as Marcia continued to talk and talk and talk and talk. Lighting a cigar, sitting back in his chair and blowing a plume of smoke towards the Mediterranean sky, he glanced out at the midday view of Via Veneto that sprawled below the balcony. It had been his suggestion that Marcia should join him for lunch in his suite at the Excelsior, and he had ordered the hotel's staff to prepare a romantic meal for two on the balcony. As always, the dark one was paying Todd's account and so he made sure no expense was spared in creating the right setting. The lunch was served with fresh roses for the lady, there was a bottle of one of the more pleasing local wines, and the cuisine would have been a credit to any of the city's most acclaimed trattoria.

Marcia was very attractive, her beauty made striking by her youth and the arrogance of her haughty deportment. She dressed with more style than any of her contemporaries in the choir, and although her nubile young figure would have looked desirable in rags, her wardrobe of designer chic transformed her into a goddess. Sitting across the table from him, the sunlight shone like freshly spun gold in her hair and the radiance of her smile came close to burning just as brightly.

With the ambience of La Boheme playing in the background, Todd thought it should have made the ideal setting for a smooth, sophisticated seduction. But he hadn't counted on Marcia bringing her mouth. And he hadn't expected her to use it so maliciously.

'…told me they only accept gold card customers…'

He watched the bustling traffic below, envying those drivers who were yelling at each other, honking their horns and flicking offensive hand signals. At least, he thought, they were only listening to threats and vicious obscenities. They weren't having to endure a comparison of apricot and salmon voile, or the second outing of Marcia's platinum credit card anecdote.

A bitter smile crossed his lips when he remembered the dark one asking him to kill Faith. He had said no because it seemed immoral to murder a defenceless young woman. However, he thought, it would only take another half hour of Marcia's self-indulgent chatter and he might reconsider his stance on that particular crime.

'...so I told the shop assistant that platinum is obviously better than gold...'

'May I just say something?' he asked quickly.

The flexing of Marcia's frown indicated that she was unused to having her monologues interrupted. She tested a terse-but-patient smile and sipped at her wine before nodding. 'Sure,' she relented. 'What do you want to say?'

Todd grinned, almost apologetically. 'I had an ulterior motive for inviting you to this lunch,' he began. 'As interesting as it is to hear about whatever bollocks you were saying, I wanted to discuss your role in the production.' He held up his hand to stop her from breaking into the conversation and said, 'We can probably discuss this better if you don't use words. In fact,' he added, warming to his theme, 'from this point on, you'd be well advised to either shake your head or nod rather than speaking. I make the suggestion because, if you do say another word, I swear I'll throw you over this bloody balcony.'

She pouted, clearly unhappy with his rudeness, but Todd was beyond caring. He had intended seducing her slowly with the magic of a romantic meal, a little too much frascati, and possibly the bribe of some gold or diamond jewellery. Yet now, although it put the remainder of his plans at risk, he saw no other option except to offer a large incentive and see if Marcia was willing to be swayed. The alternative was to sit and listen to her monotonous rhetoric and that was a prospect Todd couldn't contemplate.

'You're currently singing the role of the sacristan, aren't

you?'

She replied with a sullen nod of her head, and he couldn't work out if her surliness came from a dislike of the minor role, or if she remained peeved by his abrupt manner. Because Todd was still smarting after listening to her inane babble for the previous hour, he didn't really care. 'Would you like to stop being the sacristan?' he asked softly. 'Would you like to stop being the sacristan and take the lead role, instead?'

Her eyes glinted and her smile widened greedily. Whatever animosity she had harboured was clearly banished by the promise of this unexpected promotion. 'Would I like the lead role?' she repeated. 'I'd *love* the lead role. I'd do anything for the chance to play Tosca and...'

He held up a hand to prevent her from continuing and used his cigar to point at the balcony. 'Either nod or shake your head,' he said gruffly. 'I won't warn you again.'

It was almost comical watching the emotions struggle for control of her face. He could see she didn't like being treated with such contempt, but as he had expected the chance to play the lead was something Marcia had been coveting. She tried to fix him with a look of reproach, mixed with sycophantic adulation, and then seemed to realise neither expression was going to properly convey her mood. Vexed, yet anxious to accept, Marcia nodded.

'There are two things I need you to do for me,' he started.

In truth, there was only one thing he needed Marcia to do for him. As a member of the choir, and as a person who shared a dormitory with Faith each evening, Marcia was in an ideal position to help him make the virtuous one vulnerable. He hadn't worked out all the details of his plan but he knew it would be invaluable to have an ally who could work against Faith when her defences were down. The other reason he claimed to need Marcia was simply an act of concealment. He didn't want her to speculate on his motives and thought her less likely to do that if she believed she already knew what was going on in his mind.

Coolly, he fixed her with a lecherous grin.

The subtle nod of Marcia's head told him she was familiar with this sort of exchange and he didn't get the impression she was offended. He appraised her with his gaze, aching for her body and trying not to think how contemptible he found her personality. It was something of a first for him to hesitate at the chance to wield control over an attractive younger woman, but Marcia managed to nurture equal measures of desire and revulsion. Coming to a swift decision, unwilling to let any opportunity pass him by, Todd decided that as long as she kept her mouth shut he could pretend there was more inside her head other than empty space and the fading memories of magazine pictures.

'You can start by stripping,' he said flatly. 'I want to see you naked.'

Her knowing smile suggested that she understood his motives, and that thought warmed him more than the promise that gleamed in her eyes. Reaching for the button at her throat she leant across the table and opened her mouth.

Todd placed a finger over her lips before she could mutter a word. 'Strip in silence,' he said firmly. 'Do everything I say and don't speak, and I promise you the role of Tosca. Try speaking, just once more, and we'll be rehearsing Tosca's leap from the battlements at the end of the third act.'

Her ice-blue eyes were sharp with fury, but that didn't stop her from undoing the buttons. She exposed a full cleavage, her plump breasts encased in a silky black bra, and continued unfastening her blouse until she had revealed her sun-bronzed stomach. Her build was surprisingly athletic and, without the nuisance of her banal chatter, Todd found his longing for her returned quickly, then escalated.

He watched her shrug the blouse from her shoulders, pleasantly surprised that she was untroubled by the openness of their balcony. A part of him had expected her to shrink from the idea of exhibitionism and he half-anticipated that they would take this aspect of their afternoon into the sanctuary of his suite's bedroom. But, just as she had startled him with her absence of a likeable personality, she was also surprising him with her sophisticated responses to his instructions.

Slowly, Marcia stood up and slipped the skirt from her hips. Her silky black panties matched the bra, as he had known they would, and they dropped to a deep, inviting 'V' at her crotch. The smooth look to the flesh at her cleft told him she regularly depilated, and he smiled at her commendable attention to detail. He would have been happier if she was wearing stockings – the caress of a sheer denier stretched taut over smooth thighs was one of those sensations he adored – but he didn't allow the small disappointment to sour his rising excitement.

'Turn around,' he snapped. 'Let me see all of you.'

She turned away from him, revealing that her panties were a thong design. The strip of black fabric at the back was invisible between her buttocks and he felt the first stirrings of genuine arousal shift inside his trousers. When she started to bend, and parted her buttocks, he could see the fabric tapered to a string barely wide enough to cover her anus. The slender crotch clung to her sex and Todd saw the shape of her pussy lips pressing against the silky gusset. Marcia wriggled her hips and her buttocks shivered enticingly.

Drawing on his cigar he maintained a façade of impartiality and said, 'Now, undress completely.'

Marcia turned around and met his stare with a secretive smile. She folded one arm across her chest and used her other hand to reach behind her back and unfasten the bra. Managing the clasp easily, she brushed the straps from her shoulders and allowed her breasts to fall free from the cups. When she pulled her arm away both orbs were exposed to him.

Todd rubbed the heel of his hand against his growing erection.

Her breasts were full and round and tipped with cerise areolae that stood shockingly dark against the rest of her lightly tanned skin. Neither nipple was hard until she crossed her forearms and stroked each bud of flesh between finger and thumb. Gradually they grew fatter.

He had expected to spend the afternoon seducing a naïve young woman, but with every action Marcia was revealing herself to be exceptionally experienced. Todd had watched professional strippers who didn't have her finesse for undressing or exposing themselves, and when she began to sway her hips while showing him the gusset of her thong, he began to suspect she was more than adept in the art of being a sexual tease. It was almost a disappointment to discover she wasn't the inexperienced conquest he'd been hoping for, and he tried to console himself with the assurance that she would provide proficient entertainment for the afternoon. As Marcia continued to tweak her breasts, teasing each nipple to a state of full hardness, he vowed that the next member of the choir he corrupted would be chaste before they began. Hopefully it would be Faith, his yearning for her burnt like a fever, but if he had to use another girl from the dormitory he was determined she would be an innocent virgin.

Marcia hooked her thumbs under the hips of her thong and began to peel them down. Then stopping herself, she smiled coquettishly and stepped around the table to Todd's side. Without needing her to speak, grateful she had chosen to obey that command, he could see what she expected from him: she was presenting him with the opportunity to remove her thong, so putting his cigar aside, he pulled on the hips of the underwear and began to draw them slowly down her thighs.

Marcia shivered.

He glanced at her face, wondering if she was genuinely aroused or simply trying to excite him with a brief show of theatrics. It was impossible to read anything from her pretty smile and he decided he didn't care what had caused her response. His immediate concern was slipping the thong past her knees and revealing the expanse of her smoothly shaved sex.

Unable to resist, he stroked his fingers against the bare skin.

Her sex lips were flushed, glistening with a film of arousal. When he touched a finger against her pussy he knew that, this time, her shivers weren't for effect. Anxious to have her, but careful not to appear too hasty, he grabbed her buttocks and pulled her closer to his face. Pushing his mouth over her sex he drove his tongue against her smooth labia and tasted the rich musk of her excitement.

She inhaled deeply as he carried on stroking his tongue back and forth. Had she been a virgin he would have savoured the moment, but because he was sure Marcia had bedded as many lovers as he'd enjoyed, he couldn't find the enthusiasm to treat the moment as something special. He unzipped his trousers, pulled out his erection and said, 'It will need lubricating before we do anything.'

She fell to her knees and her head moved over his lap. Her mouth was a sultry haven around his glans, sucking lightly as her tongue smoothed over the swollen dome. She kept her fist wrapped tightly around the base of his shaft, stretching his foreskin tight and making him painfully aware of every pleasure she was bestowing. When her head began to bob up and down, and he could feel her trying to squeeze his helmet past the back of her throat, Todd decided she was progressing things too quickly for what he wanted, so he used a fistful of her hair to pull her face away and made her stand up. Her smile glistened with a lustre of his pre-come.

From the street below he could hear the faraway hubbub of congested traffic, raised voices and fraying tempers. The intoxicating smell of the city was brought up to the balcony on an indolent breeze. He supposed there was little true exhibitionism in what they were doing; a voyeur would have needed x-ray vision, a pair of binoculars and possibly a rooftop vantage point. But it still felt daring and he always tried to enjoy every sweet pleasure.

'I'm lubricated enough,' he told her. 'Straddle me.'

She stepped over his thighs and began to lower herself onto his hardness. They were face to face, their mouths close enough to kiss should either of them have wanted, but Todd couldn't find the enthusiasm to show such affection for Marcia, and she seemed content to continue without that particular intimacy. Using one hand to splay her pussy lips, she guided his glans to the centre of her sex.

Todd reached into the space between their thighs and grabbed his erection, and pushing the tip away from himself he watched Marcia's eyes widen with surprise when he held it against the ring of her anus. She tried to feign hesitancy, but he could see she wasn't a very good actress. There was eagerness lurking beneath her expression of surprise, and when she did start to lower herself he sensed an air of controlled urgency governing her slow descent.

The muscles of her anus clutched him and squeezed, and she gripped his shoulders for balance and impaled herself fully on the entire length of his shaft.

Todd held himself still, savouring the sensation of her forbidden muscle as it squeezed around his erection. The pleasure was enormous, enough to engulf him, and it only continued to grow when she began to ride up and down.

'You and I aren't that much different,' she murmured. 'Are we?'

Relishing the tight squeeze of her rectum, he didn't bother to acknowledge Marcia's remark or remind her that she was forbidden from speaking. Closing his eyes, relishing the ripple of tender muscles throbbing around his shaft, it was easy to ignore everything except for the moment's pleasure.

'We're not that much different,' Marcia repeated, her voice dropping to a slow, seductive whisper. 'We both know what we want,' she explained. 'And neither of us cares what we have to do to get it. I'd say that makes us very much alike.'

Todd smiled to himself, easily able to understand how her mind was working. She had decided this was one of those mutually beneficial arrangements directors often placed on their cast: her using him to land a better role; him using her for the pleasure she could give. He felt certain she had no idea about his plans for Faith and remained positive she would never suspect as much.

He continued thrusting into her anus, studying the chill ice of her eyes as her warmth encircled him. 'I agree,' he said quietly. 'We're not that much different. But not for the reasons you suggest. I think we're not that much different because I own a car with twenty cubic metres of interior space, and the inside of your head can boast a similar figure.'

She raised a hand to slap him but he caught the wrist before she could catch his face. Then pushing himself deeper, smiling when she grimaced with discomfort, he said, 'Remember our agreement, Marcia: You don't talk and I don't throw you off the balcony.'

Pouting, she began to ride him with renewed vigour. Her enthusiasm surprised him and her pace left him breathless. She tightened her hold on his cock and began to slide up and down with a speed that made her breasts jiggle. He placed a hand against each orb, enjoying the weight of her stiff nipples pressing into his palms, and savoured the control he had over her. Perhaps she wasn't the innocent he had hoped to exploit, but he was never one to dwell on the negative aspects of a situation. As expected she was riding him with a skill that bordered on being professional, and he knew she would easily be able to wring the climax from his hardness. But that didn't change the dynamics of which one of them was in control and which one of them was subordinate, and he revelled in his position of domination.

Marcia reached down and began to play with herself. Todd's erection remained buried in her backside and he continued to tug on her nipples, but she seemed in need of more stimulation and determined to have it. Watching her spread the pink flesh of her pussy lips, then slide a wet finger against the pulsing nub of her clitoris, he couldn't help but compare her to the many female vampires he had used. Invariably they were sultry temptresses and practiced lovers, as hungry for their own pleasure as they were for the taste of blood, but he didn't think many could boast Marcia's greedy desire for physical and sexual gratification. If any man had insulted a female vampire as rudely as he had hurt Marcia, he knew they would have fed from him and drained his life's blood rather than continuing to sate their appetite. Yet Marcia seemed able to put antipathy aside in her quest for a climax and the personal gain Todd had promised, and rather than reinforcing his dislike, it made him think that she might just be a spirit after his own heart.

She wrenched the climax from his cock with a brisk twist of her buttocks. The explosion startled him, making him squeeze her breasts tighter as his length pulsed repeatedly into her arse. He caught a brief glimpse of her cruel smile, was almost hurt by the contempt he could see in her eyes, and then realised she was going to keep his flailing shaft inside her anus while she squeezed an orgasm from her clitoris.

He dropped his hands from her breasts and watched her with mounting appreciation. Her cheeks were flushed, her nipples remained hard, and her entire body trembled with the encroaching climax. Retrieving his cigar from the table – lighting it and blowing the smoke thoughtfully away from her face as she inched herself closer to release – he decided he had misjudged Marcia when he derided her for being vacuous. She was goal-oriented and self-obsessed, but Todd thought it would indicate a double standard if he boasted about those traits in his own personality and then pinpointed them as the flaw in Marcia's.

'Coming,' she grunted.

She hadn't needed to say the word because he could

feel the first pre-climactic tremors tingling through his lessening length. He considered reminding her that she wasn't supposed to be speaking, and then decided that in the light of his newfound affection for her it would be unnecessarily cruel. The muscles on her thighs became taut with exertion, her breasts swelled as she pushed out her chest, and then she was groaning with bitter satisfaction as the orgasm struck. Her pelvis bucked spasmodically, tearing Todd's shaft from her anus, and then she pressed back hard against him.

Drawing lazily on his cigar, Todd regarded her with fresh respect. He could imagine her maturing into one of those women with a chain of wealthy lovers supporting her excessive lifestyle. If she ever fell in league with anyone from the vampire community he could see her filling a role similar to his, but most likely with a lot more success. Surprised by the way his affection for her was blossoming, he regarded her with fresh respect when she glanced coyly at him.

He jammed the cigar in the corner of his mouth and glared at her. 'You've leaked your pussy juice all over my cock,' he pointed out. 'Lick me clean and make me hard. I want to fuck you again.'

Obediently she lowered her head and worked her tongue against his limp shaft. She seemed unmindful of where his erection had been and used her mouth to coax swift stiffness back into it. To make the act easier she climbed off his lap and knelt by his side. He caught a brief glimpse of her backside, enjoying the sight of his spend dribbling from her anus, then he closed his eyes and allowed her to bring him to full hardness.

'When we've finished,' she began tentatively, 'what else will you want me to do?'

He considered cautioning her for speaking, and then

decided that this time it would be counterproductive. 'How do you mean?'

'You said I could have the role of Tosca if I did two things for you,' she reminded him. She kept one hand around his erection as she spoke, drawing his foreskin delicately back and forth over his glans. The tip hovered enticingly close to her mouth and the breath from every word was a light breeze against his growing arousal. 'I know we haven't finished the first of those things,' she said quickly, 'but I just wondered if you were ready to tell me what you expect for the second thing? What else did you want me to do?'

Moving his gaze to meet hers, he spoke with deliberate slowness. This was an exchange he needed to make without arousing her suspicions, and he knew the slightest slip could upset his plans before they had properly begun. 'The girl who's currently singing Tosca,' he began, wafting his cigar through the air as though struggling to remember. 'What's her name?'

'Faith?' Marcia supplied.

'Faith,' he repeated, nodding. 'That's right.' Not meeting her gaze, wary she might see through his charade if she caught a glimpse of his concentration, he asked, 'Do you have access to her possessions?'

Marcia raised her eyebrows in surprise. 'In the dormitory? Of course. Why? Do you want me to plant something in her case? We could put drugs in there. Or do you want me to steal something from her?'

The eagerness in her tone made Todd realise that Marcia would have no qualms about helping. He nodded and allowed his smile to spread slowly. 'That's a good idea,' he said. He had toyed with several ideas for usurping Faith's vulnerability, from tempting her with the offer of whatever it was she found irresistible to slipping a crushed viagra tablet into her morning orange juice. But ultimately, he thought his goal could best be achieved if he had a fuller control over the situation. 'Maybe you could steal something from her,' he agreed. 'That would be a start.'

Marcia's hand continued to slide up and down his erection. 'Should I take anything in particular?'

He shrugged again, savouring the promise of what they would do next, and forcing his tone to remain indifferent. 'It doesn't matter,' he said. 'Maybe you could get some of her jewellery, a ring or a necklace or something. Just so long as it's an item that's important to her.'

'Okay,' Marcia agreed eagerly. 'And do you want me to bring it back here once it's in my possession?'

He lifted her from the floor and encouraged her to straddle his lap again. This time he pushed into the slippery confines of her flushed sex and steeled himself against the rush of excitement as her pussy muscles clenched around him.

'We'll talk more about Faith when we're finished,' he assured Marcia, and with a grim smile he added, 'I don't believe either of us needs to be thinking about her while we're doing this.' Yet, despite his words, when Todd closed his eyes it was all too easy to envisage the satisfaction he would enjoy when in this position with Faith's pretty face in front of him.

Faith

Act II, Scene I

Faith stood in Ms Moon's chalet, shifting from foot to foot as the foreboding sense of déjà vu grew stronger. She supposed her anxiety wasn't helped by the nightly demands of her onstage suicide – the performance had gone well but it was an intense role, both emotionally and physically exhausting – and she suspected that the choir mistress's severe frown was also contributing to her mounting apprehension. Ms Moon wore the same furious expression that Faith had seen the night before, and it was all too easy to remember the humiliation that followed that encounter. Intimidated and trying to hide the nerves the choir mistress inspired, she struggled to think how best to explain that she had made alternative arrangements for this evening. Claire had repeated her supper invitation and Faith was convinced it was a meal her friend shouldn't attend alone. But before she could broach the subject of her plans, Ms Moon rounded on her and was pointing an accusatory finger.

'Did you enjoy your punishment last night, Faith?'

Faith blushed and studied the floor. The humiliation of being spanked still cut deep and she was shocked that the choir mistress could phrase her question so callously. The pain had been bad, the embarrassment hurt worse, yet she only remembered those as minor aspects of the ordeal. The worst part, the element she was still trying to understand, was the arousal induced by the discipline.

Sure her expression must look guilty, certain Ms Moon would be able to read her damning thoughts if she didn't make a quick and vehement denial, Faith shook her head. 'No,' she said. 'Of course I didn't enjoy it.' Subconsciously rubbing her bottom, she added, 'It was a punishment and it hurt. It hurt a lot.'

Ms Moon continued to pace back and forth in front of the guttering fireplace. She looked as elegantly dressed as ever. The high throat of her long-sleeved blouse was starched and pristine and the smooth-flowing lines of her outfit accentuated her willowy figure. Clearly vexed, she shook her head from side to side and occasionally lifted her gaze so she could fix Faith with a disappointed scowl. 'You're telling me the punishment didn't excite you?'

'No, it didn't.'

'You didn't enjoy the experience?'

'No.'

'You haven't been longing for it to happen again?'

'Of course not!'

Ms Moon stopped and glowered. Her eyes reflected the dark orange flames from the fireplace. 'In that case I'm thoroughly confused,' she admitted. 'I'm confused because the idea that you might have enjoyed your punishment was the only explanation that made sense to me. I can't imagine any other reason why you would leave here last night, after being disciplined for travelling alone in this strange and dangerous city, and then make directly for the same Trastevere cemetery I'd told you to avoid.'

Faith opened her mouth, not sure if she was going to apologise, attempt to deny the accusation, or try to explain her motives for making the illicit journey. But she didn't get the chance to speak before Ms Moon was raising her finger again, and this time she used it to beckon.

'Come here and bend over, Faith,' she growled. 'I can see I'm going to have to make this evening's lesson a lot more severe. I can't think of any other way to make you realise that you're supposed to obey my instructions.'

Shaking her head, not wanting to submit to the punishment again, Faith started backing towards the chalet door. 'Please don't,' she cringed. 'You can't make me go through that for a second time.'

Ms Moon advanced, and when she stepped off the rug the click of her heels resounded from the chalet's wooden floor. 'I'll make you go through it as many times as is necessary.' She marched closer with every word. 'I'll make you go through it again and again until you realise that your virtue is of paramount importance to me,' she declared. 'Now, do as I tell you and bend over.'

Miserably, Faith could see she had no option. She had been unable to refuse the choir mistress's demands the previous evening, and she could see that tonight would be no different. Shuffling unhappily to the centre of the room she glared at her tormentor and whispered, 'This isn't right. This isn't right and it isn't dignified.'

Ms Moon settled in her chair and nodded agreement. 'You're absolutely correct, Faith,' she said. 'Punishment is seldom right, and it's rarely dignified. But neither is disobedience.' Smoothing her long skirt across her knees she gestured for Faith to bend over.

Grasping a final opportunity to escape, Faith said desperately, 'I've made plans for this evening. I've promised Claire I'll accompany her to a late super with her sister.'

Ms Moon raised a sceptical eyebrow, and then nodded. 'In that case, if you have other plans you'd better not delay this lesson any longer,' she said, patting her lap as though making an invitation. 'I'm sure you won't want to keep Claire, and her sister, waiting.'

Faith silently cursed the choir mistress as she bent over her knee. The shame of the position returned with frightening clarity, but the pounding pulse in her temples drowned her thoughts out. She wanted to ask how the woman had discovered about her excursion and why she waited until now to exact her punishment. Although she hadn't seen the choir mistress all day there must have been plenty of opportunities when Ms Moon could have called her to her chalet. But it was impossible to articulate any question and she knew, if she attempted to say anything, the sound of her own weak voice would make the predicament seem even more unbearable.

'I hope you don't think I like administering this punishment,' Ms Moon said stiffly, although as she spoke she raised the hem of Faith's skirt.

The familiar tingle of dark excitement stole through the girl, starting as her thighs were tickled by the caress of the fabric, and burrowing deeper as the choir mistress reached for the waistband of her panties. She held herself rigid, trying to ignore the whisper-soft sensations of arousal that made this torment so unbearable. The underwear was drawn away from her buttocks, the chill air of the chalet stroked her bare flesh, and her stomach churned with crushing dread.

Ms Moon drew the panties down Faith's legs and instructed her to lift her feet from the floor so the underwear could be slipped over her shoes. That moment seemed to make the humiliation complete. The feeling of exposure was heightened by the way her upper thighs were able to brush against her bare sex and Faith tried to shrink from the fact that she was submitting to this indignity for a second time.

The choir mistress stroked Faith's bottom, and as before

her touch was icy-cold and she could feel both cheeks bristling with gooseflesh. She squeezed her eyes closed against the threat of tears and tried to brace herself for the torment she was about to suffer.

There was a slight whisper through the air and Faith glimpsed quick movement from the corner of her eye, but the landing of the first smack still caught her by surprise. She sucked startled breath, clenched her buttocks tight together and tried to distance herself from the insidious heat the punishment generated. Both cheeks burnt from the crisp clap of Ms Moon's hand and Faith was shocked by the ease with which she was almost brought to tears. She swallowed thickly, suddenly sure she could voice all her arguments, and half-turned to tell the choir mistress why this was wrong and should be stopped.

But before she could say anything Ms Moon was landing another spank. This one was harder than the first, smarting cruelly against one cheek, and Faith was aggrieved to feel the sly caress of the woman's fingertips press briefly against her pubic curls. She couldn't decide if the touch had been deliberate, or if it was an inevitable accident for this sort of chastisement, but the intimacy shocked her into silence. The knowledge that her bare pussy lips had been caressed, even if the touch had been unintentional, made her feel as if she was surrendering herself to something darker and more sexual than a simple spanking for disobedience.

Ms Moon was infuriatingly swift, delivering blow after blow until Faith's buttocks blazed. The punishment didn't just redden her backside, and she was sickened to feel the invidious heat radiating between her legs. Hating every moment of the ordeal, she couldn't bring herself to imagine the view the choir mistress would have. She knew her buttocks would be the burning crimson of a painful blush, and her sex lips would be glistening as if she was in the first stages of a lewd arousal.

The torment might have been easier to tolerate if not for the other symptoms that plagued her, but they made themselves known with far too much power. Her breasts ached to be touched and her nipples stood taut and needy inside her bra. Each breath seemed harder to draw, and as she noticed this she realised she trembled with the effort of inhaling. She stiffened every time the choir mistress slapped her but that only seemed to make the stages of her growing excitement more defined. Following each blow she could feel herself inching closer to a delicious, explosive release.

Ms Moon stopped and rested her palm on one of Faith's aching cheeks. Her hand was a cooling balm against the seared flesh, and while she told herself she wanted to be away from the chalet and the hateful choir mistress, she knew that she yearned for the woman's touch to again brush against the burning lips of her sex. It was wrong and immoral, and she couldn't understand why she would desire such a caress, but her ignorance didn't stop her from trying to squirm her sex closer to the tips of Ms Moon's fingers.

'Why did you return to the cemetery last night?' the choir mistress asked.

Faith swallowed twice before finding the words. 'I'd lost my necklace there,' she explained. 'I had to return to get it back.'

'If you'd told me, we could have gone there together to retrieve it.'

'I didn't realise until after I'd left here last night,' Faith explained. 'I didn't really notice it was missing until… until someone asked me where it was.' She rushed the last part of the sentence, uncomfortable with the memory of Claire's intimate caresses and the embarrassment of what she and her friend had been doing prior to that discovery. She was thankful that she was still bent over the choir mistress's knee, because she knew her guilt would have been obvious.

Ms Moon's hand stroked lightly across Faith's rear. 'You could have come to me and told me it was missing,' she whispered. 'I could have made arrangements to have it retrieved for you.'

Her careless caress was infuriating and Faith had to tense every muscle to stop herself from shivering. She held her breath, fighting hard to resist the arousal while longing to succumb.

'I take it you found your lost necklace,' Ms Moon said softly.

Keeping her answers simple, scared the excitement would be audible in her voice unless she kept every response short and quiet, Faith said she had. The woman's hand was drawing light circles against each raised buttock, her fingers constantly threatening to stroke the bristling flesh near Faith's sex. The perpetual tease was proving more unbearable than the indignity of the spanking, and Faith wanted to scream with frustration.

But clearly oblivious to her mounting distress, Ms Moon said, 'Since you found your jewellery, and managed to return to the dormitory unharmed, I assume nothing remarkable happened to you while you were in the cemetery?' She raised her voice at the end of the sentence, turning it into a question.

Faith closed her eyes, trying not to think of all she endured in the depths of the dark one's lair. It was still easy to remember the kisses she had enjoyed, the furious arousal that swept over her and the way she nearly submitted to the hateful charms of the masterful vampire and his coven. Every second of her encounter with them was etched indelibly in her memory, and closing her eyes and relishing Ms Moon's hand against her punished buttocks, she could easily recall the magical thrill they had generated.

She couldn't decide if the choir mistress would be angry or understanding, and not wanting to risk another bout of the woman's wrath, she let the question remain unanswered. Rather than wait for her to force the issue, and either repeat her enquiry or present it in a way that had to be answered, she asked quietly, 'How did you know I'd been to the cemetery? Did one of the girls tell you I was gone?'

Ms Moon pulled her hand away from Faith's buttocks. 'There'll be time for your questions later,' she said firmly. 'But right now I'd like you to undress so we can conclude your punishment.'

Faith glanced up over her shoulder, shocked to think there were more indignities still to come. She tried to think of all the arguments she could raise to make the choir mistress reconsider, but Ms Moon's stern frown silenced her before she could open her lips.

'Undress,' she repeated, 'and then stand in the corner.'

Faith levered herself away from the woman's lap and studied her uncertainly, then started reaching for the buttons on her blouse when the embarrassment of the situation made her stop. 'I have a supper invitation,' she reminded the choir mistress. 'I promised Claire I'd go with her and meet her sister, and I don't want to renege on that promise.'

Ms Moon nodded. 'You're virtuous, so I'm sure you won't want to go back on your word. But you'll make that supper invitation a lot faster if you stop wasting time and start obeying my instructions. Now, undress and stand in that corner.'

Seeing no alternative, appalled that she could be so easily controlled, Faith went where Ms Moon was pointing and began to take her clothes off. She was surprised to see a length of bamboo cane resting in the shadows of the corner and wondered why the choir mistress would have something like that in her otherwise uncluttered room. It was easier to dwell on that anomaly, rather than concentrate on the crushing shame of stripping, and she fervently studied the limited scope of the room rather than think about what she was doing.

She dropped the blouse to the floor, and then removed her bra and skirt. Facing the wall, wearing only a plain pair of shoes and simple white socks, she wondered if the choir mistress expected her to remove those last remaining items.

'Pass me that cane,' Ms Moon instructed, pointing into the corner, and not daring to think why the choir mistress would want the implement, Faith handed her the length of bamboo. She hadn't been able to understand the choir mistress having such a thing, but now a thousand possibilities sprang to mind and none of them made her feel comfortable.

'I said that this lesson would have to be more severe,' Ms Moon reminded her, 'and I intend to make sure you obey all my instructions in future.'

'I will,' Faith promised, her voice in danger of rising to a pitiful wail, but she was beyond caring about how she sounded. 'I will obey your instructions,' she insisted. 'I'll do everything you tell me. I promise I will.'

Ms Moon grinned. 'I'm sure that's true,' she agreed. 'I'm sure that's true because you'll be aware, the next time I have to punish you, I'm going to make it a much crueller ordeal than this.'

Without another word she sliced the cane against Faith's backside. The blow was swift and sharp and stung with the severity of an electric needle. Faith pushed herself against the corner of the room, containing her cry and struggling not to fall to the floor.

Unhurriedly, exacting her discipline with methodical patience, Ms Moon swiped another stripe across Faith's rear. This one cut lower, scoring the crease of flesh where her upper thighs met her buttocks. It landed with the same cutting impact as its predecessor, but because the cane was striking such a sensitive area it bit with twice the ferocity.

Faith pressed her hands against the walls and put every effort into stopping her knees from buckling. She could feel herself teetering on the verge of tears and couldn't bring herself to acknowledge the base arousal that broiled beneath her punished flesh. Lowering her head, steeling herself for the next slice, she inhaled and exhaled with deliberate slowness.

'You won't go back to the cemetery alone, will you, Faith?'

As she asked the question, the choir mistress drew a third stripe against Faith's buttocks. Faith coughed back a groan, not sure if the sound was borne from excitement or anguish. Her body trembled before she had regained enough control to answer properly. 'No, Ms Moon,' she whispered quietly. 'I'll never go back to that cemetery alone.'

'And you'll obey my instructions in future?'

The choir mistress's voice had turned shrill and Faith thought it was reminiscent of the same cruel whistle that preceded each strike from the cane. She gritted her teeth as another blistering shot kissed her bottom. Speaking quickly, no longer caring if her words revealed her upset and arousal, she said, 'I'll obey your every instruction in future, Ms Moon. I'll do whatever you say.'

'That's what I wanted to hear,' the choir mistress told her.

Faith closed her eyes, unsure what she had agreed to but certain it was damning. She didn't know why she felt indebted to Ms Moon – all the woman had done was offer her punishment and cruel discipline – but she felt as though she owed her devotion and gratitude. She knew the choir mistress was silently gloating – it was almost possible to feel the triumphant glee radiating from her – but Faith still intended to stand by the promise she had made. In future she would obey all the woman's instructions.

'Now, turn around,' Ms Moon said. 'I think we ought to conclude this lesson.'

Faith wanted to cry at the suggestion that there was more suffering to come, but she contained the urge. She didn't want to endure any more discipline, but if Ms Moon thought it necessary, she knew she would have to suffer. So obediently she turned from the corner.

She was no longer troubled by the fact that she was naked in front of the choir mistress, and although Ms Moon still held the bamboo cane, Faith barely noticed the torturous implement. She was more unsettled by the glint of licentious appreciation she could see sparkling in the woman's eyes. Since enduring the previous night's punishment, Faith had worried that Ms Moon might be inflicting the chastisement for her own pleasure, but eventually she dismissed the idea as being spiteful and unkind. It was the sort of accusation that could be levelled against anyone who wielded authority over others, and she thought it was just an easy way to account for her own response.

But now, uncomfortable beneath the woman's approving

smile and not liking the way she avariciously licked her lips, Faith began to wonder if Ms Moon might be some sort of sexual predator. For an instant, as she turned around, Faith had thought the woman's hand had been pressed between her legs. She couldn't be sure if she had seen that, or if it was a trick caused by the threat of tears that welled on her eyelids, but she knew it wouldn't have surprised her. Trying not to make her attention too obvious, she studied the front of the woman's skirt for some sign of disarray.

'Kneel down,' Ms Moon said sharply, and Faith obeyed before she realised what she was doing. Her knees pressed uncomfortably against the wooden floor and the position made her feel more vulnerable than ever. Her face was level with the choir mistress's waist, and she couldn't help thinking there was something overtly sexual about kneeling at the woman's command. She stared helplessly up and cringed when Ms Moon grabbed a fistful of her hair. The pain in her scalp was sudden and enormous, and when the choir mistress pulled her head back she barely had the chance to realise that the shift in posture made her breasts more accessible.

Ms Moon raised the cane, and as the woman slashed it down Faith closed her eyes. The bamboo landed brisk and hard and scored a line across both nipples, and the pain of every previous blow was forgotten in the rush of agony that tore through her breasts. Faith heard herself squeal and tried to pull herself away from Ms Moon's hold, but she didn't manage to effect an escape before the second shot struck her breasts. This one wasn't as true as the first and only drew a scarlet weal across the underside of both orbs. It hurt – Faith felt as though a molten barb had branded her – but it was nothing like the exquisite pain that still sang from her nipples.

Dumbfounded, she stared up into the choir mistress's cool smile.

Ms Moon sliced a final stripe, catching both nipples again, and then released her hold on Faith's hair. She left her crumpled on the floor, breathless and confused. It was instinctive for Faith to cup her hands over her beaten breasts, needing to touch herself and try and do something about the throbbing ache, but she couldn't bring her fingers against her nipples. The shocking pulse that pounded in her breasts wasn't just pain, and she knew it would take little more than a light caress and she would be lost in the rush of an orgasm. She couldn't understand where that reaction came from, or why such cruel discipline should affect her in such a manner, but she didn't doubt that the fear would be proved right. For an instant she was tempted to test the theory, suddenly greedy to experience the thrill of a punished climax, but she couldn't bring herself to indulge that appetite in front of the austere choir mistress. Breathing slowly, telling herself the arousal was beginning to fade, she started to lever herself from the floor.

'Are you all right now, virtuous one?'

Faith met Ms Moon's gaze, noting the woman's smile no longer looked lecherous. She wondered if she had really seen that appetite in her expression, or if it had just been a figment of her excited imagination. 'Why do you keep insisting that I'm the virtuous one?' she asked meekly. 'What makes you think I have a special claim to virtue?'

Ms Moon smiled and stroked her face, and after the harshness of the punishment it was a disturbingly exciting caress, and Faith could have melted into her embrace there and then. She found she no longer cared whether Ms Moon had improper designs on her; all that mattered was that she continued to meet with the woman's approval and never again merited her punishment.

'You don't have a special claim to virtue,' Ms Moon whispered. 'But you do resist the temptations of sin. You don't steal or revel in vice, but you aren't pious about your accomplishments. You practice temperance and patience, and you have a kind heart. But you don't have a special claim to virtue. And you won't be virtuous forever. Sin is the one fact of life that none of us can avoid and eventually, like the rest of us, you will succumb. However, for now you remain truly virtuous.'

Not sure she accepted or understood the explanation, Faith could only nod. The greedy heat that seared through her nipples felt far from virtuous but embarrassment prevented her from raising the argument. Her cleft still ached for the satisfaction the punishment hadn't provided, but she knew that was a secret she couldn't tell the choir mistress. Standing naked, save for her shoes and socks, she waited until Ms Moon told her she could dress.

'Go on, then,' the choir mistress said. 'We can postpone your training until tomorrow night. To be truthful with you, I have an engagement this evening that would have to be broken, so if you've made arrangements to go with Claire and her sister you'd better get going.'

Hurriedly, Faith began to pick her clothes from the floor and put them back on.

'I expect you to travel directly there together,' Ms Moon added. 'And I want you to come back exactly the same way.' Placing her cane back in the corner she sighed and said, 'I wasn't lying when I said it before, Faith. I don't like having to punish you.'

And, seeing the wicked shine in the choir mistress's eyes, Faith suspected that was true. Ms Moon didn't like administering corporal punishment: Faith believed the woman *loved* administering corporal punishment.

Faith

Act II, Scene II

'About last night,' Claire began.

They sat in a discreet booth of the cosy osterie con cucina where they had arranged to meet Claire's sister. It was late but surprisingly busy, and the clatter of cutlery and the chatter of exotic conversations was as rich in the air as the fragrance of wine-scented cooking. The inn was unpretentious, its wooden floor and simple furnishings implying a rustic ambience that was matched by the informal service and hearty fare. Because Helen and her boyfriend had yet to arrive for their supper date, Faith had ordered the house speciality for herself and Claire. Her command of the language wasn't great, but she was pleased the staff had followed her simple instructions and added extra seasoning to their pomodori fettucine and a side order of funghi l'aglio.

Faith was savouring a mouthful of the delicious pasta when Claire's hesitant words made her start. She glanced up sharply and fixed her friend with an uncomfortable frown. The previous evening had been rich in discoveries, and in the space of a few short hours Faith had learnt that the undead really did exist and that she was destined to defeat an evil vampire leader. She also found out that she enjoyed the punishing pleasures of being spanked, as well as the magical thrill of being kissed, caressed and fondled by a group of predatory strangers. Consequently, she didn't think Claire's phrase was narrowing the conversation down to one specific life-changing event. 'What about last night?' she asked sharply.

'When we kissed,' Claire prompted, then hurriedly snatched her wine from the table and drained its contents. Then without saying anything further she reached for the half-carafe and refilled her glass.

She looked a little flustered and Faith could sympathise; her own feelings on the subject were an identical turmoil. She nodded her understanding and continued to eat the fettucine.

Claire was referring to the kiss they shared. It was a kiss that had left her wondering if there were undiscovered lesbian tendencies within her make-up; a kiss that made her doubt the great store that Ms Moon was investing in her alleged virtue; a kiss that made her face burn each time she allowed her thoughts to touch against its torrid memory. Not looking up, trying to focus her concentration on swirling ribbons of pasta around her fork, she whispered, 'Could we talk about something else, please?'

Claire shrugged, trying to mask her upset. 'I guess. If you like. We can talk about what Marcia was doing, rifling through your suitcase. Or we can discuss why you spent so long in Moonie's chalet this evening.'

Faith stiffened momentarily. The bench seat was uncomfortable against her buttocks and a constant reminder of the indignity Ms Moon had made her suffer. Inside her bra, straining painfully against her nipples, the wicked torment of the cane still burnt as though it had only just landed. The idea of mentioning what had happened in Ms Moon's chalet was enough to make her cringe and she made up her mind that she wasn't going to discuss that with Claire. 'Marcia was going through my suitcase?' she said quickly. 'Why? What did she want? What was she doing?'

Claire waved the matter away as if it were unimportant. 'She said she was looking for an eyeliner and a lip pencil. She's got some big date tonight and I think she was trying to goad someone into asking about the new fella she's seeing.'

Uncomfortable with the explanation, sure that Marcia had brought more make-up with her than Faith had ever possessed, she tried to brush her worries aside but they refused to shift. She couldn't accept that Marcia would want to borrow make-up from any of her colleagues in the choir, yet Faith found it impossible to imagine what else she might have been doing in her suitcase. 'Does Marcia have a new boyfriend? Who is he?'

Claire shrugged again and speared one of her mushrooms with her fork. 'He could be anyone. There are plenty of guys out there who like their women as shallow as spit.' Her eyes narrowed sharply as she studied Faith and said, 'Are you trying to divert the subject away from Moonie? Did she give you another dressing down?' She swallowed her mushroom quickly, reached across the table, and touched Faith's hand. 'Is that why you're currently auditioning for the role of the PMT Ice Bitch? Moonie didn't try and spank you again, did she?'

Faith forced a laugh that she hoped didn't sound too strained. 'I'm not auditioning for the role of the PMT Ice Bitch,' she said, trying to smile. 'I'm just a little uncomfortable with the subject of our kissing.' Using her fork to gesture, she added, 'But it doesn't seem very discreet to be talking about what we did last night while sitting in a public place like this.'

Claire glanced out of the booth and pulled a face. 'No one here is listening and none of them speak our language. How discreet do you want things, Faith? Would you be more comfortable if I found us an underground concrete

113

bunker? Maybe we could have separate nuclear fallout shelters, and then send our conversation over radios using encrypted messages?'

Faith replenished her glass of water from the jug in the centre of the table and sipped a little. 'Sarcasm isn't an attractive quality.'

Claire grinned and squeezed her hand. 'If you don't want to talk about it, I understand. Helen will be along any minute, and then we're just going to hear her raving about the marvels of her new boyfriend. If he's Italian, considering how conceited they all seem to be, he'll probably join in with her adulation and then orchestrate an operatic chorus so we can all sing his praises.'

That wasn't how Faith expected the supper to go, but she kept those thoughts to herself. Forcing herself to relax, preferring to talk about anything rather than tell Claire about the cruel punishment Ms Moon had administered this evening, she asked, 'What did you want to say about last night?'

'Did you enjoy the kiss?'

For an instant Faith couldn't think how to respond. She considered eating another forkful of pasta whilst deliberating a tactful answer, then realising she was just trying to avoid the question, she stopped hesitating and decided Claire deserved an honest reply. 'Yes,' she said eventually. 'I did enjoy our kiss.'

The corners of Claire's eyes creased as a smile illuminated her face.

'It excited me,' Faith went on, her voice low and urgent, audible over the background chatter of the other diners in the osterie con cucina, but not loud enough to escape their cosy booth. 'It excited me more than I would have believed and our kiss has been in my thoughts all day. Was that all you wanted to ask?'

'No.' For an instant Claire looked almost shy, her confident and sarcastic veneer stripped to reveal the shy young woman beneath the façade. 'That wasn't all I wanted to ask.' Her eyelids fluttered as she switched her glance from the tabletop to meet the challenge of Faith's bold stare. 'I also wanted to know if you'd like to do it again.'

Faith considered the invitation seriously. It was all too easy to remember how much excitement she experienced when kissing Claire. Her loins smouldered with libidinous hunger and her entire body ached to take that sweet exploration to the next stage of discovery. Although the previous day had proved a relentless revelation in arousing new experiences, she believed that her kiss with her friend was the only one that could be described as wholesome. And, seeing she was being given the opportunity to repeat that thrill, she knew there was only one answer she could give.

'Yes,' she said firmly, and making the statement was enough to release countless butterflies fluttering in the pit of her stomach, but she was determined not to retract the word. 'Yes, I think I'd like to do it again,' she decided. 'Yes.'

'Tonight?' Claire asked eagerly. She put her fork down, her partly eaten meal all but forgotten. 'Would you like to do it again when we get back to the dorm?'

Faith glanced around the busy osterie con cucina, aware that no one was watching, then amazed by her own daring she interlaced her fingers with Claire's. Her heart thumped heavily and the butterflies in her stomach heightened her anxiety. 'Why wait until we get back to the dorm?' she asked carefully. 'Why don't we do it now?'

Claire's smiled blossomed and she held Faith's hand tighter. Careful to avoid the candle that fluttered on their table, she leant closer. Pushing her plate aside, Faith raised her face to meet her friend's. Their lips touched in a brief caress that almost sizzled. It wasn't the breathless passion she had experienced while Claire lay nearly naked in bed against her, but she didn't think it was so far from that level of arousal. Their tongues briefly collided as each pushed their mouth closer and Faith became lost in the mesmerising enchantment of the way Claire was watching her. Her friend's eyes shone with adoration and Faith could see her own elated features reflected in her sparkling smile.

Her emotions were a conflicting battle of relief and frustration. The taste of another girl's lipstick, and the exciting intrusion of a tongue between her lips, crippled her with mounting arousal. She was grateful they were kissing in a comparatively public place, sure that common decency wouldn't allow them to do anything bolder. But she wished they were alone so she and Claire could progress their intimacy further. It was almost too tempting to think she could steal a hand against her friend's leg, possibly push her fingers beneath the hem of her skirt, and maybe caress the bare flesh of her thigh. Inspired by the thought, her arousal growing with every heartbeat, she wondered if she would have the courage to stroke the warm gusset of her friend's panties.

'Gosh, Helen!' Close by a male voice gasped with faux-surprise. 'You never told me your sister's a lezzer! I'd consider it a singular honour if you allowed me to be the man who cures her. Perhaps I could even cure this virtuous little friend of hers.'

Faith and Claire pulled away from each other in unison. Claire's elbow caught her plate and there was the crash of a fork landing sharply against crockery. Faith managed to avoid the candle but the back of her hand nudged a glass and the deafening tinkle of crystal shattered on the floor. Claire had caught hold of the half-carafe but in her trembling hand it looked ready to spill blood-red wine all over the white linen tablecloth. A handful of diners glanced in their direction, but the accident was forgotten as soon as a waitress with a dustpan and brush arrived to sweep the broken glass from the floor.

Claire mumbled an apology, half-standing and never once lifting her eyes to meet her sister's. Her cheeks blushed madly as she struggled against her embarrassment and tried to make polite introductions.

Faith sat back in her chair and appraised Nick and Helen. He was as handsome as ever, his cruel smile and swarthy good-looks making her resist the pull of her natural mistrust of him. In spite of his English vocabulary, he had the look of a self-assured native from the city. His smile was infuriatingly confident and he fixed Faith with an expression that seemed somewhere between mockery and contempt.

'Helen,' Claire said thickly, 'this is my best friend, Faith.'

'I'm pleased to hear she's your best friend,' Helen remarked slyly. 'I wouldn't like to think you kiss casual acquaintances with such passion.'

Claire blushed furiously and started to stammer as she concluded the introductions. 'Fuh-Fuh… Faith…'

For an instant Faith remained oblivious to her friend as she studied Helen. The woman was as attractive as her sister, her beauty only slightly flawed by her pale complexion, the pallor of her skin accentuated by the wavy brunette tresses that framed her face and curled down to the inviting valley of her cleavage. Helen's low-cut dress hugged her hips, waist and breasts, and Faith tore her gaze away before her treacherous appetites could get the better of her. She held up a hand to stop the embarrassment of Claire's stammering and said, 'There's no need for introductions; I know them both. These are the pair of vampires I met in the Trastevere cemetery last night.'

Claire looked momentarily shocked, and then shook her head. 'No,' she assured her, 'I think you might be mistaken.' She looked bewildered and Faith couldn't decide if her confusion was caused by the kiss they had been sharing, the rude way the intimacy had ended, or her reluctance to accept what she was being told. 'This is my sister, Helen,' Claire said, extending a hand. 'And, I'm assuming, this handsome gentleman is her boyfriend, Nick.'

Faith nodded and reached for a fresh glass of water. 'Nick's a vampire,' she insisted simply. 'And he turned Helen into one last night. As I recall, he turned Helen into a vampire after she promised him he could have you.'

Claire gaped, her embarrassment disappearing as disbelief and the threat of upset fought for control of her features. Clearly bewildered she dropped onto her chair and stared from Nick, to Helen, then to Faith.

Helen remained nonplussed, and it was Nick who took advantage of the silence that hovered between them. 'That's right,' he told Claire. 'Your sister promised you to me in exchange for the pleasure of my dark kiss.' His smiled broadened as he slid onto the chair next to her and glanced at Faith. 'But aren't you going to tell your friend everything else about last night?' he asked.

His gaze remained intent on Faith but he was reaching for Claire and he pulled her closer. She leant into his embrace without any protest.

'Do you want to tell her about the group tease you provided in the dark one's lair? Do you want to tell her how you went from one member of the coven to another; letting us kiss your virtuous lips; letting us fondle your virtuous tits; letting us finger your virtuous pussy?'

He was presenting her with a challenge and she knew she would have to respond, but before she could stand and defy him Helen was sitting next to her.

She placed a hand on Faith's arm and shook her head, her eyes glimmered a devilish red and her ruby lips peeled back to reveal a lethal smile. 'Don't let Nick taunt you,' she whispered, trailing a fingertip against Faith's arm. 'I thought you were wonderful last night. I know I said you were a slut, but I thought your kisses were redolent with innocence. I'm hoping we'll get the chance to repeat the experience soon and teach you a more fulsome flavour.'

Swiftly Faith reached for her crucifix and was shocked to discover it wasn't at her throat. She had replaced the broken chain with a length of ribbon, and remembered taking the jewellery off before leaving for the performance at Castel Sant' Angelo. But she thought she had placed the crucifix safely in her suitcase. It seemed absurd that she could have forgotten such an important accessory, but she could see little point in fretting about the oversight now. The immediacy of the situation called for action and not recriminations, and she quickly scoured the table for something she might be able to use.

Nick pulled Claire closer, pressing his lips over hers. Claire didn't struggle as he kissed her, melting against him and pressing eagerly against his exploring hands. Nick's fingers traced the swell of one breast, inspiring the shape of a stiff nipple to thrust against the fabric of her top, and then his hand was dropping lower. From her chair across the table Faith had a perfect view as he touched Claire's thigh and pushed his fingers up and under her skirt. Claire sighed, a soft sound that promised her swift surrender.

Nick's hand continued to slide upward and Faith could see the tips of his fingers brushing the brilliant white crotch of Claire's panties. She remembered thinking she might want to touch her friend in the same way, and was torn by the fear that she was driven by the same base force that motivated the vampire. Telling herself that her appetites were different – convinced that what she had been intending would have been affectionate and consensual – she watched Nick graze a nail against the fabric.

Claire shivered eagerly and made no protest when he pulled the gusset to one side, and Faith was shocked to see her friend's sex lips being exposed and she fought to quell the rush of arousal that touched her. She knew she ought to act quickly, needed to do something to stop Nick from inflicting this cruel torment, but she couldn't think past the idea that Claire's submission was infuriatingly arousing.

She stiffened on her chair, ready to take some action even if her mind was still idling. Helen reached beneath the table and put a hand on Faith's leg. Her touch was surprisingly intimate and the coldness of her hand reminded Faith of the excitement Ms Moon seemed to generate with her icy caress. She glanced into the woman's glowering eyes and willed herself not to be excited.

'Leave Nick and my sister to get to know each other,' Helen said quietly. 'Surely you won't deny her the pleasure of a vampire's kiss? You know that nothing is more exciting. As I recall, you seemed to be enjoying that particular pleasure to its fullest last night.'

Hesitant, Faith glanced across the table. Nick and Claire's faces writhed together as though they were devouring each other. Between her thighs, invisible to the rest of the osterie but frighteningly obvious to Faith, Nick's touch was growing more adventurous. He raised and lowered his fingertips, easily exciting Claire's pussy lips and forcing the flesh to part. Her thighs were already sticky with excitement and Faith was sickened to find the sight fuelled her arousal. Inching his reach higher he tested an exploratory finger against the pulsing centre of her flushed, pink sex, and eased it inside.

Claire moaned and pushed against him. Faith was appalled and excited, knowing she needed to end her friend's torment but unsure how to begin. She drew a deep breath, scared it awoke the memory of every sexual thought she had harboured over the past two days.

Nick worked a second finger alongside the first and then slipped them both into Claire's tight hole. Her sex lips suckled against him as he burrowed them deeper. She parted her legs, obviously eager for more, and he tried to press a third digit alongside the first two.

Writhing against him, clearly eager for his penetration, Claire moaned. It was a soft sound, not loud enough to be heard outside their booth, but Faith didn't doubt her friend's next cry would be far more forceful. Unable to just watch, needing to stop Nick from bending Claire to his will, she tried to push away from her chair.

But Helen's hand pressed tighter against her leg. The pressure of her nails bit hard into Faith's thigh and the pleasurable rush of pain surprised her. She couldn't decide if the response was expected, but the sting made her secretly covet the enjoyment of some cruel hurt.

'Don't move,' Helen whispered, enough authority in her voice to let Faith know it was an instruction. 'Don't move, stay here beside me, and let them get acquainted.'

Nick moved his mouth from Claire's and smiled rapaciously. 'What's wrong, virtuous one?' he sneered. 'Are you jealous? Does it worry you that I can excite your little girlfriend more than you could?'

Faith forced her features to remain indifferent. She made no attempt to remove Helen's hand from her thigh and tried to look like a picture of cool composure. 'You can kiss her,' she told him. 'But you'll never make her into one of your kind.'

He barked a bitter laugh and extracted another kiss from Claire's eager mouth. The fingers at her cleft plunged momentarily deeper, and then he was sliding them back and forth as he frigged her. His knuckles were soaked with the viscous smear of Claire's arousal and the scents of her musk were suddenly stronger than the funghi l'aglio and the pomodori fettucine. Claire wrapped an arm around him, pulling him closer, and she began to buck her hips so her sex was greedily accepting his forceful invasion.

He moved his face away and fixed Faith with a triumphant leer. 'You're wrong, you virtuous slut,' he told her. 'I can take her. And I'm going to take her.' Smiling wickedly he added, 'I want you to get yourself good and hot while you're watching, and then I might decide to finish my evening by feasting on your virtuous pussy.'

Faith remained stiff on her chair. 'If you're so confident you can do it, why don't you just bite her?' she challenged, and Helen drew an excited breath, her hand squeezing harder against Faith's leg.

Nick's brows narrowed suspiciously and Claire stared at Faith from behind his frown, her expression a mixture of gratitude, disbelief and horror.

'Go on,' Faith encouraged. She felt like a poker player making the biggest gamble of the night. She met Nick's inquisitive gaze with defiance and willed herself to look relaxed and untroubled by nerves. 'If you think you've got such a control over Claire, if you think you're so irresistible, why don't you go ahead and bite her?'

'I will,' he decided, and swiftly pulled Claire from her chair and placed his mouth to the side of her throat. His eyes glistened with scarlet malevolence and his teeth pressed into her yielding flesh. Then staring at Faith, his piercing gaze never leaving her eyes, he began to bite into Claire's throat.

'Yes!' Helen hissed triumphantly. Her hand squeezed briefly tighter against Faith's leg, and then relaxed.

There was a moment of pain, a pang that made Faith wish she was suffering the same pleasure that was clearly being visited upon Claire, and then she realised Helen had finally dropped her guard.

Claire gasped, her eyes growing wider and her features straining in an expression that looked disturbingly close to orgasm. She was fixing Faith with a look of hurt and disappointment, but those emotions were almost lost beneath the joyous lilt of her satisfied smile.

Helen moved her hand away from Faith's leg and pressed against her own groin. Like Nick's, her eyes glowed red with vampiric intent and her colour sat high with arousal. Not seeming to care that they were in an osterie con cucina, obviously caught up in the thrill of the moment, she raised her skirt and rubbed vigorously between her thighs.

A ribbon of blood trickled against the pallid flesh of Claire's throat. It was a shocking vermilion, disturbingly wrong against the porcelain pallor of her skin, and Faith was relieved when she watched Nick lap the blood up with his tongue.

His eyes had been focused firmly on Faith, but as he tasted the trail of crimson his expression changed to a disgusted grimace. He pushed Claire away and stood up, spitting and wiping at his mouth, and rather than looking like an aroused predator he now wore an expression of near-nausea.

'What have you done to her?' he demanded. 'What the fuck did you do, you virtuous bitch?'

Faith didn't bother to reply.

This was the moment she'd been waiting for, and while Helen was watching events with confusion, and Nick was still trying to spit the taste of garlic-sweetened blood from his mouth, she acted without hesitation. She reached for Claire and pulled her from her seat. Helen made to grab her but Faith knocked the candle from the table and it landed in her lap. There was no chance to see if the flames caught hold of her dress, or if the candle simply died in a puddle of wax, because she was busy making her hasty escape. Hurrying to take advantage of the moment she pushed her way past a confused Nick and dragged Claire with her, and they ran through the silence of startled diners as they made their way into the safety of the night.

Interlude

Part III

'Lilah,' Todd said, grinning his wholehearted approval. He moved the bullwhip to his left hand and reached out to greet her. 'I'm glad you decided to accept my invitation.'

She regarded him with a disparaging scowl, but it was an expression that only heightened his arousal. He had seen her in costumes that hid her true nature, clothes that masked her vampiric beauty, and disguises that allowed her to walk unnoticed amidst the mortals. She managed to look alluring and exciting in any outfit, but when she was Lilah, dressed in leather and looking at her most beautiful, lethal best, he didn't think a more desirable creature had ever walked the earth. The black leather basque clung to her contours, accentuating her cleavage and glistening provocatively with every fluid step. Her tight pants hugged her hips and defined the coltish muscles of her long, slender thighs. There wasn't an inch of her that didn't exude captivating charm and he was, as always, mesmerised in her presence.

'Toad,' Lilah murmured. She didn't bother to keep the disdain from her voice and sneered at him with obvious contempt. She had an ability to spit his name, or her bastardised version of his name, as though it was something unpleasant in her mouth. 'Why has my brother's pet bitch summoned me here?'

The insults stung but, because they came from Lilah, Todd was willing to forgive. She had ignored his offer of

125

a handshake, but overlooking her coldness he linked her arm in his. She stiffened and tried to pull away, making no attempt to disguise her dislike, but he still took great pleasure in guiding her along the Coliseum's lower tier.

Grudgingly, Lilah allowed him to lead and they walked towards the two figures that wrestled near the side entrance. A large cross on the opposite side of the arena overlooked their progress. It was the remnant from a papal order to prevent pillaging, and Todd noticed Lilah deliberately turn her face so as not to be troubled by the sight. He silently cursed himself for not having thought to cover the symbol of Christianity and save her distress. 'I haven't summoned you here,' he corrected carefully. 'I made an invitation.'

Moonlight illuminated the amphitheatre, silvering the marble columns and the brickwork reconstruction, and deepening the myriad shadows that populated the rising levels. The Coliseum's acoustics added a hollow resonance to their every footstep, making Todd feel dwarfed by the vastness of their surroundings. The sounds of distant traffic were a world away and nothing more than a buzz beneath the mewing of the Coliseum's vast feral cat population.

'Whether it was an invitation or a summons,' Lilah said, 'you told me to be here but you haven't said why. What do you want, Toad?'

He held her tight against him, relishing her frigid aura. Ignoring her question he pointed to the shapes of exposed cells and subterranean corridors that lurked in the lake of darkness beside them. 'There used to be a tremendous wooden floor covering the arena,' he confided. 'And the argument still rages about whether this place was regularly flooded to stage mock naval battles, or if that was done in the Circus Maximus between the Aventine and the Palatine.

Titus threw a hundred-day-long fete to commemorate the opening of this building in eighty AD, and five thousand wild beasts perished during that celebration. It's almost certain that Christians were never slaughtered in this arena, but there's no question that this was the site for the most bloodthirsty hunts and the most savage battles between gladiators.'

'I'm beginning to understand why you summoned me here,' Lilah said stiffly, snatching her arm from his grip. 'My brother no longer requires you as his errand boy, and you've taken a job as a tour guide. Thank you, Toad. It's nice of you to keep me informed about what you're doing with your pathetic, mortal life. Perhaps you can update me again in a century or two?'

He laughed, took her arm again, and managed to pat her hand without losing his hold on the bullwhip. It didn't escape him that her eyes flashed with red fury for the condescending gesture and he knew, unless he placated her swiftly, he was only a matter of heartbeats away from suffering the full brunt of her deadly wrath. In truth, the lithe perfection of Lilah's body excited him, but it was her potential for vicious and barbaric cruelty that truly inspired his arousal. More than the thrills of stockings or corruptible young virgins, it was the allure of being with someone remorselessly sadistic that made him bask in the pleasure of Lilah's company.

'I think you misunderstand me,' he said conversationally. 'I'm still your brother's errand boy. I was only thinking of you when I extended my invitation for this evening. Last night I watched the dark one's favourite defeat an attractive young challenger and I was saddened that you weren't there. I know the tournaments have always entertained you and I thought it a cruel injustice that you were hiding amongst mortals for your brother's benefit, and missing out on your favourite diversion.'

'Is there a point to what you're saying?' Lilah asked wearily. 'I know we vampires are blessed with immortality, but listening to you makes that seem like a curse.'

Untroubled by her rudeness, savouring her mounting antipathy, he continued to smile and said, 'I brought the tournament to you, Lilah.' He gestured at the stark interior of the unlit amphitheatre. 'We've got the Coliseum for the night – the most magnificent arena ever built – and I've organised a pair of attractive female gladiators to battle for your pleasure. I thought you might enjoy a night off from your selfless pursuit of the virtuous one.'

Her brow wrinkled with obvious suspicion, but she made no objection when he gently guided her towards the pair of wrestling figures. It was just possible to discern that they were both female, and Todd could see the struggle had already progressed beyond the stage where each was ripping at the other's clothes. They remained in shadows – naked hips glistening silver with sweat, bared breasts visible as black silhouettes against the midnight background – but their grunts, groans and angry exclamations were audible over the crisp click of Lilah's heels.

'They don't look like they're putting much into the fight,' she observed.

Todd handed her the bullwhip. 'Things will pick up when you throw that in,' he said confidently, leading her closer, allowing her to take her first proper look at the pair. 'Marcia's never fought before. But the mulatto is your brother's current favourite and she's something of an expert.'

Lilah rounded on him. 'Is this some sort of joke, you pathetic little man?' Before he could blink she was holding him by the throat and pushing him back against a marble column. He had imagined he was close to death before, but now that moment seemed finally upon him. Her hand squeezed tighter around his throat. The swell of her breasts pressed against his chest as she leant closer and he could see the fire that gleamed in her outraged features. The bullwhip he had passed her was instantaneously unfurled and she threw it back ready to strike its cruel length down on him with a vicious, angry blow. In the expectant silence that hung between them even the feral cats seemed to have finally fallen quiet.

'How badly have you jeopardised my plans?' Lilah demanded. 'Both of these women know me, and one wrong word from either will spoil all the hard work I've done over these past months. How badly have you fucked things up, Toad?'

With enormous effort he pushed her hand away from his throat. 'You're not wearing your disguise, Lilah,' he reminded her. 'And since you're out of your disguise, Marcia won't stand a chance of recognising you.'

Her anger remained unchanged. 'That takes care of one of them,' she growled. 'But the mulatto will be—'

'The mulatto will be able to tell your brother that you're still in Rome,' Todd broke in, pressing his face close to her ear, keeping his voice low so neither Marcia nor the mulatto could hear. 'Your bother knows you're still in Rome.' Each time he inhaled he was intoxicated by the scent that perfumed her flesh; rather than being a synthetic fragrance designed to imitate sugars or flowers, he knew he was drinking in the bouquet of a cruel, sadistic excitement. It was a rich aroma, reminiscent of sexual musk and poignantly, frustratingly, arousing. 'The dark one knows you haven't left the city,' Todd continued. 'He just doesn't know why you're avoiding the coven. But trust me when I tell you he's oblivious to your plans.' Sensing he might be on the verge of winning her over, he pressed, 'Your brother will remain oblivious to your plans regardless of what happens during this tournament. All I'm asking you to do is trust me.'

She pushed him back against the wall and he saw the arm that held the bullwhip stiffen. 'Trust you?' she sneered. 'How foolish do you think I am?'

'This is a challenge where you can have the victor, Lilah,' he said, speaking slowly, determined that she wouldn't make him resort to a panicked babble or the indignity of begging. 'I know your brother usually demands that spoil for himself, but with this tournament *you* can have the champion.'

For a drawn out moment he knew his life hung in the balance. Lilah was still considering her options and he could see she was sorely tempted to kill him. He didn't want her to end his life; the pleasure of facing her glorious fury was not a joy worth dying for, and he didn't doubt she would hurt him before she drank every drop of blood from his body. She still held the whip and he imagined she was trying to gauge the most painful spot where she could land the first shot.

'My brother remains oblivious to my plans?' she hissed.

Todd nodded. 'He thinks you've gone off because you're scared of the repercussions from some gypsy curse. I haven't told him any different. Even if the mulatto tells him every detail about tonight, he'll still be no wiser about where you're hiding or what you're doing.'

Slowly, Lilah lowered the whip. She turned her back on him and fixed her attention on the two women. 'They'd better put on a good fight, Toad,' she growled menacingly. 'Or I might just decide to drink you for the fun of it.'

Not replying – his heart still racing from the near-death experience and his arousal aching more than ever – Todd stepped to her side.

The mulatto was the dark one's favourite and not without good reason. She circled Marcia, using the speed of the undead to tear the remaining scraps of clothes from her opponent's body and, at the same time, methodically disorientate her. Carrying herself low, unmindful that her breasts were bared and undulating in the moonlight, she darted this way and that as she tried to wear Marcia down.

'Mr Chalmers,' Marcia called, her voice reedy with nerves, and she sounded lost in the darkness, 'is that you, Mr Chalmers?'

Todd said nothing, not sure any comment he could make would help. At best he knew he could lie to her and offer false hope, but he saw no benefit in adding unfair torment to her predicament.

'The mulatto will eat her alive,' Lilah sneered.

'I expect you're right,' he agreed. Being honest with himself, he thought Marcia was doing better than should have been expected. Although the mulatto was faster and more practiced in combat, he had seen Marcia trip her opponent on a couple of occasions. He also knew that the mulatto wouldn't have undressed herself, and realised her near nudity was testimony to Marcia's surprising skill. But he doubted her advantage had been won by anything more than luck and good fortune, and he thought it only a matter of time before the mulatto proved Lilah right. That glum thought was strengthened when the mulatto pushed Marcia to the floor.

Laughing wickedly, Lilah settled on one of the stone seats. She placed her elbows on her knees, her chin resting on her hands, and fixed her attention intently on the struggling females. Her sharp gaze flitted from Marcia to the mulatto, and Todd watched a smile spread slowly across her lips. With growing relief he began to hope she might show some appreciation for the effort he had made.

The mulatto pushed herself over Marcia, a knee beside each ear, her buttocks pressing down on the blonde's chest. Marcia struggled and tried to twist free, cursing and hitting with unexpected fury, but the mulatto simply laughed and pressed home her advantage. Inching herself forward she pushed her crotch closer to Marcia's face and grabbed a fistful of hair. Then pulling the blonde's mouth closer to her cleft she screamed, 'Drink me, you little bitch! Tongue my pussy and drink me!'

Putting every effort into resisting, Marcia shook her head from side to side.

Lilah shifted on her seat and Todd saw she was absently coiling the bullwhip, and not wanting her to throw the weapon into the fight so early, anxious to see the tournament progress a little further, he placed a hand on her leg. 'How are you progressing with your pursuit of the virtuous one?' he asked.

She glared at him and he couldn't work out if she resented the impertinence of his touch, the question, or the interruption of her sport. 'Don't pretend you're not trying to win the virtuous one yourself, Toad. You know my plans, and I'm fully aware of your twisted little schemes.'

Todd tried to feign innocence. 'I was just asking—'

'Keep your questions to yourself,' she spat, glaring at the fingers that remained on her thigh. 'And keep your hands there as well.'

He did as she asked and turned his attention back to the tournament.

The mulatto was moving ever closer to a victory, pushing her sex over Marcia's face and smothering the blonde's mouth and nose. The shimmer of the mulatto's juices glistened on Marcia's chin and cheeks, adding a glossy sheen to her expression of disgust and fury. Todd had seen enough tournaments to know that the battle was now in its final stages, and he made no complaint when Lilah tossed the bullwhip towards the two women.

'Did you really expect a choir girl to stand any chance against my brother's favourite?' Lilah asked.

Todd didn't get the chance to reply. He had expected the mulatto to snatch the bullwhip out of the air but Marcia seemed full of surprises, reaching out and catching the handle. Taking tight hold of the weapon she smacked it hard against the mulatto's head and used the opportunity of the confusion to wriggle free.

Todd thought she might run, drop the bullwhip and hurry frantically through the maze of marble, stone and shadow that made up the Coliseum's interior. But instead she turned to her fallen opponent and raised the bullwhip high in the air.

For an instant she looked formidable and Todd could understand a part of the reason why Lilah had a yearning for victorious challengers. He had considered Marcia to be vacuous and insipid before, then thought of her as obliging and convenient once she had satisfied him. But now she looked powerful and truly desirable, and his appreciation only increased when she jabbed the bullwhip down.

The mulatto shrieked, and her pained cry echoed around the Coliseum.

Lilah sat forward on her seat and Todd saw her lips were the deep, hungry red of a vampire preparing to feast. Her smile shone brilliantly as she stroked her tongue against her overlong canines.

Marcia cracked the whip a second time and Todd saw its tip bite sharply against one coffee-coloured buttock. The mulatto howled, pushed one hand against the ground and tried to pull away from danger. Todd had seen the dark one's favourite wield her control over countless opponents and enjoyed the vindictive malice with which she tormented unfortunate challengers, but he had never heard her scream before and he didn't think he had ever seen the expression of terror that glimmered in her scarlet eyes.

Beside him Lilah stroked a hand against her thigh.

Todd thought Marcia was showing a surprising aptitude for hand-to-hand combat. She stopped the mulatto rising and lashed the whip down a third time, striking directly between her buttocks, making her shriek and arch her back as she tried to escape the blistering attack.

Then while her opponent was still squealing Marcia wrapped the length of the whip around her body, securing the mulatto's arms, and squatting over her face, pressing her sex hard against her opponent's mouth, she roared with triumph. 'Now, why don't *you* drink *me*?' Marcia demanded. The muscles of her thighs strained with exertion as she forced her sex against the vampire's head. Her words were strained with exhaustion and delight. 'Why don't you drink me, you little bitch?' she mocked. 'Why don't you tongue my pussy?'

Todd shifted position as his erection made it awkward to sit comfortably. From the corner of his eye he could see Lilah had stopped stroking her thigh and now had a hand pressed between her legs. The fingers trembled with brisk movements and he knew she was enjoying the tournament as he had hoped. Her breasts swelled ever so slightly, making the pink flesh above her basque look ready to spill free. Her wrist began to bend back and forth as her hand worked more vigorously against the gusset of her leather pants.

'Tongue my pussy, you little bitch!' Marcia shrieked. 'Or do I need to get you excited first?'

Todd wondered if she had assumed the position deliberately, or if she was simply making best use of the way circumstances had worked for her. The mulatto's arms remained bound against her torso and the length of her body stretched out in front of Marcia's squatting view. Marcia still held the handle of the bullwhip, but there was enough play in the length for her to move it down to her opponent's groin. Keeping her sex against the other female's face, maintaining her position of control now she'd won it, Marcia pushed the rounded handle of the whip between the mulatto's thighs.

'She's better at this than a choir girl ought to be,' Lilah murmured, and attentive to every word, Todd caught the undercurrent of arousal that deepened her approving tone.

Marcia stiffened, and for an instant it looked as though the mulatto might have a chance to secure an eleventh hour victory. Todd could see half of the vampire's face and he noticed her teeth were biting into the sensitive flesh of Marcia's labia. There was too much shadow for him to see if the kiss had penetrated skin, and it was impossible to tell if he was looking at the glossy sheen of Marcia's arousal, or the cruelly spilt droplets of her blood, but he felt certain the blonde was on the brink of having her triumph overthrown.

But Marcia arched her back and then plunged the bullwhip's handle into the mulatto's sex. Her pussy lips easily accepted the thick phallus and her attempts to inflict pain were banished as Marcia pushed deeper.

'I told you to tongue me, you bitch,' Marcia grunted, working the handle in and out, twisting her wrist and making no deference for the female's sensitivity. 'I told you to tongue me, and you'd better do it well.'

Beside him Lilah gritted her teeth and spat a brief string of incomprehensible expletives. Todd glanced at her, saw her face was flushed with colour and that her body was rigid, and knew he had missed seeing her climax.

'Thank you, Toad,' she whispered, and he stared at her, amazed by the acknowledgement. 'This has been an entertaining diversion, and I don't think any woman could ask for a more romantic gesture than having her own gladiatorial combat organised in the Coliseum. I owe you for this.'

'You don't owe me anything,' he said, amazed and unsure of how to treat her gratitude.

She nodded. 'I do. And I've already decided how I can return the favour.'

Intrigued, he raised an eyebrow and encouraged her to continue, but Lilah wouldn't be drawn. So not wanting to make the moment uncomfortable, and consoling himself with the knowledge that she had at least appreciated his endeavours, he pointed at Marcia.

The blonde remained on top of the mulatto, continuing to work the bullwhip's handle in and out of her defeated opponent. Todd could see that the dark-skinned vampire was obediently licking Marcia's pussy, and was no longer making any attempts to extricate herself.

'Marcia's yours now, if you want her,' he said. 'I've used her for everything I need. And I said you could have the victor. Why don't you take her…?'

Lilah grabbed the blonde before the echo of his words died. She pulled Marcia from her position astride the mulatto, twisted her head to one side and took a moment to savour the sensation of cupping the blonde's breast. The nipple stiffened between Lilah's elegantly manicured fingertips, Marcia opened her mouth in a soft sigh of arousal, and then Lilah bit. Her lips pressed against Marcia's throat and the skin dimpled as her teeth broke the flesh. Regaling each other with eager sighs, the two lost themselves in a furious, passionate clinch.

Todd tried to remain unmoved as Lilah tore her mouth away. The bloody holes on Marcia's throat dripped with the same crimson that tainted Lilah's smile. 'Sweet,' she murmured. Her eyes flashed with momentary gratitude and then she returned her mouth to the blonde's throat and continued to drink. They groaned together, both of them making sounds that could have come from sadistic pleasure or sexual pain. Marcia was pushing herself against the vampire and Lilah writhed in response as though they were locked in a lovers' embrace.

Lilah finally broke the dark kiss, staggering back a little as she allowed Marcia to fall to the floor. The blonde clutched her bloody neck, staring up at Lilah with a mixture of shock, excitement and gratitude.

'Take her back to my brother,' Lilah told Todd.

She walked on unsteady legs and he guessed she had been affected just as profoundly as her victim. Although he knew he would never be an expert in Lilah's behaviour, he strongly suspected that the act of making Marcia had brought her to an orgasm.

'Take them both back to my brother,' she said, pointing at the fallen mulatto. 'And tell him to have them prepared for another tournament tomorrow night.'

'Tomorrow night?' Todd asked doubtfully. 'But they've just fought each other. There'll be no question about which of them will win.'

She glared at him with undisguised contempt. 'They won't be fighting each other,' Lilah growled. 'I'll be bringing a contender for them both to go up against.'

He regarded her sceptically. 'Who?' he demanded. 'Who are you going to bring?'

Her smile glinted softly in the moonlight. 'I'll bring the virtuous one.'

Faith

Act II, Scene III

'How did you know?' Claire asked. 'How did you know Nick would react like that?'

They had arrived back at the dormitory after a breathless cab journey through the busy streets of Rome. Faith's heart still thundered with an adrenaline rush from the encounter at the osterie con cucina and she could tell Claire was equally excited. Putting a finger to her lips, determined that they wouldn't wake those members of the choir who were now sleeping in their cots, Faith pulled Claire to her bunk and they sat comfortably close to each other.

Out of consideration for the rest of the girls they hadn't flicked the main light switch, but Claire turned on the peach lamp that sat beside Faith's bed. Its warming glow made it possible for them to see each other without disturbing anyone else in the room. The muted hues of the lamp made Claire look lovelier than ever, and gave her beauty the ethereal quality of an old photograph with the edges softened. Uneasy with the emotions that stirred inside her, Faith glanced around the stillness of the dorm hoping it would prompt her to say something that took the conversation away from their growing affection. Seeing the silent TV in the corner she murmured, 'I'm surprised Marcia's not watching her porn programmes. She seems quite smitten by the adult channels.'

Claire glanced along the row of beds and sniffed. 'The

snotty bitch isn't even back yet. I expect she's still out with her mysterious fella.'

Faith nodded and took Claire's hand in hers. She felt a little more composed and better able to deal with the excitement her friend aroused. Assuring herself that she was only touching her in a platonic way, determined to believe that there was nothing sexual about holding Claire's hand, she asked solemnly, 'Are you all right about all that occurred this evening? You haven't mentioned how you feel about what's happened to your sister.'

Claire's smile turned momentarily bitter. 'I haven't let myself think about that,' she confessed. 'It's sad that she's become a vampire; I don't think that could be a good life decision for anyone. But I think it was pretty low that she was going to sell me out to that boyfriend of hers, even if he was kind of sweet looking.' Rushing the words quickly, speaking before Faith could interrupt, she went on, 'And I know I can't blame that on her being a vampire, because he said she'd agreed to it before he changed her.'

Faith tried to find appropriate words of sympathy or condolence, but the situation was so new that she couldn't think of anything that wouldn't sound glib or facile. The best she could manage was a tight smile of understanding and squeezing Claire's hand.

Brightening, leaning closer, Claire said, 'And you still haven't told me how you knew I'd be safe. For a moment back there I thought you'd sold me out to Nick as quickly as my sister.'

Faith laughed, muting the sound before it could disturb the others, but still feeling absurdly pleased with herself. 'I'd listened quite carefully to what Ms Moon had to say about vampires,' she explained. 'And I'm glad I put my trust in her. She told me that vampires are attracted to particular things in blood.'

'Go on,' Claire encouraged, inching closer on the bed.

Their thighs were touching, and even though they were both fully dressed, Faith couldn't ignore the frisson of excitement that stole through her leg. Trying not to be uncomfortable with the contact, reminding herself that Claire was her best friend and they had sat this close on countless asexual occasions before, she took a deep breath and tried to summarise all that Ms Moon had told her on that aspect of vampire lore.

'Excitement, fear, pain and arousal all give blood a distinctive flavour,' she began. 'It's something to do with pheromones and endorphins and the other things they talk about in A-level chemistry.' She shook her head, knowing she was doing a poor job of reiterating Ms Moon's carefully worded explanation, but unable to recall the exact phrasing. 'The myth that vampires are repulsed by garlic comes from the effect that garlic has on your body. It's a purifying agent, it cleanses the blood and it gets into your circulation within minutes of being ingested.'

'That's why you ordered garlic mushrooms?'

Faith nodded, grinning. 'And why I asked the waitress to add extra garlic to the pomodori fettucine.'

Claire gawped with unconcealed admiration. 'You knew what was going to happen when you were ordering the meal?'

'I had an idea it might. I wasn't a hundred percent sure, but I figured a little extra garlic was a reasonable insurance policy. I'd have let you in on my worries, but I couldn't think of a way to tell you without sounding like a lunatic.'

Claire shook her head. 'I could never think you a lunatic.' Looking like she was about to say more – another compliment, Faith suspected, or a declaration of her growing feelings – she suddenly hesitated and said, 'But, if garlic cleanses the blood, surely that would make it taste better?'

Faith nodded, relieved they had passed the moment of intimacy she'd feared. 'That's what I thought, but Ms Moon says it doesn't work that way,' she explained, thankful to be able to continue talking about something that was unlikely to lead to kisses, or anything else. 'She compared it to the difference in taste between a cold slice of dead pig and a rasher of grilled, smoky bacon covered with ketchup.'

Claire's nose wrinkled with mild disgust.

'When a vampire bites,' Faith continued, sounding more knowledgeable than she felt, 'they go for the blood, but they stay for the flavour. Sexual arousal is supposed to be the favourite seasoning, and the thrill of fear comes a close second. Pain is meant to be pretty high up there too, so I guess if you combine the three you've got the perfect vampire meal.'

Claire took Faith's hand and placed it against her breast. 'What flavour do you think mine is?' Holding the hand in place, resisting Faith's slight attempts to pull free, she went on, 'If a vampire tasted me right now, what flavour do you think they'd find in my blood? I think I know what it would be.'

Faith blushed and lowered her gaze. She could have pulled her hand away but she didn't want to spoil the moment. Wanting to say something else, uncomfortable with the heady silence that stretched between them, she said, 'Ms Moon explained it all a lot better. And I was putting a lot of my trust in everything she'd said.'

'I'm pleased you decided to trust Ms Moon,' Claire said, squeezing Faith's fingers against the supple mound of her breast. 'I think it's important that we know who we can trust.'

'Do you think this could be the wine talking?' Faith asked quietly. 'I ordered it for you so Nick wouldn't smell the garlic on your breath. I'm surprised he didn't taste it when he kissed you, but maybe he was thinking about other things.'

Claire shook her head. 'It's not the wine talking,' she said firmly. Her eyes were glassy with adoration but Faith could see they were clearly focused and unaffected by drink. 'You excite me, Faith. You excite me and you make me want to…'

'My necklace!' Faith suddenly remembered. She pulled her hand away and turned to the case she kept stored under the bed. Her heart was racing, and although she knew the necklace wasn't as important as what she and Claire had been sharing, she was glad of the respite the distraction gave. Turning away from her friend, rummaging through the untidy collection of clothes and accessories, her consternation began to grow as she continued to search for the crucifix.

'Why don't you forget the necklace for now?' Claire suggested. She closed the gap that had separated them and placed her hand on Faith's shoulder, the swell of a breast moulding against Faith's back. 'I'm sure it's in your case somewhere, and if it is it will still be there in the morning.'

The hand on her shoulder felt too inviting to ignore, and the pressure of the breast was more intoxicating than any bottle of wine could ever hope to be. Faith half-turned, and was unsettled to see Claire's face very close, her lips parted in a pout that begged to be kissed.

'I was going to use my crucifix to save you this evening,' she explained.

'And you saved me without it,' Claire reminded her. 'You saved me from my sister. You saved me from her boyfriend. And you saved me from their nasty, evil schemes. I want to repay you for that.'

Faith tried to wave the gratitude away, but before she could find the necessary degree of modesty, Claire's mouth was enveloping hers. It was the passionate exchange she had feared it would be. It was a penetrating kiss that rekindled the perpetual arousal that had tormented her since they arrived in Rome. Faith struggled to find the willpower to resist, searched deep within herself to find the strength to pull away, but Claire's passion so perfectly reflected her own that she could do nothing except yield. She allowed her friend to caress and tease, letting exploratory fingers brush against her, and making no objection when she was pushed back against her bed. Claire leaned over her, a nervous smile faltering on her lips.

'I don't think my crucifix is in my case,' Faith said solemnly, voicing her worst fears. 'I think it might have been stolen.'

'We'll search for it in the morning,' Claire whispered. 'I think there are more important things we could be doing right now, don't you?' Rather than waiting for a reply, she lowered her face, and this time Faith responded eagerly. She revelled in the touch of Claire's hand against her face and marvelled at the excitement that came from their bodies pressing together. Her previous reservations – worries about the wrongness of what she was doing and fears for her prized virtue – were banished in a wave of deep, wonderful longing. She made no complaint when Claire began to pluck at the buttons on her blouse, eager to expose herself and surrender further to her friend's desire.

Claire's light caress brushed the fabric from her shoulders and she placed a gentle kiss against Faith's bare throat. Still touching, her hands exciting swirls of arousal from every casual contact, Claire moved her lips to the lacy cup of Faith's bra and stroked her tongue against the breast.

The pleasure was so strong that when she raised herself away, Faith gasped in frustration. The need for her friend to continue had never been stronger, and if she hadn't feared it would seem too demanding she would have forced her face back to the aching swell of her breast. She glanced down, surprised that Claire had suddenly stopped, and she was shocked to see her friend's expression of dismay. 'What's wrong?' Faith asked.

Gaping, Claire stroked a finger against Faith's chest. The touch was only soft but Faith felt a prickle of sharp discomfort, which continued as Claire traced a line down from her shoulder to the lacy cup of her bra.

'Jesus, Faith,' Claire gasped, 'what are these marks? Where did they come from? Has someone been hitting you?'

Embarrassed by their presence as well as Claire's obvious disapproval, she tried to brush the lingering welts away as unimportant. 'They're just marks,' she began defensively. 'Ms Moon…'

'I might have known Moonie would be behind this,' Claire growled.

Faith shook her head, putting a protective hand over her chest. 'She's teaching me all I need to know about vampires,' she explained. 'They're harsh lessons, I'll admit that. And her punishments are very strict and painful. But the penalties are going to be a damned sight more severe if I fail.'

'She's a sadistic bitch,' Claire said, pulling Faith's hand away and cringing at the sight of a blazing red stripe that lay across her breast. Releasing the front-fastener, gently allowing both breasts to spill from their confines, she winced sympathetically when she saw the weal continued unbroken in a line across Faith's nipple.

Faith saw the bud of flesh was rigid, and didn't know if it was the evidence of the punishment or the sight of her own arousal that made her turn away. When Claire's finger teased lightly against the nub she drew a sudden, startled breath. It was impossible to tell if she had experienced pain or pleasure, but she knew it was a sensation she could happily enjoy again.

'I don't know how you can defend her,' Claire complained, holding the tip of the breast between her thumb and index finger and gently rolling it from side to side. Each time she lightly squeezed a flurry of dark pleasure seared through Faith's chest.

'Ms Moon is one of the two people I trust in this city,' Faith said, lowering her voice, meeting Claire's eyes cautiously. 'You said yourself, it's important that we know who we can trust. I trust her and I trust you. Don't put me in a position where I have to choose one of you over the other because you know what I'm like. I'll make the wrong choice.'

Looking like she was biting back the rest of what she wanted to say, Claire lowered her mouth to Faith's breast. She placed a gentle kiss against the punished red line, and in that instant Faith knew she was going to surrender. Electricity charged her body and every nerve ending tingled with her need for Claire to continue. She languished beneath the sensation of her friend's tongue against her nipple, and when Claire pulled her head away Faith wanted to urge her to carry on.

'What else did Moonie do to you?' Claire asked. 'Are you going to tell me now, or is this evening just going to be one surprise after another?'

Faith didn't miss the trace of bitterness in her friend's voice, and knowing better than to argue or pretend that things were otherwise, she lowered her gaze. 'She spanked my backside too,' she confessed.

Claire drew a deep breath, and then seemed to decide not to voice her opinion. 'Are you going to show me?' she asked, not making any move to unfasten Faith's skirt, keeping her hands deliberately by her sides.

Faith reached for the waistband and popped the button. She pushed the zipper down, and then wriggled the skirt over her hips and off. After the punishment she had endured from Ms Moon, and considering the intimacies she and Claire had already shared, she thought there would be no embarrassment in revealing herself to her friend. But her cheeks burnt brightly and she cringed with the same low-grade shame that struck her when Ms Moon demanded she strip. Trying to disguise her reaction, Faith turned on the bed so she could bury her face in the pillow while Claire studied her bare buttocks.

'Jesus, Faith,' Claire hissed, but Faith barely heard the words, her temples pounding with adrenaline as Claire slowly pulled her panties away. The crotch was damp with arousal and Faith was repulsed by the sensation of the gusset sliding wetly away from the flesh of her pussy. She could imagine her labia looking flushed and dark pink, and knew the lips would be shining with the telltale moisture of sexual excitement.

Claire's fingers stroked her, and although her hands were warmer than Ms Moon's, Faith thought the touch still felt cool against the ravaged heat of her backside. 'Is it bad?' she mumbled.

'It looks uncomfortable,' Claire said quietly. 'But it's okay.' Faith could hear the smile in her friend's voice. 'It's okay, because I can kiss it better.'

Unable to stop her, not sure she would have tried even if the opportunity had presented itself, Faith lay still as

Claire began to kiss the punished cheeks of her bottom. The caress of her lips was a sweet balm against the warming red, and the rush of excitement that embraced Faith amazed her. She wanted to turn over, anxious to see her friend and return the affection in some way. But just as Faith had been in control during their adventure at the osterie con cucina, she knew Claire was in control here at the dorm.

'You shouldn't let her punish you like this,' Claire murmured, the breath from each word tickling against Faith's sensitive flesh. 'It's not good for you and it's not right.'

'I trust her,' Faith said simply.

'And do you trust me?'

'Yes.'

'Then turn over.'

Not sure what to expect, but eager to show Claire that she valued her friendship, Faith rolled onto her back. Claire remained sitting on the edge of the bed, her eyes briefly flitting over the sight of Faith's exposed sex. The sting of embarrassment was no longer there when she caught her friend studying her, and she could only admit to a heightening of her excitement, and when Claire gave her a reassuring smile, then began to lower her head, Faith was overcome by desire.

She tried to relax but it was impossible to remain still. Claire was placing her lips gently against her inner thighs, kissing lightly and slowly moving her head higher. Each movement made Faith squirm, and when Claire touched her tongue against the febrile heat of her pussy lips, she wriggled with undiluted joy.

Claire put her hands on Faith's thighs and held her face directly between her legs. For one awful moment Faith felt sure, if she glanced down, she would see her friend's features transformed into a mask of undead menace. She felt certain she would see the characteristic glimmer of red in Claire's eyes and her pouting lips parted to reveal too many teeth. It was a disquieting thought because, even though she knew the most sensitive part of her body was exposed, she would have still happily relented to her friend's vampiric assault.

But instead, when she looked, she only saw Claire's pretty face smiling hesitantly. The sight was such a relief she nodded her acquiescence without a second thought. Pushing herself into the mattress, savouring the balm of Claire's tongue as it stroked against her pussy, she basked in the rush of unbidden pleasure.

It crossed her mind that they were in a dormitory, that any of the girls could wake and catch them, or that Marcia could come flouncing through the door and see what they were doing, but she pushed the worries aside. Rather than fretting about what might happen, she was happier to submit to the moment.

Claire's tongue slipped fluidly against her sex. The warmth and wetness combined to provoke a delicious swirl that rushed up and out to fill her entire body. The outer lips of her pussy were teased and tasted and the delicate inner folds were gently titillated. But it wasn't until Claire trilled her tongue against the pulse of Faith's clitoris that she really began to savour the experience.

Until that moment Faith had felt confident she could end their experiment whenever she chose. She was enjoying the thrill Claire was giving her but she felt certain she could tell her to stop and force an abrupt end to the liaison. But with Claire's mouth lightly devouring her sex, and so many new and unbearable pleasures flooding her body, Faith knew she would have to remain there until Claire brought her to a climax.

She twisted and turned, buffeted by joy and tormented by rising excitement, but she made sure her sex remained motionless beneath Claire's mouth. She slapped her hands against the mattress, not sure if she should be trying to contain her response or surrender to its siren call. By the time the first tremors of her orgasm had started to well inside her she realised she wasn't going to have a choice. She bucked her hips against the bed, trying to move away before the climax struck. She didn't know why she wanted to distance herself from the encroaching joy – her body ached for the release she knew would come – but she struggled valiantly to escape Claire's teasing tongue.

And yet, before she could invest any proper effort into escaping, the delight was washing over her. A sparkling rush of pleasure made her writhe as the orgasm took its hold. If she hadn't clasped her hands over her mouth her scream would have woken every one of the girls in the dorm. Her body exploded with wave after wave of climactic release and she briefly fretted that she was going to drown in a blissful sea of sensory overload.

Claire shifted position and moved beside her on the bed. She stroked a stray lock of hair from Faith's sweat-soaked cheek and grinned. Her lips glistened with moisture and Faith was darkly excited to think that she could see the wetness of her own arousal on her friend's lips. She watched Claire's fingers gingerly caress her breast, surprised that there was no longer any hint of discomfort when the contact was made. Silently she beseeched Claire to continue teasing the stiff nub.

'I'd best get off to my bed,' Claire whispered, but Faith shook her head, unable to think that Claire could consider leaving her alone now. After what they had shared, after the joy she had just received, Faith wanted to know if she could give the same pleasure, and how it would feel to make Claire moan with the same triumphant arousal. Also, although the climax had been satisfying, Faith felt sure she could suffer another taste of the previously undiscovered bliss.

'Don't go to your bed,' she pleaded, but it was Claire's turn to shake her head.

'I don't want us to rush things,' she explained. 'We'll have time to do more tomorrow night, and lots of nights after that. For now, I'm just happy I was able to say thank you for saving my life.'

Faith frowned. 'Is that all you were doing?'

Claire kissed her lightly on the cheek. 'No, I think I was doing a lot more than that. I think we both were. But this is as new to me as it is to you, so let's not rush things.'

In the shadowy light Faith watched her go back to her bed, smiling at the sight of her voluptuous, sexy body, and trying to imagine what it would look like naked. The thought threatened to reawaken her satisfied libido and she quelled it before it could continue on its licentious spiral. Wrapping herself in her bedding and closing her eyes, she willed herself to purge the sexual thoughts from her mind and go to sleep, but it didn't take long before she realised her appetites weren't fully satisfied and, intending to coax her way into Claire's bed, she tiptoed across the dormitory floor.

But it was a disappointment to find that Claire was already asleep. Feeling peeved, annoyed that she would have to wait to find out what it was like to make love to another girl, she turned and started back to her own bed, when the twinkling of silver caught her eye.

Faith glanced at Claire's bedside cabinet, seeing the jewellery lying in a casual heap with her friend's mobile phone and purse. She was touching it before she realised her fingers had moved, and when she pulled it into the light she knew for certain she was holding her own crucifix.

Admittedly, Hope hadn't picked a piece of jewellery that was unusual or distinctive – the cross was plain silver and the martyred Christ figure wasn't fashioned in a way that would make him look particularly different to any other – but Faith had laced the strip of ribbon through this one to replace the broken chain.

She stared down at her friend's slumbering form, trying to think of a reason why the jewellery would be amongst her possessions. Every explanation that occurred to her seemed contrived, and somehow wrong, and she felt sure the most obvious solution had to be the correct one.

Faith remembered Claire saying she thought it important that they knew which people they could trust. And staring at the missing crucifix that had mysteriously turned up amongst Claire's possessions, Faith wondered if she should heed that advice. It didn't seem possible to consider her friend as a potential thief, especially after the intimacy they had just shared, but with no plausible explanation coming to mind, she thought it might be prudent to afford Claire a little less trust in future. Remembering she had said there were only two people in the city she did trust, she realised that number had just been reduced by half.

Faith

Act II, Scene IV

'Faith!'

The knot of arousal remained heavy in her stomach and sat there like an undigested supper. Every time she changed position, shifting restlessly and willing herself to succumb to tiredness, the unsatisfied urges made her shiver with longing. The hours dragged slowly by, her gaze grew used to the all-pervading blackness of the room, and sleep refused to take her in its embrace. Several times she thought about teasing herself to climax – and reached beneath the sheets to the wet, pink split of her sex – but at the last moment she always refrained. She fretted that a bout of self-pleasure would spoil her last hope of being the virtuous one, but that was only part of her reason for resisting the impulse. On some level she hated to acknowledge, Faith felt certain her own hand wouldn't give the true relief she craved, and she didn't think the exercise would get her any closer to sleeping.

'Faith!'

She couldn't decide whether the real cause of her unrest came from the excitement of the confrontation in the osterie, the passion she had shared with Claire, or the festering doubts that rankled each time she thought about her friend and the stolen necklace. Memories of each incident bounced around her thoughts in a perpetual, unceasing loop, and she was sure she would still be awake when dawn's first light crept stealthily into the dorm.

'Faith!'

She glanced towards the door, wondering if she could hear someone on the other side calling her name. It was whispered in an urgent hiss, not so loud as to wake the others but repeated often enough to finally catch her attention. Glancing down the row of beds she could see that Marcia had still not returned, and idly wondered what the choir's resident bitch was doing that prevented her from coming back to the dorm. She supposed there was every likelihood it might be Marcia at the door, calling her name for some reason, and decided she ought stop languishing in her bed and see who was there. Grabbing a loose robe from her case, tying the cord around her waist and pushing her toes into a pair of fluffy slippers, she started hesitantly through the silent rows of beds.

'Faith!'

She wasn't wholly convinced it was Marcia, because the voice was indistinct and only vaguely recognisable. Her main worry, niggling at the back of her mind and rekindling thoughts of shameful arousal, was that it might be Ms Moon. She could almost picture the choir mistress standing outside, wielding her cane once again and insisting that Faith needed to receive another session of discipline. The image was horribly easy to fix in her mind's eye and it made the knot in her stomach tighten. Glancing down at her silk robe she could see the shape of her hard nipples thrusting against the fabric, and she grimaced at the base appetite that fuelled the response.

'Faith!'

She pulled the door open and looked hesitantly out into the darkness.

Helen smiled at her. Her teeth glistened wickedly in the moonlight and her eyes sparkled with a greedy, ruby gleam. And before Faith could think to act, before she could find

153

the footing to step back and slam the door closed, Nick appeared at Helen's side and two pairs of hands grabbed her. Helen held her right wrist, Nick snatched her left, and they pulled her out of the chalet and into the night. Resisting and kicking, fighting with as much energy as she could invest in the struggle, Faith quickly realised she did not have the strength to escape. She briefly thought of shouting for help, and then stopped herself for fear of putting anyone else in danger. The idea of crying out only briefly returned when the two vampires brought her face to face with the dark one.

'Hello again, virtuous girl,' he grinned. He reached a finger under her chin, traced down her chest and pulled her robe open.

She made another attempt to wrestle free but it proved futile and embarrassing. Nick and Helen held her arms behind her back, only relenting their hold while the dark one slipped the robe from her shoulders. The fabric slid away from her body and her bare flesh was caressed by the night's chill air. The cord from the robe was wound around her wrists and panic struck when she realised she was bound and naked in the presence of the three predatory vampires. An icy shiver tickled down her spine.

'What do you want?' she demanded.

The dark one's laughter was as seductive as a velvet caress. His crimson gaze studied her nudity with coarse approval. 'How decent of you to give me a choice,' he mocked. 'I'm not sure I would know where to begin.'

She blushed and tried to pull out of her bindings, but the cord around her wrists remained secure. Still chuckling, the dark one shook his head and nodded at Nick and Helen, Faith had the impression he was giving them a predefined signal, and she wasn't wholly surprised when they passed her into their leader's hands before entering the chalet.

She couldn't recall if Ms Moon had said that the undead had to be invited before they could enter a room, or if that was one of the many myths she had picked up from watching vampire films.

'What are they doing in there?' she demanded. The dark one was behind her, holding her bound wrists in one hand, and she struggled to glance over her shoulder and see his face. 'You have to tell me. What are they doing in there?'

'They're acting on the instructions of my advisor,' the dark one murmured.

He pulled her closer, fixing an arm around Faith's waist in a disturbingly intimate embrace. The cuff of his jacket brushed her breast, sparking the nipple back to erection. His cold hand was gentle yet uncompromising against her stomach. The pressure of his body rested against her back and her bound hands lay over the hard lump at his groin. Its weight, thick and long and sickeningly desirable, remained inside his trousers but its shape pressed against both her palms.

'Would you like to see what they're doing?' he suggested affably, and taking her acquiescence for granted, exerting an absolute control over her every movement, he encouraged her towards the dorm's window. 'Come with me, virtuous one. Let me show you.'

Faith glanced through the glass, sure the curtain had been closed before and certain that Nick or Helen had opened it so she could watch. The pair were gathered in the centre of the dorm, their eyes glowing dull crimson as their heads bobbed in whispered discussion. As well as drawing the curtain aside they had also opened the window and Faith could hear a dim murmur of their conversation. She couldn't make out anything coherent from what they were saying, and only suspected they had reached a decision when they nodded curtly and then went to opposite ends of the dorm.

'What are they doing in there?' she said indignantly. 'They shouldn't be touching the rest of the choir. I'm the virtuous one. I'm the one you want.'

'How right you are,' the dark one confirmed. 'And I don't think you know how badly I do want you.'

The lust that carried his words sank a deep spike of arousal into her stomach, but she told herself to ignore the response. Her position in front of the window showed the inside of the dorm and her own frightened reflection. The vampire behind her was invisible in the glass surface, but she didn't need to look back to confirm he was still there. His arm remained across her stomach and the pressure of his erection continued to swell against her hands.

'You'll see what they're doing soon enough,' he promised. He brushed the hair away from her neck, and when he next spoke the movement of his lips trembled against her skin. 'My advisor assured me you'd get a lot out of this,' he whispered. 'So why don't you just relax and enjoy the show?'

She made another attempt to pull away from him, but it was only a token gesture and they both knew it wouldn't get her any closer to escape. The dark one's mouth remained against her throat and Faith had no choice but to suffer his attention and watch what was happening through the dormitory window.

Helen stepped past the unoccupied bed where Marcia should have been, and walked towards the end bunk where Brenda Lace slept. Brusquely, she pulled the sheet from Brenda's sleeping form and her eyes grew wide with avid appreciation. Faith had a chance to glimpse Brenda, no pyjamas but wearing bra and panties, and then Helen was climbing over the girl. She tugged her skirt up to allow her legs more freedom to move, and straddled over Brenda's unsuspecting body. There was something overtly sexual in the way she assumed the position and Faith watched with a mixture of disgust and intrigue as Helen stole a kiss from the sleeping girl.

Her obvious enthusiasm was disquieting, and Brenda's eager response was equally hard to accept. Faith thought that if anyone had been looking through this window earlier in the evening they would have seen her and Claire in an identical liaison, and she tried to shrink from the comparison. Uncomfortable with her growing unease, she deliberately turned away from Helen and studied the opposite corner of the dorm.

Nick stood over Deborah Cummings, caressing her cheek with his fingertips. Her sleep remained unbroken but she responded to his touch with an eager sigh. Turning towards him she made no complaint as he slipped the sheet from her bed and began to unbutton her nightshirt.

Caught up with growing arousal, worried for her fellow members of the choir but also envious of the pleasures they were enjoying, Faith licked her lips.

Nick exposed Deborah's breasts and then smiled with vampiric appreciation. Both orbs were ripe and full, the nipples standing erect. He lowered his mouth over one throbbing tip and Faith could see his teeth pressing into the stiff flesh.

She clenched her legs together, stung by sudden excitement, and understood exactly why Deborah arched herself towards his bite. Her own breasts ached for a similar sinister kiss, and when the dark one's wrist brushed against her chest as he adjusted his hold, she was treated to an echo of how she imagined that thrill would feel. It was enough to make her want to squirm against his erection and she had to use all her willpower to resist the urge.

Then movement from the other end of the dorm made Faith turn away from Nick.

Helen had either lost interest in Brenda or satisfied her depraved appetite. Whatever the reason she had moved on, past Marcia's empty bed and Faith's own vacant one, to where Jenny Foulkes lay. She wasted no time in stripping the sheet away from Jenny's body and knelt hungrily between her legs, and from her position at the window Faith had a perfect view of Helen's mouth working furiously against the choirgirl's sex. Jenny didn't look as though she was awake, her movements had the guileless lethargy of slumber, but that wasn't affecting her obvious enjoyment. She writhed beneath Helen's tongue and Faith could see the choirgirl's mouth parting. Her low moan trailed through the open window.

'Why aren't any of them waking up?' Faith asked.

The dark one brushed a soft kiss against her neck and pressed his body more forcefully against hers. The thrust of his erection swelled against her palms and she secretly relished its obscene presence. She knew she would only have to part her hands slightly to feel the vampire's hardness against her naked buttocks, and suspecting that he could satisfy her unfulfilled arousal, she valiantly fought the urge. The idea left her breathless but she wouldn't bring herself to surrender so easily.

'Why aren't they waking up?' she asked again. 'What have you done to keep them asleep?'

'We vampires are very familiar with the night,' the dark one explained, his tone a rich, intoxicating syrup. Each word caressed her ear as intimately as his fingers stroked her bare flesh. 'We move in shadows, we live alongside dreams, and we know how to take best advantage of sleeping innocents.'

Jenny shifted position on her bed, bucking her hips to meet Helen's mouth, and made a clumsy attempt to wrap her thighs around the vampire's shoulders. Clearly in control of the situation, determined to dominate rather than submit, Helen pushed the girl's legs back to the bed and devoured her sex. Faith could see the vampire's mouth was glistening wetly, but because there was no light in the dorm she couldn't work out if the moisture was blood or sexual arousal. She supposed there was every likelihood it could be both, but wouldn't let her thoughts follow that avenue.

'Watch them,' the dark one insisted, and Faith obeyed the instruction, wrenching her gaze from Helen and turning to see what Nick was doing. He had moved along the dormitory with the same swiftness as Helen and been through two other beds since exposing Deborah Cummings. Laura Smith's sheet had been stripped away from her skinny frame and she moaned and writhed softly in her sleep. One hand clutched her own sex and her wrist worked vigorously back and forth. Kelly Welles twisted her legs together, one hand grasping her own breast, while Nick moved onto where Tanya Sharpe lay.

He placed his hand in the mop of her loose perm and held her against the bed as he extracted a kiss. Tanya remained asleep but she still reached out for him, and they held one another in a brief but passionate embrace. Nick's hand slid against her hip, caressing the flesh before moving towards her thigh, then Tanya was gasping with obvious, urgent need.

Mesmerised by the scene, her excitement more inflamed than she dared admit, Faith rubbed her thighs together. The friction produced an infuriatingly dry warmth, a pale shadow of the attention she desperately craved, but she supposed it was better than nothing and a lot safer than the alternative of surrendering to the dark one. Trying to keep her movements surreptitious she prayed the vampire behind her wouldn't notice her arousal.

'Not her,' the dark one growled. He rapped on the window, a deafening sound after the expectant silence, and Faith saw he was pointing at Helen. 'He told us not to touch that one,' the dark one reminded her. 'And we're going to adhere to that instruction.'

Faith glanced at Helen and saw she was standing over Claire's bed. Helen had pulled the sheet away from her sleeping sister and smiled longingly at her throat. The vampire glared at the dark one, petulance obvious in the way her brows knitted together, and there was no question that she had heard what he said even though he hadn't raised his voice. Tilting her chin defiantly, Helen said, 'She's my sister.' Her voice was lowered to a vicious whisper as she added, 'She's my sister and I should be able to take her if I want.'

'I don't care who she is,' the dark one grumbled. 'He said we weren't to touch her, and we're going to do exactly as he said.'

Glaring angrily at the leader, making her annoyance obvious, Helen stepped away from Claire's bed and moved on to Wendy Byrne.

Faith tried to rationalise what the dark one had said but it made little sense. From what she had learnt it was hard to imagine the dark one following the instructions of any advisor. Ms Moon had said that the black-hearted vampire behind her and his sister, Lilah, led the coven. And the choir mistress had indicated that it was a cruel dictatorship. But the dark one spoke as though he was acting on the instructions of a greater power, and Faith wondered if there were other opponents for her to face who held greater positions within the vampire hierarchy.

She was still puzzling over the statement as Helen pulled Wendy Byrne from her bed and bit into her shoulder.

'No!' Faith protested, but the dark one's lips moved into a smile against her neck and Helen made no attempt to stop what she was doing. She buried her teeth into Wendy's throat and began to drink gluttonously. Trails of blood spilt from her mouth, drawing dark lines down Wendy's throat and over her breasts as she gasped with climactic pleasure. The sheet had fallen from her body, exposing the fact that she slept naked, and her nipples stood furiously hard. Even as her skin paled, and the blood was drained from her body, Faith noticed the tips of her breasts remained painfully taut.

'She can't do that to Wendy,' Faith hissed.

'I think you'll find she can,' the dark one assured her. 'And even if she were awake, I don't think Wendy would complain. Would you?'

Just then Wendy's eyes opened wide and she stared at Faith with an expression of perfect understanding. She didn't seem to mind that Helen was drinking from her throat, or that one of the woman's hands was cupping her breast and squeezing cruelly tight. Moreover, judging by the sparkle in her eyes, Faith thought Wendy looked on the verge of an orgasm and was about to be visited by that blissful release.

'Make her stop,' Faith begged.

'What on earth for?'

'Please,' Faith insisted. 'Please make them stop.' She glanced at Nick and saw he was sucking on the nipple of Charlotte Fry. 'Please,' she pleaded.

'Are you suggesting an exchange of favours?' the dark one asked. 'Are you proposing that I should do this favour for you and make them stop, and that you'll do something for me in return?'

Faith twisted her head around so she could see the leer of his smile. 'Is that why you came here?' she asked. 'Are you trying to force that sort of bargain from me?'

He shook his head. 'I was just trying to take advantage of an opportunity,' he confessed. 'But you don't need to watch me while we're talking. You'll be more comfortable if you keep looking through the window.'

She didn't do as he instructed, preferring to defy his order. 'Aren't you supposed to fear me?' she asked. 'Aren't I supposed to be the bringer of your ultimate downfall? Shouldn't you be trying to avoid me, rather than turning up at my dorm and tormenting me like this?'

His laughter was edged with contempt. 'You think I'm supposed to fear you? I've lived for more than four centuries and fed from the strongest women that ever roamed this earth. Do you really think I'm going to fear some nuisance of a choirgirl?'

'I'm the virtuous one,' Faith reminded him. 'I'm the virtuous one and it's my destiny to—'

'You're no more virtuous than that slut,' he said, pointing towards Helen.

Faith glanced in the direction he indicated, disturbed to see that Nadine Brown was now responding eagerly to Helen. She couldn't decide if the girl was awake or acting in her sleep, but there was no chance of missing the enthusiasm she put into returning Helen's passion. She raised her hips so her sex could meet the attention of the vampire's tongue, and buried her face greedily against Helen's sopping pussy. Their exchange was so torrid Faith could hear the wet lapping of one drinking eagerly from the other.

'I'm the virtuous one,' she said weakly.

The dark one continued to chuckle. 'I'm beginning to doubt that,' he confided. 'I think your virtue is all but spent.' Shifting his gaze momentarily, rapping on the window, he called for Nick and Helen to stop what they were doing, and with grudging obedience they both walked to the dormitory door. Faith suspected they had been ready to leave the room anyway because, aside from Claire's bed, they seemed to have visited every other occupied bed in the dorm. She also realised this was another prearranged part of the evening because the dark one didn't need to offer any further instructions to either of the vampires.

Helen rushed to the dark one's side and placed her mouth over Faith's right breast. Nick did the same at her left and Faith was treated to the gorgeous pleasure of having both nipples sucked and teased simultaneously. She complained, told them both to stop and demanded the dark one should let her go, but she could feel herself responding to the rushing swell of pleasure. No longer able to resist, giving in to the heady joy of each new experience, she parted her hands and allowed the weight of the dark one's erection to press against her buttocks.

'How are you supposed to vanquish me, you fucking harlot?' the dark one whispered vehemently, reaching down and placing his hand against Faith's pussy. His fingertips were a shock of icy cold, instantly quashing the heat that had nestled there. She begged for him to stop, insisting that he couldn't – and shouldn't – be so intimate, but she still parted her legs to make herself more accessible.

Nick knelt on the floor with one hand smoothing up her left thigh. His mouth repeatedly sparked slick delight from the tip of her left breast and she could feel herself rushing towards the climax she needed.

Still suckling against Faith's right breast, Helen slipped her fingers between the dark one's groin and Faith's buttocks.

Faith partly expected to feel the cheeks being delicately caressed, or possibly scratched by Helen's viciously long fingernails, but instead she was appalled to realise that the vampire was unfastening the dark one's trousers. His erection was released from its confines and Faith could feel every inch pressing eagerly against her. She glared at the three of them, tears threatening to blur her vision. It was impossible to work out if her distress came from the fact that she was helpless, that she was being tormented by their kisses, or if she was fighting the urge to admit her own excitement. And the issue didn't become any clearer when the dark one's erection pushed against her pussy lips. The hand against her stomach moved lower and his icy fingers spread her sex open.

His touch remained freezing against her growing heat, and she knew she should have been repulsed by his hateful, unsolicited attention, but she couldn't deny he was on the verge of sating her unfulfilled need.

'You're fucking close, aren't you?' he whispered.

There was no point in lying. Sobbing miserably, Faith nodded.

He pushed Helen's hand away and moved his erection so the glans rested over the centre of her sex. Faith wondered if this would be a chance for her to escape, but it was a distant thought and she knew she was really beyond resisting her base instincts. She made no complaint when the dark one rubbed a finger over her clitoris, and only shivered with anticipation. The arousal that pushed at her sex was long, thick and deliciously hard. She had thought there might be some sort of heat coming from his length, but like his touch and kisses his erection only radiated an icy chill. Nevertheless, she was stung by the sudden need to know how that hardness would feel if she could take it between her pussy lips.

But instead of penetrating her, instead of pushing into her needy sex, he pressed his mouth against her throat. Faith stiffened in his embrace, hoping he would decide to bite her. The pressure of his teeth on her neck was an exquisite agony that made her yearn for more, and she could imagine the euphoria of feeling his mouth suck the blood from her.

'Do you know,' he mused thoughtfully, 'I could take you now, if I wanted?'

She contemplated pushing against him, anxious to have his length penetrate her sex and desperate to feel the painful pleasure of his kiss. It was only because she didn't know which she wanted most that she didn't succumb to either impulse. The mouths at her breasts were exciting whorls of swirling arousal and the promise of a climax was closer than it had been since Claire thanked her for what happened in the osterie con cucina. She glanced down at the two vampires and wasn't surprised to see them leering up at her.

'I could take you now,' the dark one breathed. 'I could do it without my advisor's contrived plans and without any worries about curses and insipid gypsies. I could bite your sweet little throat and drain your virtuous fucking body here and now.'

She swallowed thickly, her need for him so strong it almost hurt. 'Why don't you?' she asked weakly. She couldn't decide if she was defying him or begging him. 'If you think you can do it, why don't you?'

He chilled her with his nasty laughter and pushed her away, and with her hands tied she fought for balance, lost her footing, stumbled and fell to the floor. The cruel way he discarded her made her feel used and sordid, and the unsatisfied knot in her stomach only made her feel more degraded.

'You had your chance,' she gasped. 'Why didn't you take it?'

'I've been told I'll see you fight tomorrow night,' he declared. 'It's a form of entertainment I enjoy, and I think the promise of that pleasure can make me defer my gratification for twenty-four hours.'

Faith stared at him, not understanding but reluctant to expose her ignorance. Shivering, and more determined than ever that he wouldn't see her upset, she said, 'I'm going to defeat you.'

He laughed again, seeming to find something in her response genuinely amusing. Nick and Helen stood on either side of him and they joined his mirth.

Hating the way the three of them stared at her, determined to force some reaction other than the dark one's contemptuous laughter, Faith added, 'I'll defeat you, and I'll rip the cold black heart from your body.'

His amusement ceased as if flicked like a switch. 'I don't think you will do that,' he said, stepping closer, pushing his terrifying frown into her face. 'You can say the words, you can repeat them over and over from now until tomorrow night, but I promise you this much: they'll be the last words you hear before I've drained the blood from your virtuous body.'

She expected him to say more, but he took one glance towards the brightening horizon, and then he, Nick and Helen all disappeared.

Interlude

Part IV

'Eat my pussy, you filthy bitch!' Marcia roared.

Todd rushed into the suite unable to believe it had happened again, and so soon.

The mulatto lay with her back on the floor and Marcia straddling her face. The former choirgirl held her opponent in place, securing her arms with the bullwhip. She squashed her sex against the mulatto's mouth and clearly revelled in the pleasure of demanding each kiss. Her pussy looked swollen with need, the lips dark pink and flushed. Todd could see her flesh was sodden with viscous arousal and smears of the wetness daubed against the mulatto's cheeks and chin.

'Eat my pussy,' Marcia demanded again, and obediently the mulatto did as she was told. Her tongue snaked greedily against the wet slit of Marcia's cleft, then plundered the glistening pink folds. The wicked gleam in her vampiric smile was dulled and Todd remained dumbfounded that the dark one's champion could be so easily cowed. He watched the scene a moment longer, enjoying the way the blonde relished her triumph. She put so much effort into bucking her hips and forcing her opponent to surrender, that she looked like a different female to the prim and vacuous choirgirl he had first encountered. He supposed part of the change was due to her newly acquired status as a vampire, but that explanation didn't tell him why Marcia had been able to succeed at the Coliseum or how she had done it so easily.

'Let her go, Marcia,' he said, clapping his hands as he entered the suite. 'You've confirmed another success.' She fixed him with a vicious glare but he ignored the expression's venom. 'There's still a lot more training to do before you face tonight's challenge,' he said firmly. 'Let her go.'

Grudgingly Marcia levered herself away from the mulatto. She made no attempt to help her opponent from the floor, instead sauntering to Todd's side. Rather than playing the role of the vicious harpy she tested a coquettish smile for him. It sat incongruously with her dishevelled hair, scratched skin and near nudity, but he saw no reason to let her think she didn't remain charming. Because one breast was peeping from her rent blouse, the cerise tip standing rigid beside him, he found it easy to smile for her.

'I beat her again,' Marcia said, pointing as the mulatto struggled to release her arms from the bullwhip and then get up from the floor. Then lowering her voice to a conspiratorial whisper, pushing her face close to his ear, she added, 'I don't think she's very good.'

'She is very good,' he said, stepping cautiously away. 'But I think you might just be better.' Now she was a vampire, Todd thought Marcia appeared more desirable than ever. The gaunt pallor suited her better than the sun-bed tan she had worn, and the flush of colour in her cheeks gave her face vivacity. She seemed genuinely pleased by his praise but he was prudent enough to be wary of the newly made undead. The acquisitive taste for blood, and the conviction that everyone should enjoy the same revelatory pleasures they were now experiencing, made them uncommonly dangerous. Even if she believed him to be her best friend in the world, Todd knew there was always the risk that Marcia might still decide to make him or take him and he wanted neither. There were fortunes to be made from doing the dark one's work, and Todd didn't believe they could be accomplished or appreciated if he was either dead or undead. As the dark one's closest mortal advisor he was afforded protection from those in the coven under penalty of their leader's strongest wrath. Even Lilah obeyed her brother's insistence on this point, but Marcia was newly made and still sure that she could feast on anyone she desired. And considering the way she had repeatedly defeated the dark one's favourite, Todd didn't think her confidence was misplaced and he treated her with a good deal of caution. 'Drink from her for a little while,' he said, pointing at the fallen mulatto. 'I don't want you tired out before tonight.'

He could have blamed the mulatto's defeat on a number of aspects. It was midday and, although they were all protected from the sun by the heavy curtains at the window, he knew that vampires never operated at their best during daylight. But that same argument could be raised against Marcia and she wasn't allowing the hour to spoil her consistent record of victories. He supposed the mulatto had been initially surprised by Marcia's first win, and reasoned that she might have fallen into the mindset of believing her opponent unbeatable. But he wasn't ready to discount the idea that the mulatto had lost simply because Marcia was the superior challenger.

'What's happening tonight?' Marcia asked with veiled curiosity. 'I thought I was going to take the lead in Tosca this evening?'

Since Lilah had told him of the night's impending fight, Todd had been testing and training Marcia, trying to prove that she was worthy to replace the dark one's favourite. In every trial so far she had proved herself the victor, and even when he had stacked the odds against her, and forced her to stand facing a wall while the mulatto whipped her bare backside, Marcia had pulled a surprise defeat from nowhere.

'Mr Chalmers?' Marcia called, snapping him from his reverie. She knelt beside the fallen mulatto, her mouth against the woman's neck. Her lips were bloodied, he could see her teeth were stained dark pink when she glanced up to talk to him, and her eyes shone with a wicked scarlet glint. Her cerise nipples stood as hard as bullets. 'What's happening tonight?' she asked. 'I thought I was going to take the lead in Tosca this evening. That's still going to happen, isn't it?'

He shook his head and tried to find a diplomatic expression. 'There's been a change of plan,' he confided. 'You're needed for something far more important than mere singing.'

Marcia did not look pleased. 'What change of plan?' she demanded indignantly. 'You promised me, if I stole that necklace for you and placed it with Claire's possessions, the role was mine. You promised me, Mr Chalmers. You promised.'

He didn't get the chance to respond.

The mulatto had looked dazed and dumbfounded while Marcia fed from her, but she managed to recover with starling speed. Kicking Marcia's legs from beneath her, knocking her to the floor then pinning her down, she pushed her sex over the blonde's face and nuzzled her mouth against Marcia's.

There was a brief but vigorous struggle. Marcia tried to kick and wrestle her way free but the mulatto fought valiantly to maintain control. Her head was lowered to Marcia's cleft and she pushed her tongue deep into the inviting wetness. Keeping her hands fixed on Marcia's thighs, holding her hard against the floor, she didn't stop licking until Marcia had finally ceased protesting. Eventually the mulatto sat back on her haunches, a smile playing on her tired features as she forced a defeated Marcia to lap at her pussy. Shivers of pleasure rippled through her and made her breasts tremble enticingly.

Todd blinked, wondering if that was all it took to defeat Marcia. The mulatto had caught her off guard, the blonde's attention elsewhere, and she had finally been overpowered. Amazed that it could happen, wondering if this should affect the advice he had intended to give the dark one, he clapped his hands to signify an end to the fight.

The mulatto shook her head defiantly. 'I'm the dark one's favourite,' she growled. 'You should let me feed from this bitch until she's drained,' she added, wriggling her hips, squirming her pussy hard against Marcia's mouth.

Todd stepped closer to the curtain, his frown deepening at the threat of insurrection. The mulatto did finally climb away from Marcia but she fixed him with a mutinous glare. He had seen vampires preparing to feast before and knew, despite his status as the dark one's advisor, the mulatto was ready to risk her leader's anger and bite him. 'Don't make me destroy you,' he warned. 'I'd regret having to do that.'

The mulatto sneered as though the suggestion was ridiculous. 'I've just beaten that vicious bitch,' she said, pointing at Marcia. 'I've been the dark one's champion for countless years. What makes you think you could destroy me?'

Marcia watched the budding confrontation with a hungry leer. Slyly, almost as though trying to keep the action a secret, she pulled the bullwhip from the floor and began to coil its length in her hands. Todd only needed to glance at her eyes to know she would side with the mulatto if she thought it could work to her advantage. It was all too easy to recognise the traits of an opportunist because he saw one each morning when he stood before the shaving mirror. Acting quickly, not allowing indecision to leave him in jeopardy, he tugged at the curtain and allowed a brief shard of sunlight to pierce the gloom.

Marcia turned her face away, shielding her eyes as she roared with pain.

The mulatto shrieked and dropped to her knees.

The bullwhip fell forgotten from Marcia's hand and skittered along the floor.

The cries of both vampires were echoing around the room before Todd had pulled the curtain back into place. Determined to drive home his advantage while he still had the chance, he walked between the two and retrieved the bullwhip. 'Both of you bend over,' he growled softly. 'Before we have any more training, I think you both need a lesson on proper respect for my authority.'

The prospect of rebellion still remained in the mulatto's eyes, but he could see her appetite was no longer as strong. Still smarting from the dose of sunlight, yet seeming determined to show some defiance, she waited until Marcia had bent before she deigned to obey Todd's instruction.

He took a moment to collect his thoughts, his heart still racing from the mortal threat the mulatto had posed. If there had been a cigar close to hand he would have taken it to steady his nerves. It briefly crossed his mind that his job as the dark one's advisor would one day prove his downfall. And, not for the first time, he wondered if he should dissolve the unwritten partnership he had with the vampires and their coven.

But when he saw the mulatto and Marcia bent over for him, their perfect backsides thrusting into the air, he decided the job had enough fringe benefits to merit the risks.

They stood so close together their hips touched. It was something of a contrast to see the mulatto's coffee-coloured skin against the alabaster of Marcia's, and as he studied them both, Todd realised he had no intentions of willingly leaving the dark one's employment. As long as the vampire needed an aide who could walk in sunlight, Todd knew he would have a lucrative income and a lifestyle that was replete with opportunities like this one.

Without thinking about what he was doing, he coiled the whip into a large loop. The desire for a cigar remained with him, but this time it was less to steady his nerves and more to congratulate himself on the success of holding court over two grudgingly subordinate vampires. Drawing his arm back, throwing all his strength into the blow, he slapped the whip across both pairs of buttocks.

Marcia gasped and the mulatto released a low growl of protest. A perfect line of red blossomed across all four cheeks.

'Who's in charge?' Todd asked simply.

'You are,' Marcia said quickly, but the mulatto grunted something incomprehensible.

Todd raised the whip and slashed it down hard against her rear. It struck with a resounding crack and he had the satisfaction of seeing her tremble. Two cords of the coiled whip had sliced her buttocks and the welts blazed viciously.

'Who's in charge?' he asked again. 'I didn't hear you.'

'You are,' she spat angrily.

He placed a condescending hand against her bottom and patted the punished cheeks. His fingers lingered against her, delighting in the smoothness of her behind and itching to brush closer to her sex. Because she was bent double her pussy lips were visible and infuriatingly accessible.

But he resisted the urge to touch. He knew her inviting wetness would be frigid against his fingertips and the thought excited him greatly. Yet he felt it important that she recognised him as her superior before he gave into the temptation of his libidinous impulses. There would be no chance to use sunlight against her later in the day, and while he did have other weapons within his arsenal he knew none would be as effective as the burst of sunlight had proved.

Sharply he swept the whip down again. It struck with uncompromising force, and as he expected it slapped against the mulatto's pussy lips.

Hearing the crisp retort, Marcia flinched as if she had received the blow, but Todd didn't notice, his attention fixed on the mulatto as she tried to cope with the explosion of pain. The muscles of her thighs were tense with exertion and tremors of disquiet undulated through her buttocks. It didn't worry him that the discomfort might be more than she could handle. All the vampires he had ever known seemed to have a greater tolerance for pain than any mortal, and he had met a lot, like the mulatto, who took bitter satisfaction from receiving punishment. As he had expected, her exposed pussy lips began to pout with a lustre of wanton wetness.

'Tell me again,' he growled. 'Who's in charge?'

'You're in charge, Mr Chalmers,' the mulatto snarled. 'You're in charge.'

He grinned to himself and rubbed the stiffness at the front of his trousers. He felt confident that he could have either of them and knew his only problem was the decision of which he should take first. Marcia's pussy lips gaped and were wet from the mulatto's tongue, and he didn't doubt she would appreciate having his cock inside her. Previous experience had taught him the mulatto was always receptive after the exertion of a challenge, and he idled over the choice. Trying to gauge if one was more responsive than the other, he slapped the whip against Marcia's arse and then the mulatto's. They both bit back their sounds of complaint and he watched the fresh marks blossom on their cheeks.

'One of you will be facing the dark one's nemesis tonight,' he explained. 'And I want you both in your best condition so that your leader's victory will be assured. But I need to know which of you feels ready to defeat the virtuous challenger. I need to know which of you will be best able to win if you have to go up against Faith.'

Marcia turned to stare at him, her servility all but forgotten. 'Faith Harker?'

He nodded. 'You wouldn't have a problem fighting her, would you?' Her response wasn't the one he expected, and he had wondered if her concern came from the camaraderie for a fellow choirgirl, but Marcia was full of surprises. Her smile gleamed brightly as she grabbed at him and began to beg.

'Let me fight against Faith,' she implored him. 'I've been wanting to sort that bitch out since before we left England.' Grunting the words with her eagerness she went on, 'Please, Mr Chalmers. I want the chance to hurt Faith, I really do.'

'Are you telling me you don't like Faith?' he asked.

She laughed as though he had made a ridiculous joke. 'That's the understatement of the century.' Marcia held the lapels of Todd's jacket, pressing her bare breasts against him and writhing her groin against his hip. The movement was lewd and seductive and he could have enjoyed it for the remainder of the evening. He was still wary of her, mindful that she might be trying to lull him into a false sense of security, but the passionate spark in her eyes

175

seemed to ridicule that idea. For the first time since meeting Marcia, Todd felt as though he had discovered her true motivation.

'I hate that sanctimonious bitch,' Marcia confided, and as she writhed against his leg he could feel her pussy lips splaying and rubbing over the weave of his trousers. It was easy to imagine the silvery trail of arousal she was leaving against him, but he didn't lower his gaze from hers. 'I'd do anything to see her suffer,' Marcia promised.

'Anything?' he repeated doubtfully, whereupon she acted faster than he would have believed, and it was only afterwards that he thought himself lucky she hadn't decided to attack. Rather than feeding from him, she snatched the bullwhip from his hand and unfastened his trousers in the same fluid motion. Releasing his erection, stroking it to full hardness with one careless caress of her fingertips, she turned around and impaled her pussy on his shaft. They groaned in unison. Marcia's cry sounded as though she was already close to the brink of a powerful release. Encouraging him to fondle her, riding back and forth on his erection, she took advantage of the position and began to snap the whip hard at the mulatto's rear.

Todd marvelled at the way her sex muscles clenched around his stiffness, the ferocity increasing every time she was able to hurl another blow at the other woman. He didn't think Marcia was hurting her opponent out of spite, sure she was only anticipating the joy that would come if she got the opportunity to exact this discipline on Faith.

'Let me fight her,' Marcia insisted in staccato bursts, her words growing faster as her arousal became more urgent. Even the briskness of each whip crack seemed fractionally faster as she edged closer to the pinnacle of orgasm. 'You have to let me fight her. You simply have to.' Chasing her climax with single-minded determination, she snapped the whip repeatedly against the mulatto's rear. The echo of each shot sang shrilly from the suite's walls but the vampire's grunts of discomfort were inaudible beneath Marcia's rising cries of excitement. 'Please let me, Mr Chalmers. Please.'

She squeezed her pussy muscles as she delivered another blow, and it was almost enough to wring the climax from Todd's shaft. He gasped, shocked that she had brought him so close to ejaculating so quickly, and pulled himself free from her confines. But she seemed unmoved by the fact that he was no longer penetrating her sex and continued whipping the mulatto with the same clinical abandon she had been enjoying before. Each crack of the whip inspired a moan from the mulatto, and Todd was appalled to notice it also brought a sigh from Marcia.

Todd watched with undisguised admiration. He loved strong females, and they excited him so fiercely he compared his need to an addict's compulsion. With the exception of Lilah, whose strength was almost the equal of her brother's, Todd felt sure Marcia was the most dominant girl he had seen in a long time. Knowing he couldn't resist her power, he caught her arm before she could whip the mulatto again.

Marcia whirled to face him and for an instant he thought she would try to strike. But instead, seeming to sense something in his stern expression, she lowered the weapon and allowed it to fall to the floor.

'You want the chance to go up against Faith Harker,' he said solemnly, and she nodded, struggling to suppress an eager smile. 'And you said you'll do anything in exchange for that opportunity.'

For a moment he didn't think she would understand his intimation, but when his meaning finally registered she fell to her knees and began to devour his erection. He smiled to himself, savouring the sensation of her tongue sliding against his hardness and her lips sucking his swollen helmet. There was no warmth in her kiss, but Marcia easily compensated for that with the greedy way she lapped at him.

Snapping his fingers for the mulatto's attention, he pointed to the bathroom. 'Go and get yourself cleaned up,' he barked. 'The dark one will want to see both of you at your best tonight.'

She fixed him with a brief glower of resentment before storming away. Todd realised he had made a dangerous enemy in the mulatto, but that knowledge didn't stop him enjoying the pleasure that Marcia bestowed. He relaxed and stared at the ceiling as she slipped her mouth and tongue wetly over his rigid length. Repeatedly she tried to swallow his erection, forcing the tip of his glans past the back of her throat, and he knew his eruption was inching closer each time she practiced that particular trick.

'Will you let me go against her, Mr Chalmers?' she asked softly. 'Will you let me have a chance to settle some old scores with Faith?'

He glanced down at her and had to restrain himself from exploding. The contrast between the faux-innocence of her wide-eyed smile, and the way her lower lip trembled against his glans, made him yearn to erupt and he knew he wouldn't be able to refuse any request she made. 'You really want that?'

Marcia nodded and pushed her mouth over him, and she was sucking with furious abandon before he realised he had agreed to her request. The climax came in a sudden rush and he held her head tightly as his shaft continued to pump into her mouth. Marcia swallowed with the greedy appetite he had come to expect, and she didn't stop even when it was obvious he was spent. He pulled her face away from his dwindling shaft and she smiled adoringly up from the floor.

'You'll fair well as the dark one's champion,' he assured her. A dribble of his semen trailed from her lower lip and he wiped it absently with the back of his finger. Holding his hand under her nose, waiting for her to lick the ejaculate before continuing, he added, 'You have the appetites and drives that the dark one looks for in his favourites.'

Marcia didn't seem to care whether or not she met with anyone's approval. 'There's just one thing I don't understand,' she said, frowning uncertainly.

'Only one thing? With your IQ I'm sure it must be more than that.'

Her curt smile spoke more eloquently than she could ever have hoped. It said she didn't understand his remark, it said she suspected the comment was meant to be rude or hurtful, and it told him that she didn't care. 'Why did you have me steal Faith's necklace just to give it to her best friend? That's not proper stealing. That's just losing something and finding it with someone else's...'

He raised a hand to stop her from speaking. Marcia had a beautiful body, she was a fantastic lover, and had been a joy to watch when fighting the dark one's mulatto. But her rambling questions irritated him. 'The dark one employed me to find out about Faith,' he explained. 'And I did that to the fullest extent possible. I didn't just compose a report on her from the information of private investigators and mystical shaman. I also employed a team of psychological experts to give me a breakdown of her personality and some indication of her strengths and weaknesses.'

Marcia looked as though she wanted to say something, but she remained silent.

Todd smiled inwardly, surprised that she was showing

so much restraint and wondering if her reticence came from a genuine desire to obey him, or her heartfelt need to remain in his favour so she could confront Faith. He wanted to believe it was the former, but he had never been a great one for fooling himself. Taking a deep breath, he said, 'Those profiles told me that Faith is very reliant on others. She surrounds herself with family and friends and relies on her trust in them to support her through life's obstacles and challenges.'

Marcia nodded. 'I could believe that,' she agreed. 'After the opening night she wanted to phone her sisters and tell them how well she'd done.'

The news confirmed what the psychological reports had told him. 'She gets her strength from friends and family,' he reiterated, and unable to stop himself, he smiled at his own cleverness. 'Her closest friend over here has been the girl, Claire. Finding the necklace amongst Claire's belongings is going to make Faith think her best friend is a thief, and she won't be able to fully trust her now.'

Marcia shook her head. 'But there are two-dozen of us in the choir, and Faith's the sort who will have a new best friend before the end of the day.'

He was surprised she had noticed so much about Faith's personality. Two of the profilers had missed that small detail, and Marcia's natural cunning shifted higher in his estimation. 'Ordinarily Faith would have a new best friend by the end of the day,' he agreed. 'But I instructed the dark one to rectify that matter.' Smiling tightly to himself he explained, 'After last night, Faith won't dare trust any of the choir for fear that she might be confiding in a vampire.'

'You've thought of everything,' Marcia complimented him.

'I have,' Todd agreed. 'And the icing on the cake will

come tonight when Faith invests the last of her trust in her one remaining ally and then finds out she's been led into a trap.' His enjoyment felt unnecessarily Machiavellian but, after all the hard work he'd invested in the project, he couldn't resist congratulating himself. 'That's going to be the crowning glory of defeating the virtuous one.'

Marcia nodded emphatic agreement. 'It will be good to see that bitch get what's coming to her.'

'You really don't care for her much, do you?'

'I hate her,' Marcia assured him. 'And if you let me go up against her tonight I'll wipe the smug look off her sanctimonious little face.' Her crimson eyes glistened with mischievous intent as she added, 'I'll feed from her. But before I do that, I'll have seen that pious face of hers struggling against my pussy.'

The union of their malicious laughter echoed from the suite's walls.

Faith

Act III, Scene I

Another night, another suicide, Faith thought despondently.

Her pleasure at completing the choir's penultimate performance was easily quashed by Ms Moon's foreboding frown. The choir mistress remained at the back of the girls' dressing room, arms folded, brow knotted and lips pressed tightly together. She didn't speak to congratulate, complain or acknowledge. She simply stood, fixedly glaring at Faith.

The usual after-show exuberance of the choir seemed unnaturally muted, and Faith wondered if the events of the previous evening were the cause. Wendy Byrne wore a roll-neck sweater, so it was impossible to see if her throat bore any of the marks Helen might have left, and Faith wracked her brains to remember if Laura Smith and Tanya Sharpe were in the habit of turning up the collars of their jackets. She was also struggling to recall if it was usual for either Charlotte Fry or Deborah Cummings to wear their hair down to their shoulders without plaits or ponytails. But the more she puzzled over the details, the more she thought the entire troupe looked like a conspiracy of concealed necks.

'Taxis for all you girls,' Ms Moon declared crisply. 'That was the most lacklustre performance you've given so far,' she proclaimed. 'I'd use the word dire, but in this context it sounds unnecessarily like praise. I want you all to go straight back to your dormitory and rest. Hopefully our final show might see an improvement.'

There was a general murmur that was too lethargic to be called agreement or denial. The mood of the entire choir was subdued and they were all oblivious to the glaring daggers the choir mistress steadfastly hurled in Faith's direction. The ferocity of her gaze was unsettling, but regardless of the discomfort it caused, Faith found herself constantly glancing at the woman.

Claire stepped between Faith and her intermittent view of Ms Moon, her smiling face a welcome contrast from the severity of the choir mistress's narrow frown. 'Do you want to share a cab back with me?' she asked eagerly. 'We haven't had a chance to talk all day, and I've been so wanting to chat.'

Faith glanced at her friend, torn between feelings of affection and doubt. The idea of sharing a cab was tempting because it meant she could give Claire a chance to explain why she had stolen the crucifix. Amongst the many other concerns that had weighed on her mind, and there had been an inordinate amount throughout the day, Faith had been particularly fretting about the theft.

The stolen crucifix would have been easier to dismiss or overlook if Nick and Helen hadn't made a point of deliberately avoiding Claire when they went through the choir's chalet. Ms Moon's initial mention of the coven's daylight staff – the unscrupulous mortals who were happy to work for the undead – made Faith wonder if Claire might be employed by the dark one. She told herself it was a ridiculous idea, and that she was taking paranoia to absurd levels, but she couldn't think of any other explanation.

'You may take a cab back with Faith, Claire,' Ms Moon said sharply. 'But you'll have to wait. I need to have words with her before we leave here this evening.'

Claire opened her mouth to protest, and Faith knew her friend was going to make some complaint about Ms Moon's regime of discipline and punishment, so holding up a silencing hand, stopping the confrontation before it could begin, she shook her head and glared at Claire with silent meaning. 'Do as Ms Moon says,' she said quickly. 'Wait for me and we'll share a cab back once Ms Moon and I are done.'

Claire cast a meaningful glare in the choir mistress's direction, then turned to Faith. 'Are you sure?' she asked, her tone sombre.

Faith had spent most of the day deliberately avoiding Claire, and she silently cursed herself for the unkindness. Her doubts about her friend remained, but she couldn't miss the genuine concern that now etched her features and she was touched to think her friend was so willing to defend her. She wanted to believe she had misjudged Claire, and hoped they might be able to resolve their differences before the night was over.

But Ms Moon's impatient frown was growing more severe and Faith realised this wasn't the time to deal with that particular issue. She didn't want to cause embarrassment for any of them, and gave her friend a reassuring smile. 'Wait outside the dressing room for me,' she said. 'I'm sure, whatever Ms Moon wants, it won't take long.'

Claire cast a glance around the dwindling group of the choir as they casually filed past the choir mistress, and her brows narrowed as she asked, 'Why wasn't Marcia playing the role of the sacristan tonight? I haven't seen the bitch all day. Where is she?'

'It's not polite to refer to fellow members of the choir with that particular term,' Ms Moon said stiffly.

Claire gave an insincere apology before asking, 'So where is she? Do you know?'

'Mr Chalmers informed me that Marcia was doing something for him this evening,' the choir mistress said simply. Ordinarily the remainder of the choir would have laughed at the statement – wolf-whistled or joked about the connotations that could be applied to the innocent remark – but Faith was amazed to observe that none of them even smirked. The lack of merriment disturbed her.

And her unease deepened when Claire mumbled a brief, 'See you soon,' and then walked past Ms Moon, the last of the group to leave the dressing room, casting a final, reluctant glance over her shoulder as she went. When she closed the door Faith was chilled to realise she and the choir mistress were alone, and she could sense waves of barely controlled anger radiating from the woman.

'Don't you want my help, Faith?'

'Of course I want your help.'

'Do you lack trust in me?'

'No!' Faith could hear herself saying the word too quickly, but it was out and she couldn't retract what she had said or the way she said it. Trying to soften the way her reply had sounded she said earnestly, 'No, Ms Moon, I do trust you. Honestly, I do.'

Ms Moon's nod was little more than a perfunctory movement of her head. She stepped away from the door and began to walk in a slow circle that made Faith uncomfortable. 'You've been keeping secrets from me, Faith. You wouldn't do that if you trusted me.'

Faith shook her head, anxious to refute the allegation. 'That's not true, I've been trying to contact you all day,' she returned indignantly. 'I've been wanting to keep you updated about everything that happened in the dormitory last night, but I haven't been able to get hold of you.

There was no answer at your chalet and Mr Chalmers had no way of getting my message to you.'

'What about the osterie?' Ms Moon asked softly, the click of her heels against the linoleum floor punctuating every syllable. Watching her, Faith could imagine the tense muscle control that was flexing the choir mistress's strong, shapely thighs and calves. 'Were you going to tell me what happened at the osterie as well as what occurred in the chalet?'

Faith blushed, thinking of the kiss she and Claire had shared over their pomodori fettucine. By the time she realised the choir mistress was talking about her encounter with Nick and Helen, Faith realised she had all but admitted to being guilty of something. 'I was going to tell you everything!' she blurted, and even to her own ears the exclamation sounded like a lie. 'I was going to tell you everything that happened. Honestly I was.'

'Get down on your knees and bend over that stool,' Ms Moon said stiffly. 'One way or another we'll teach you a lesson, Faith. And this time I'm determined it will sink in.'

Faith shook her head. 'No more lessons.' She struggled to sound adamant but her voice had already begun to falter. 'I don't want you spanking me any more.'

Ms Moon moved with frightening speed. She reached out and took a fistful of Faith's hair in one hand. Pressing herself close, she placed a leg behind Faith's bottom and stepped nearer. The modest swell of her breasts was obvious against Faith's arm and the weight of the woman's sex was pronounced against her hip.

Faith struggled not to be bent to the choir mistress's will, but it was taking all her efforts to resist the intoxicating effects of the woman's presence. With a moan of self-disgust, Faith consented and allowed the choir mistress to force her to her knees. She was positioned over a convenient stool and then Ms Moon raised the hem of her skirt.

The familiar spikes of shame and embarrassment pierced Faith's stomach. She clenched her thigh muscles tight and was warmed by a fluid rush of anticipation.

'Don't defy me,' Ms Moon warned softly. 'You'll be facing the dark one all too soon and my help is all you've got.'

'You don't need to spank me,' Faith insisted and tried to pull away, but the choir mistress was quick and surprisingly strong. Every attempt she made to break free was easily countered. 'There's no need for this at all.'

'You've been playing with vampires,' Ms Moon growled. 'I think I need to do something.'

Her fingers had slipped under the waistband of Faith's panties and the choir mistress's icy touch invoked a hateful thrill of arousal. Faith's palms grew sweaty with nerves, her heartbeat raced, and the flesh between her legs became sickeningly wet. When she drew a deep breath, intending to make one final plea for leniency, she could smell the syrupy fragrance of her own musk, the scent as damning as an admission of guilt.

'The dark one isn't scared of you, the way I would have expected,' Ms Moon continued. 'And each time you've faced his subordinates, there's been a grave risk of your being tainted. Learn from the discipline this time, Faith. Try to understand what I'm telling you.'

Faith didn't want to hear, or have any part in the punishment. She made another attempt to tug herself away but it was a futile struggle. As the panties were pulled from her hips, and drawn slowly down her thighs, she knew she was going to have to suffer the choir mistress's discipline again. The punishment might have been easier to bear if she hadn't known a part of her wanted to feel Ms Moon's hand slapping her bottom, and she realised it was her fear of that dark, inexplicable need that made her try to escape.

Ms Moon stroked the rounded flesh of Faith's behind. Every nuance of her fingers seemed to make some impression, exciting Faith's arousal and increasing her desire. She silently willed the choir mistress to land the first blow, not wanting to be tormented by the wicked tease of the hand smoothing her rear, her body responding with an eagerness that was mortifying. It was all too easy to picture her sex lips pouting greedily, and she could imagine the curls that covered her labia were plastered with the residue of her musk.

'Last night you promised to obey my instructions,' Ms Moon reminded her. She had lowered her voice to a husky whisper, and it was just as seductive as the palm that stroked Faith's exposed buttocks. 'Last night you promised me your unfailing obedience. Do you intend to honour that promise?'

'Yes,' Faith whispered.

The choir mistress moved her hand away, and Faith tensed, expecting to feel the sharp slap of a hand clapping against her flesh. The familiarity of the position – bent over with her bottom exposed and awaiting punishment – was almost as obscene as the indignity itself. She could have cried with self-pity when she realised she wanted to feel the smack, but she managed to contain the tears.

The moment dragged on and Faith wondered if Ms Moon had decided to show some mercy, but the facile optimism of that thought was brushed aside when she dared to glance back and saw Ms Moon retrieving something from her purse. With growing horror Faith watched the woman produce a short leather switch. Her stomach muscles tightened, her excitement burnt briefly brighter, and she quickly looked away. Disgusted by the prospect of suffering such a wicked torment, she pleaded frantically, 'I do intend to honour that promise. And I will trust you from now on. I promise I will.'

There was a short, breathless hiss and Faith knew it was the sound of the leather slicing air. Before she had the chance to brace herself – before she had the opportunity to steel her backside in readiness for the inevitable shock – the switch branded a weal against one bare buttock.

Faith gasped. The switch stung like a barb and it took every effort not to wriggle in anguish against the chair. Despising her own response to the punishment, she tried not to let her body succumb to the thrill that had followed previous chastisements. It was a valiant effort but she knew it wouldn't do her any good when the warmth spread to her sex. Shaking, she tried not to think of how that moment always made her eager for more.

'Tell me you trust me, Faith.'

'I trust you, Ms Moon,' she said hurriedly. 'I trust you.'

Ms Moon slapped the switch down harder for the second blow. It struck the other cheek and Faith had to chug her breath for fear of crying out loud. This time she didn't bother resisting the swell of excitement. It was easier to allow the shameful thrill to begin its flow so it could simply tingle through her body. She knew she was setting herself up for further embarrassment, but she couldn't resist the salacious impulse to relent.

'Tell me you'll always trust me,' Ms Moon insisted.

Faith didn't bother to think about the words before she repeated them. 'I'll always trust you, Ms Moon. I always will.'

The choir mistress raised the switch and brought it down briskly, and while Faith was still stifling her cry Ms Moon struck again. The pain was exquisite, fresh and invigorating. It blossomed quickly from the centre of the switch's tip and spread over the entire cheek that had been struck. Her bottom blazed with the fire of the punishment, but Faith knew that wasn't the only heat that warmed her. Nevertheless, anxious to keep her reaction concealed for as long as she could, she remained stoical as two further blows were wrought against her aching rear.

With pinpoint accuracy Ms Moon scored two further shots: one for each cheek.

Unable to contain the sound, needing to vent her growing response, Faith groanèd. It was a soft murmur and she muted it for fear of drawing Claire's attention from outside the dressing room. But the cry was enough to make the choir mistress study her with renewed interest. Faith glanced at the woman, appalled to see that her lascivious smile said she had heard something in the timbre of the moan. Faith knew exactly what that sound was, because she recognised the same greedy desire that had coloured her exclamations the previous evening when Claire was lapping between her legs.

'What happened last night, Faith?'

For an instant she thought the choir mistress had read her thoughts. Memories of what she and Claire did were so close to the forefront of her mind that she nearly blurted out every detail.

'What happened in the dormitory? And what happened in the osterie? The dark one was at the dormitory, wasn't he? What did he say? What did he do?'

Relief made Faith shiver. She considered petulantly dismissing Ms Moon's questions, telling her that there was no point reiterating what had happened because it was clear she already knew every important detail. Faith didn't doubt such a show of defiance would earn her further punishment, and she was shamed to find the idea tempting because of that potential result. But because she knew the situation was growing serious, and because she'd wanted to share this information with Ms Moon all day, she made herself answer properly.

She explained about the encounter with Nick and Helen at the osterie, and then the dark one's appearance at the chalet. The only points she omitted were those glorious discoveries she made when Claire shared her bed. Those were details she was determined not to reveal to the choir mistress.

Ms Moon looked perplexed. 'It seems like the dark one doesn't fear you at all,' she said solemnly. 'It won't be easy defeating him.'

'What do you suggest?'

Ms Moon's smile was briefly malevolent. Her nose wrinkled as she sneered. 'I suggest we take the fight to him. He's obviously trying to intimidate you, and cause you to either run from fear or fail because you're not fully prepared. I suggest we defy his expectations. I suggest we go to him tonight.'

The arousal she'd been enjoying was vanquished by Ms Moon's words. The immediacy of the situation dispelled all the pleasurable warmth nestling between her legs. 'Tonight?' she gasped. 'Is that wise?'

'He's preparing to face you, Faith. Every moment he has to get himself ready makes your task that much more difficult.'

'But am I prepared?'

Ms Moon's cruel smile softened. Faith briefly thought she might be seeing a tender side to the woman she hadn't noticed before, but that idea was quickly banished. The choir mistress pulled Faith back, tore her blouse open and exposed Faith's chest. She had a brief moment to bemoan the fact that she hadn't chosen to wear a bra this evening, and had to suffer the embarrassment of showing her breasts again, and then she saw Ms Moon raising the switch, and hurl it down with a swiftness that was almost brutal.

Faith howled.

The switch had stung when it bit her rear, but that pain was nothing like the anguish that now tore through her nipple. The searing heat burnt her and throbbed inside her swollen teat. Before she had the chance to pull away or protect herself, Ms Moon was slicing a second shot at her other breast.

The anguish was immense and Faith struggled helplessly to control her response. It was instinctive to want to grovel at Ms Moon's feet and beg the woman to stop chastising her, and she could imagine there would be a base pleasure in submitting so openly. But instead she forced herself to remain unmoved, and held herself rigid so the woman could use the switch again if she wanted. As the searing pain began to lessen, the broiling afterglow of arousal rewarded Faith. She blushed when she realised her nipples were standing hard and proud. Not lowering her gaze, meeting Ms Moon's inquisitive smile with stoicism, she didn't allow her features to betray the turmoil of her emotions.

'I wanted you to learn something from this discipline,' Ms Moon said gently. 'And I think you might finally be on the verge of understanding that lesson.'

Her words made no sense and Faith didn't have a chance to ponder them. The choir mistress pushed her back over the stool and slashed the switch twice against her bottom. Neither of the blows were soft, but they lacked the surprise and severity of those made against her breasts.

Faith tolerated them, enjoying something from the experience that she couldn't quite name. It was more than the warmth that came after each punishing sting; it was almost as if she had found some pleasure that came from submitting to the woman's discipline.

When the choir mistress stroked a finger against Faith's sex, her cool touch slipping against the silky folds of her labia, all rational thoughts seemed to rush from her mind. The frisson of the contact was infuriating, as delightful as the sensation of Claire's tongue against her sex, and made sweeter by its contrast to the pain she had just suffered. As insane as it seemed, Faith knew she was on the brink of enjoying the same blissful release that Claire had inspired the previous evening.

'The pain excites you,' Ms Moon observed.

Faith could feel her blushes as she answered, and was thankful to be staring at the floor rather than meeting the woman's gaze. 'Yes, Ms Moon,' she whispered. 'I think it does.'

The choir mistress slapped her lightly. The touch wasn't harsh but because it struck on top of the welts from the switch, Faith shivered. 'Don't be embarrassed about the pleasure you receive,' Ms Moon warned. 'Embarrassment and shame won't help you overthrow the dark one.'

Again Faith felt she was about to understand something monumental, but the revelation was snatched away from her. The choir mistress's fingers brushed her sex and the only thought in Faith's mind was that she needed to experience more. Her entire body itched with the maddening impulse for satisfaction, and she bit her tongue to stop herself demanding that Ms Moon make the exploration more intimate.

'Are you ready to face the dark one?'

Faith blinked to clear the confused rush of aroused

thoughts from her mind. Ms Moon was still stroking her bottom and ripples of excitement swirled around her sex. The mild tingling that touched her before threatened to grow into an insatiable urge, so forcing her thoughts back to the question, she said honestly, 'I don't know if I'm ready to face him.'

Ms Moon nodded, and encouraged Faith to her feet without allowing her to pull up her panties.

Faith felt ridiculous as she stood in front of the choir mistress in a state of semi-undress. Her breasts were exposed, the tips a flaming red with the nipples jutting fiercely. The panties around her ankles made her feel as though she was in the act of doing something degrading. But those thoughts were brushed aside when Ms Moon took Faith's hand in her own and placed it against her breast. All fears of being accused of depravity seemed somehow misplaced beneath Ms Moon's sparkling smile. 'You'll have to strike him here,' the choir mistress explained. 'Do you think you can do that?'

Faith didn't hear the question. The shape of Ms Moon's small breast sat perfectly in her hand and, through the flimsy fabric of her Victorian-style blouse, Faith could feel the firm yet supple flesh yielding to her touch. The thrust of a nipple pushed against her palm, and although she wanted to be shocked and pull her hand away, she also wanted to maintain the contact. Mesmerised, she stared into the depths of Ms Moon's obsidian eyes and saw her longing reflected in the woman's gaze. Realising some response was expected she smiled apologetically to show she needed the question repeating.

'Do you think you can strike the dark one in the chest?' Ms Moon asked. 'Is that something you think you can manage?'

'If that's what I have to do.'

'You'll have to penetrate his flesh and tear the heart from his body.'

Faith nodded. The words had the familiar ring of lessons Ms Moon had been trying to teach her over the past three nights. She found it difficult to think beyond the pleasure of holding the woman's breast and knew, at that moment, she would have happily agreed to anything. 'If that's what I have to do,' she promised, 'then that's what I'll do.'

'You'll be facing him tonight.'

'I think I'm prepared.' Ms Moon nodded sombrely and put her hand over Faith's. The nipple seemed to swell against the pressure and Faith was overwhelmed by a growing need for the woman.

'You should get yourself dressed now, then go and take that cab back to the chalet with your friend. I'll collect you from your dorm later tonight.' Lowering her voice, making no move to break the contact between Faith's hand and her own breast, Ms Moon added, 'And remember: if you don't trust me, you'll never defeat the dark one.'

And staring into the sincerity of the woman's expression, Faith knew she was right to believe her.

Faith

Act III, Scene II

'She did it again, didn't she?' Claire demanded.

Faith climbed into the waiting taxi without responding. Claire followed her into the back seat and slammed the door closed. Neither of them spoke to the driver and Faith assumed that Claire had already given instructions about their destination. As the car set off, and swept away from Castel Sant'Angelo, she noticed the driver was a mulatto woman, surprisingly pretty for a female cabbie in the city, and with features that seemed somehow familiar. Puzzled by the idea that she might know her, and sure none of the other Roman taxis she had ridden in were driven by women, Faith was about to say something when Claire broke through her thoughts.

'I'm right, aren't I? She did it again, didn't she?'

'This isn't the place to talk about it,' Faith said, lowering her voice and casting a glance at the back of the driver's head. Rolling her eyes, allowing impatience to get the better of her mood, she added, 'Jesus, Claire, why do I always have to remind you about discretion?'

Untroubled by Faith's ire Claire made a face. 'The woman can't understand a word of English,' she said, pointing at the driver. 'She even has difficulty with Italian, because Mr Chalmers had to come out and tell her where to take us.' Drawing a deep breath, trying to show that she was being reasonable, she added, 'But if the chance of her hearing us worries you…'

'Which it does,' Faith said quickly.

'…then I can do something about that.' Claire knocked on the window that separated the driver's compartment from their rear seats. 'Musica, per favore,' she said briskly, her Italian stilted, and she compensated by miming a radio dial being twisted. 'Musica alla radio. Forte, per favore.'

The taxi driver nodded, pressed a switch on the cab's console and Faith was pleasantly surprised to hear her sister's voice coming through the car's speakers.

'…*You placed your fingers against my breast; You made me think our love was blessed; Then you tore the heart from outta my chest…*'

Faith knew BloodLust were currently enjoying a run of success in America, and the United Kingdom, but she hadn't realised the group was so popular throughout the rest of Europe. It seemed that everywhere she went in Rome she was hearing snatches of Charity's songs, and she made a mental note to mention the impressive saturation the next time they spoke.

'There,' Claire said, a triumphant smile creasing her face. 'The driver can't understand and she can't overhear. Now we can talk.' Her smile evaporated as she repeated her question for a third time. 'She did do it again, didn't she?'

'Ms Moon is trying to teach me something,' Faith began tactfully. 'I don't think you're helping with adding to my guilt every time I have to suffer one of her punishments.'

'I'm not trying to add to your guilt,' Claire told her. 'I'm just being a good friend and I'm looking out for you.' She placed a hand on Faith's leg and added, 'I enjoy looking out for you. You're nice to look out for.'

Faith held herself still, willing herself not to succumb to the temptation Claire offered. The contact was infuriating because it was the exact stimulation she craved. She itched for Claire to push her fingers higher, tease the tips beneath the hem of her skirt, and she struggled to quash the need for further intimacy. Shaking her head to clear her thoughts, she knew she had to resolve the worries plaguing her throughout the day before she gave in to those urges that Claire inspired. So she made a point of firmly moving Claire's hand from her leg before reaching into the pocket of her jacket. Watching her friend closely, trying not to be moved by the flicker of hurt that flashed in Claire's eyes, she held up the crucifix and asked, 'Do you recognise this?'

Claire glanced at it and shrugged. 'It's that cross of yours, the one your sister Hope gave you.' She giggled as she remembered. 'It's the one you wanted to go looking for last night before we…'

'I remember what happened last night.' The solemnity of her voice was enough to make Claire stop giggling, and she regarded Faith with an earnest expression that dropped in and out of shadows as the streetlamps sped past.

'Where did you find it?' she asked innocently. 'You thought it was lost, didn't you?'

'I found it on your bedside cabinet.'

The air between them grew momentarily thick. Faith watched her friend curiously for a telltale flicker of guilt or remorse, but Claire's honest and open face showed neither of those expressions. 'You thought I'd stolen it, didn't you?' Claire observed.

'What else was I supposed to think?'

Claire laughed, the musical sound briefly drowning out the BloodLust refrain, and apparently not offended by the accusation she leant closer and kissed Faith on the lips. 'I wouldn't steal anything from you,' she said earnestly. 'I thought you might have guessed as much without me having to say it.'

Confused, Faith realised she couldn't argue with her friend on that point. She had known all along that Claire wouldn't steal from her, but it seemed she needed to hear the words to understand that simple truth. Without inflection, merely puzzled enough to voice the question aloud, she asked, 'So how did it get in with your possessions?'

'Maybe someone found it on the floor and thought it was mine?' Claire suggested. 'Maybe you put it there and forgot you'd done it? Maybe someone put it there hoping to make you think I'd stolen it? I don't know how it got there, but I do know I didn't take it. I wouldn't risk our friendship over something as important to you as that necklace.' She flashed a wary glance at Faith and added, 'I especially wouldn't do something as nasty as stealing now that you and I are getting so close.'

Her sincerity was enough to convince Faith that she was beyond suspicion. She still didn't understand why the vampires had left her unmolested the previous evening, but Faith knew if someone was trying to plant a seed of doubt between her and her closest friend, she wasn't going to help with its germination. So making a determined effort to put the rift behind them, she placed her lips close to Claire's and asked innocently, 'Is that what's happening between us? Are we getting close?'

Claire had her thigh pressed against Faith's and she stroked her arm as they joined in a loose embrace. The friction of their breasts connecting was a tantalising caress that grew bolder with every bump of the cab. Without hesitation, she took up the unspoken offer of Faith's mouth. 'I don't think we could get much closer,' Claire giggled, and the joke made Faith kiss more passionately. Claire sighed in response and the sound was warming.

Faith was untroubled that their intimacy might be noticed by the cab driver because the woman was watching the busy traffic and nodding her head to the beat of the BloodLust song. The nightscape of the city was speeding by so quickly that Faith didn't imagine anyone would be able to see into the rear of the cab and notice her and Claire as they became more daring.

Eventually, after the temptation of the kiss had taken her to a point where she knew the rift between them was healed, Faith moved away and sat back in her seat. Claire held her arm, and with obvious concern in her voice she asked, 'Are you going to tell me how bad Moonie hurt you tonight? Are you going to tell me what she did?'

'She striped my bum,' Faith admitted, shifting uncomfortably on the seat as if the words had rekindled the pain. 'She had a leather strap with her and it was quite...' she hesitated over her choice of words, not wanting to let Claire know she had taken perverted pleasure from the punishment but not wanting to purposefully conceal the truth, '...it was quite effective,' she concluded.

Claire winced sympathetically. 'Was that all she did? Did she just stripe your backside?'

Faith plucked open two buttons on her blouse and exposed one breast for her friend's attention. The nipple was still a feverish red and remained as hard as when Ms Moon had struck it with the switch. Claire's obvious concern was almost enough to lessen the discomfort, but her friend seemed to think she had other ways to help Faith recover from her suffering. Gently, she reached inside Faith's blouse and touched the aching orb.

Faith stiffened against the taxi seat, stung by a poignant bolt of arousal. She glanced into Claire's eyes, wondering if her friend was entertaining the same mischievous thought that had just crossed her mind. It seemed she was, because Claire took Faith's smile as a nod of consent and lowered her mouth to the punished tip. Her lips were warm and moist and acted like a balm against the throbbing pulse of Faith's nipple, and when she stroked her tongue over the stiff bud of flesh, Faith was shocked by a barrage of raw excitement. She buried her shoulders into the seat, wanting to shrink from the pleasure and bask in it at the same moment. When Claire finally raised her head her smile radiated honest, lecherous desire.

'Do you want me to carry on?' she asked softly.

'Yes…' Faith groaned, and Claire needed no further encouragement. Wrapping one arm clumsily around Faith's waist, she pushed her mouth over the breast and nibbled lightly against the pulsing teat. Faith stifled her moans, not sure if the cab driver would notice or complain, but not wanting to take the risk. Claire had an intuitive ability and knew exactly where to touch and how much pressure to apply. The gentle bite of her teeth was almost too much to tolerate, but Faith thought her friend had found the perfect balance. As the warm tongue brushed against her, exciting the tip so fiercely that its pulse felt like a beacon, Faith wallowed in the glory of Claire's skilful teasing.

'Perhaps we shouldn't be doing this here,' Claire said suddenly. She sat upright, pulling away from Faith and sitting back. Modestly, she made a brief attempt to cover Faith's exposed breast. 'Maybe it's the wrong place or the wrong time, or the wrong something.'

Faith stared at her incredulously, wondering how her friend could bring her to such a pinnacle of pleasure and then stop so unexpectedly. As torments went she thought it came close to matching the cruelty of Ms Moon's harshest disciplines. She shook her head and held Claire's hand. 'This is exactly the right place and time,' she said urgently. 'When we get back to the dormitory the rest of the choir will still be awake and we won't be able to spend any time alone.' Claire looked as though she was considering this and ready to raise an argument, but Faith hurried on without allowing her the opportunity. 'Later tonight Ms Moon wants me to go out and face the dark one, so there won't be the chance for us to do anything after the rest of the dormitory have fallen asleep.' She considered saying that there might never be the chance to do anything ever again – she knew the confrontation with the dark one would not be without huge risk – but she didn't want to taint the moment with such a maudlin revelation. 'Please, Claire,' she begged, 'if we're going to do anything, I want us to do it now. It's going to be the only chance we have.' As she spoke she lowered Claire's hand and placed it against the burning centre of her sex.

Claire made her decision without further deliberation. She pulled her hand away, but only so she could push it beneath the hem of Faith's short skirt. Her fingers were chilly but they soon took on the heat of Faith's warm thighs. As she touched the gusset of Faith's panties her eager smile widened. 'You are sure, aren't you?' she whispered.

Faith didn't bother answering with words. Instead, she put her own hand against Claire's leg and slipped her fingers beneath her friend's skirt, whose bare thighs were whisper-soft to touch, and as she moved her hand higher she felt giddy by the boldness of what she was doing.

She was amazed that the driver didn't notice the thickness of the atmosphere they generated. The air seemed so charged she was surprised there wasn't an electrical hum droning through the ozone around them. But rather than paying any attention to her passengers, the mulatto simply continued to negotiate the dwindling traffic as she nodded along to the final bars of Charity's song.

'...*You had me day and night without any rest; You said our loving was the world's fucking best; Then you tore the heart from outta my chest...*'

Faith ignored the lyrics, and her sister's voice, allowing the pulsing rhythm to wash over her as she got closer to Claire. The crotch of her friend's panties was deliciously wet, and as she slipped her fingers up and down the sodden fabric, she could feel the shape of Claire's sex lips. The contact was maddeningly exciting, making Claire sigh eagerly, and Faith forced herself not to hurry. She cast a brief glance out of the window, wanting to assure herself that they weren't entering the chalet complex, and was pleased to see they were surrounded by the unfamiliar sights of medieval streets and unlit alleys. Confident there would be time for them to do things properly, she teased the crotch of Claire's panties aside and smoothed her fingers against the slippery folds of heated flesh.

Claire gasped, and Faith found the contact so thrilling she wanted to make a similar exclamation, but she wilfully contained her response. Excited by the viscous wetness, encouraged by Claire's whispered cries of pleasure, Faith slipped a finger between the sodden pussy lips. The labia melted to her touch and the warm flesh suckled against her like a hungry mouth. Shivering with arousal, caught up in the throes of Claire's swelling bliss, Faith pushed her finger deeper.

'You bitch,' Claire hissed, spitting the expletive without making it sound like an insult. Her mouth gaped with an unvoiced scream, and Faith saw her friend was using her free hand to stroke awkwardly at her chest. Taking the initiative, still savouring the contact of Claire's fingers against her own wet pussy, Faith squeezed her friend's breasts.

It wasn't the most intimate contact – Claire's bra and blouse prevented her from caressing bare flesh – but it was enough to make Claire's smile break into a satisfied growl. She pushed her hips closer and Faith was able to ease her fingertip further into the haven of her best friend's pussy. The pad of her thumb rested over the throbbing nub of Claire's clitoris, and when Faith lightly stroked the ball of flesh Claire became a pantomime of conflicting responses. She looked like she wanted to shy from the pleasure and bask in it at the same time. She tried to pull away and push closer in the same instant, and Faith could feel tremors of mounting excitement shivering through her fingertips.

Knowing exactly what her friend was going through, Faith found the shape of Claire's nipple thrusting against her bra and blouse, and she rubbed the stiff nub of flesh between finger and thumb. Her other thumb continued to chase lazy circles against the swell of Claire's clitoris, and she constantly coaxed her finger to burrow deeper, but she felt sure it was the torment against Claire's nipple that finally induced the orgasm.

Claire held herself motionless against the seat, her features twisted into a grimace of raw pleasure. Her thigh muscles had become as taut as steel bars and her pussy muscles clenched with sporadic vigour around Faith's fingers, and she pushed a fist in her mouth to stifle a scream.

Faith moved her fingers away, settling back in the seat as she watched Claire regain her composure. She didn't pull herself too far away, not wanting to break the contact of Claire's hand as it rested between her own legs, and she didn't wait for her friend's orgasm to completely settle. Speaking while the dreamy smile lingered on Claire's pouting lips, she quietly said, 'I think you should have this.'

The BloodLust single had finished on the radio, and after a rapid and incomprehensible interjection from the Italian presenter, the strains of another thrash metal song poured from the speakers. Faith couldn't understand the lyrics and didn't know if this was because the song was being sung in some language other than English, or because the vocalist was screaming every syllable. She also supposed it could have been because she wasn't really listening.

'I'd like you to take it.'

Claire glanced at her, and when she saw what Faith was offering she shook her head. 'I can't take that,' she insisted. 'That's the crucifix your sister gave you. I know you, Faith. I know it's your most treasured possession.'

Faith nodded. 'It is. And now I'd like it to be your most treasured possession.'

Claire looked set to refuse again, but Faith was determined to make her point. She'd spent the day believing that Claire had stolen the jewellery, and could now see how wrong that idea had been. So to make matters right in her own mind she couldn't think of a better way to absolve her own guilt. 'I'd like you to take it,' she said honestly. 'And I'd like you to wear it always and think of me whenever you notice it.'

Claire held the ribbon in her fingers and passing lights danced from the silver jewellery. 'But, I thought you were confronting the dark one tonight,' she remembered. 'Won't you need all the crucifixes you can get if you're going up against the world's most villainous vampire?' she added, speaking with forced levity.

Faith pressed the cross into her friend's hand and closed her fingers around it. 'I want you to have it,' she insisted. 'I want you to think of me whenever you're wearing it.'

'Thank you,' Claire whispered. Her other hand had remained at Faith's crotch while they spoke, the fingers sliding almost absently up and down. But as she accepted the cross she teased the gusset to one side, and Faith was shaken by an intense rush of excitement and tried to steady herself as her exposed pussy was caressed.

Claire leant closer and kissed her gently on the lips. Her fingertips burrowed deeper, teasing the wet labia and gliding easily inside. Faith struggled to draw breath, sure she was on the verge of drowning in a rising tide of passion.

Claire pushed her fingers deeper and extended her tongue to explored Faith's mouth. The position was enthralling, making Faith feel as though two lovers were taking her. The girl's tongue squirmed between her lips while her fingers softly plundered her sex, and she allowed Claire's kiss to become more passionate before grinding her hips towards the pair of burrowing fingertips.

For an instant she was struck by panic, sure that the cab had stopped, that they were parked outside the dormitory, and that the choir were leering into the window and watching the exhibition that she and Claire would be presenting. It was enough to make her arousal disappear and she had to open her eyes and stare out at the passing scenery to convince herself they weren't being watched. None of the buildings outside looked familiar, but that peculiarity wasn't worrying. Each taxi driver that had taken her from Castel Sant' Angelo had managed to find a different route back to the complex, and Faith simply thought this was another of those ruses to increase the fare.

And the distraction of those abstract thoughts was banished when Claire eased her fingers deeper. She realised the lubrication was coming from her own arousal, and the thought was so wonderfully shaming she wriggled her hips to encourage Claire to probe deeper.

If they hadn't been in the taxi, or if the vehicle had been roomier, Faith knew Claire would have been kneeling between her spread legs. Memories of the pleasure that had come from having her friend's tongue at her sex inspired another rush of excitement. She wished she had been able to kiss Claire in the same way and wondered if there might still be time to do that before she had to confront the dark one. The prospect of licking the delicious folds was enough to push Faith beyond the brink of an orgasm. The flood of pleasure soared through her, inspiring small shivers that became more traumatic and pronounced. Faith snatched Claire's wrist, not sure if she was trying to pull it closer or push it away, then she held the hand against herself as wave upon wave of an orgasm crashed through her trembling frame.

They embraced, a tight and wordless display of affection, before falling back to their own seats. The flesh between Faith's legs felt hot and sticky, but in that moment she didn't care. She waited until Claire made the first attempts to straighten her clothes before she went through the undignified process of adjusting the crotch of her panties then tidying up her opened blouse. After combing her hair back to a semblance of style she gave Claire a shy smile, and saw the sly amusement was shared.

'Gosh,' Claire giggled, and because Faith couldn't think of anything to say in reply, she joined in with the laughter. It had been a brilliant climax and Faith felt content that she had managed to settle her differences with Claire. She couldn't believe she had suspected her friend of being in league with the vampires, and wondered how her paranoid mind could have twisted events to support such an insane conspiracy theory. The idea that Claire could ever have been involved with the undead was ridiculous, and she was about to apologise again for lacking trust in her best friend when the taxi pulled to a halt before she could speak, and when she glanced out of the window she was appalled to see that they weren't outside the dormitory in the chalet complex. The view was all too familiar and she realised they were parked outside the Trastevere cemetery.

'What are we doing here?' she whispered.

Claire glanced out of the window and placed a hand over her mouth to stifle a scream. Faith followed the line of her friend's horrified gaze and was shocked to see Nick and Helen appear from the shadows. When the pair lunged at the cab doors Faith struggled to keep hers shut, but it was a pointless battle. Helen tugged open the door at Claire's side and the mulatto driver helped Nick to wrench Faith's open. They pulled so hard Faith almost fell to the ground as her grip remained around the handle.

Then it suddenly came back to her where she had seen the mulatto before. There had been so many new faces at the dark one's coven that Faith thought she had forgotten most of them. But now she could remember the mulatto's glistening smile and she knew their driver was a vampire.

'Hello, virtuous slut,' Nick grinned. 'I'm so pleased that you and Claire could stop by this evening.'

Helen cried out from the darkness, and as soon as Faith saw the vampire's face she could easily work out what had happened. A blazing cross was burnt on the brunette's cheek where Claire had struck her with the crucifix. Claire stood safely away from her sister, confusion and panic spoiling her pretty features.

'Find Ms Moon and fetch her here!' Faith yelled, and could see hesitation threatening to root Claire to the spot. 'Find Ms Moon!' she screamed the command again. 'Get her here quickly!'

Claire's footsteps rang against the street and Helen looked set to chase after her, but Nick barked an instruction for her to stay. 'This is the one the dark one wants,' he said, fixing Faith with the menacing power of his evil smile.

Still clutching her cheek, Helen stumbled in front of their captive. 'Nick's right,' she agreed. 'I can have Claire any time I want. But tonight I'm going to have you.' Laughing merrily, nastiness sounding in every echo of her mirth, she vowed, 'Or at least, I'll have whatever's left once the dark one has finished with you.'

Interlude

Part V

'That was the shittiest performance we've done to date,' Todd grumbled. 'I've never heard an opera audience cheering for Scarpia before. I'd swear, if Tosca hadn't jumped off the battlements some bastard from the stalls would have come up on stage and pushed the bitch off.'

The smile in Lilah's voice sounded forced. 'You don't need to tell me how bad it was, Toad,' she reminded him. 'I was there, remember?'

He was going through the usual after-show rigmarole of removing his make-up and tidying away his props and wardrobe. His costume hung on a rail to his left, and Scarpia's powdered wig adorned a bust on his dressing table. After styling it to the courtier's pomp he thought the character deserved, he put down the brush and considered his reply. 'Yes, you were there,' he concurred. 'And now you're here.'

It was disconcerting talking to the vampire in his dressing room, because although Lilah sat behind him, he couldn't see her reflection when he looked into the mirror. Not entirely sure he could trust her, wary that she might be creeping closer while his attention was unguarded, he turned away from the glass. 'You were there,' he repeated. 'And now you're here. And neither of those places are where you really should be tonight.'

She lounged in one of the room's most comfortable chairs, freshly clad in leather, with the heels of her thigh length boots resting on the corner of a table. Her posture looked like an act of carefully studied indifference and he tried to guess what she might want from him. Her appearance was unprecedented, and because she had hardly spoken it remained a perplexing mystery.

'I thought you were going to see your brother this evening? I thought tonight was the night of the big reconciliation between you and the dark one? That is still on, isn't it?'

'Has my brother promised to pay you extra if you can engineer our reunion?'

Todd barked dry laughter, uncomfortable with her shrewd assessment of his motives. 'The dark one hasn't officially promised me a bonus,' he admitted. 'But I know how he administers his gratitude and I do expect to profit from your return when he learns how much I've helped you.'

Lilah nodded thoughtfully. 'Errand boy, bitch and now prostitute. There's a lot more to you than meets the eye, Toad.'

He couldn't be bothered rising to the insults. 'What do you want from me, Lilah? This clearly isn't a social call, and if you've just stopped by so we can share the fare on a taxi, I'd say you're losing some of your talents as a natural predator.'

She glared at him and he struggled not to show his unease. She was one of those strong women he coveted, but she was also dangerous and he knew better than to stay on her wrong side for too long. Stretching the limits of his acting skills, he tested a smile to show he hadn't meant any offence. 'Come on. Tell me. To what do I owe the pleasure of your visit?'

'I want you to do me a favour, Toad.'

He frowned, surprised to hear a note of something

unusual in her voice. He couldn't place the tone and wondered what she could be concealing. Lilah was never usually reserved when she asked for anything, her normal attitude being to treat him as if he really was her personal errand boy. But this evening she sounded reserved, and if he had heard the timbre in her voice from any other woman, he might have said she was struggling with embarrassment. 'Go on,' he coaxed with growing unease. 'What is it you want?'

She drew a deep breath before replying. Her gaze flitted briefly in the direction of his face and added weight to his belief that she appeared apprehensive. 'This is strictly between you and I. It goes no further than these four walls.'

Todd nodded impatiently. 'Of course. Discretion assured. But, what is it you want?'

She lowered her gaze to the floor. 'I want you to spank me,' she whispered. Her cheeks coloured and she raised her glance to study him with a mixture of hope and malice that wouldn't have worked on any other woman. Saying the words again, speaking with more conviction, she said, 'I want you to spank me.'

Todd suddenly understood that he had heard embarrassment in her voice. He was stunned and uneasy that she should have chosen to come to him with her request, and his mind reeled. It took every effort of self-control not to whoop triumphantly, but maintaining a poker face, not allowing Lilah to read his emotions, he said cautiously, 'I guess I could do that for you. But I have to ask, why? You've never shown any appetite to receive discipline before. What's encouraged this sudden interest?'

'I've been watching the virtuous bitch,' Lilah growled, her explanation an angry burst, as though she was trying to find a source for blame. 'I've seen the pleasure the

little slut gets from being spanked and caned, and I'm…'
she paused and he expected her to complete the sentence
with the word *jealous*. '…I'm curious,' Lilah supplied
eventually. 'I'm curious to know what she gets out of it.'

Alarm bells sounded in the back of his mind, and he
told himself to make an excuse and politely decline her
invitation. He had spent enough years working with Lilah
and her fellow vampires to know he was entering
potentially dangerous territory, and felt sure it would end
badly. But the prospect of being able to spank her – the
opportunity to excite her, punish her, and hopefully use
her – was too tempting to simply dismiss. Determined to
exploit the unexpected advantage, he pretended to consider
his answer. 'If I did that for you, you'd owe me,' he
eventually said.

'I'd be in your debt,' she agreed, 'yes.' As she spoke
she drew her ankles away from the table and eased herself
out of the chair. Walking slowly towards him she began
to tear open the buttons on her leather waistcoat. She
started at the bottom, plucking them one by one to expose
her flat stomach, the curve of her ribcage, and then the
beauty of her small yet perfect breasts.

Todd remained motionless in his chair while excitement
stirred between his legs. The only movement he made
was to lift one hand and touch the inviting swell of her
right breast. Her skin was typically cool, but he still took
pleasure from fondling the breast. Beneath the tips of his
fingers he could feel the monotonous beat of her heart
and its distant, lethargic pulse was almost enough to spoil
his need for her. He knew little about the physiology of
vampires – his interest in the undead seldom extended
any further than the profit they could generate for him –
but the echo of a bloodless heartbeat was something that
always caused a ghostly shiver to tickle down his spine.

Trying not to show his momentary unease, Todd withdrew his fingers.

Lilah shrugged the waistcoat from her shoulders and stood shamelessly in front of him. She rested one thumb on the button of her leather pants and studied him expectantly. 'Are you going to do it for me, Toad?' she asked with quiet menace. 'Or should I find myself another teacher?'

He wouldn't allow his response to be hurried by the threat that she might suddenly leave or go to someone else. Calculating the dangers, and weighing up all the ramifications, he tried to make a decision that wasn't solely governed by the single-minded greed of his arousal. But, in his heart, he knew his choice had been made as soon as she asked the question. Nodding thoughtfully he said, 'If we're going to do this, let's do it properly. Slide your pants down, Lilah. Let me see what you're hiding.'

She obeyed as best as she was able, releasing the button at her waist and slowly easing the zip open. She revealed the tight muscles of a well honed four-pack, then the dark triangle of curls that covered her mons. The thigh length boots made it impossible for her to slip the pants down her legs, and when she had peeled them over her buttocks, Todd placed a steadying hand on her arm to stop her from trying to remove them completely.

The contact was sickeningly exciting. Lilah glared at him with such obvious loathing he wondered if she had changed her mind. Her upper lip curled into a threatening sneer, revealing the deadly sharp canines beneath. Her eyes glowed with crimson malevolence.

Nevertheless, adamant that he wouldn't be intimidated, he kept his hand on her arm and said, 'Don't bother undressing any further. That should be sufficient for what I have in mind.'

214

She nodded grudgingly and did as he asked when he told her to bend over his knee. Every vampire he had touched before had been ice-cold, but Lilah seemed somehow different. He couldn't work out if it was something to do with her strength, a quality that was attributable to her being the dark one's sister, or the crippling malaise of her apprehension. Her flesh remained chilly, without the mortal warmth of blood flowing through her veins, but she radiated a nervous, sexual heat. The energy that came from her was dark and powerful and he struggled to suppress an eager shiver.

Stroking one hand over the peach-like orbs of her rear, he relished the way she stiffened against his lap. Her buttocks were perfectly smooth, their swell encouraging his touch to trace down to the valley of her sex. As soon as he caressed the velvet-soft folds, in the moment that his fingers slipped against her wetness, Lilah's spine became rigid, and he briefly fretted that she was going to change her mind and snatch the opportunity away from him before he had landed the first blow. Holding his breath, giving her the chance to voice her reservations, he raised his hand and waited.

'Don't draw it out,' she grunted. 'If you're going to do it, go on and do it, Toad. But don't draw it out.'

Todd needed no further encouragement. He slapped her bottom and the echo snapped crisply from the dressing-room walls. It wasn't the heaviest smack he could have delivered – wariness made him reluctant to put too much strength into the blow – but it was enough to make her tremble.

She bit back a sharp exclamation and glared at the floor. 'That fucking hurt, Toad,' she mumbled.

He struck her again, harder this time, and felt the force of the blow vibrate through her buttocks and across his legs. 'You won't swear while I'm doing this,' he said sternly. 'And you'll call me Mr Chalmers.'

'Like fuck I'll call you Mr Chalmers,' she protested. 'I'll call you Toad,'

He slapped with all his force, the smack weighty enough to leave a blazing red handprint against her rear. The flesh quickly paled, returning to the gorgeous alabaster of her natural vampiric state, but the fact that the livid mark had appeared told him he had hit hard enough to make an impression. 'If we're going to do this, we're going to do it properly,' he said coldly. 'You won't swear, and you'll call me Mr Chalmers.'

She was shivering and he couldn't work out if he was feeling the echo of her arousal, discomfort or frustration. Not dwelling on the dangers, simply languishing in the pleasure of having the beautiful, powerful woman stretched across his knee, he spanked her backside again.

'Mr Chalmers!' she exclaimed.

Todd was thankful that she couldn't see his face because he knew his expression of surprise would have spoilt the moment. The arousal between his legs twitched to full hardness and he marvelled that this opportunity had presented itself without any machinations on his own part.

'I'll call you Mr Chalmers,' she conceded.

He placed his hand on her rear, stroking his fingers against the wet folds of her sex. 'You'll call me Mr Chalmers,' he agreed. 'And you'll thank me every time I spank you.'

He knew it was an audacious demand, and he expected her to protest or argue, but she remained steadfastly silent. And when he slapped her backside for a fifth time she surprised him by hissing, 'Thank you, Mr Chalmers.'

His hand lingered on her rear as he glanced around the dressing room for a convenient accessory with which to continue. There was a silver-topped cane resting in a hat stand by the door – Scarpia's only prop for act one – but he didn't want to spoil the mood by getting Lilah to climb off his knees while he retrieved the item. The same problem plagued him when he saw a leather belt dangling from the clothes rail. But glancing closer, smiling when his gaze flitted over the dressing table, he picked up the hairbrush he'd been using on Scarpia's wig.

The tips of his fingers had slipped into her cool wetness and he was disquieted by the urgent arousal she evoked. His greedy need for her had never been stronger, and when he reluctantly pulled his hand away, he imagined he heard her gasp with the same frustration. Trying not to think that she might be harbouring a desire that matched his own, he lifted the hairbrush high then slammed it down against one cheek.

The bristles freckled her buttock with uniform rows of red spots, and as Lilah hissed her grudging gratitude, Todd raised the brush then struck again to mark her other cheek with an identical rash.

'Thank you, Mr Chalmers,' she growled. 'Thank you.'

Her servility was invigorating, and he repeatedly landed the brush with wicked glee. The cruel tips of the bristles peppered her cheeks, but after each impact Lilah dutifully thanked him.

She shivered with the force of every blow. Her responses came through clenched teeth and sounded more like threats than gratitude, but she obeyed his instructions flawlessly.

His erection strained unbearably inside his trousers, and he knew she had to be aware of the length pressing into her ribs, but she simply accepted her punishment and made no deference to his excitement. Believing he would have to instigate every development, Todd put the brush back on the dressing table and stroked his hand over the desirable expanse of her bottom.

The naturally cold flesh had been warmed by the punishment, and when his fingers slipped into the gaping split of her pussy he was amazed to feel a feverish heat emanating from her sex. The lips were glossy with arousal and smears of the wetness quickly coated his fingertips.

Lilah moaned. Todd knew it was the closest she would give to encouragement and plunged his fingers into her confines. The muscles of her sex clenched greedily around his hand, and as he slipped his fingers back and forth her sigh became a low, urgent groan.

'Do you want to feel the brush again?' he asked quietly. 'Do you want me to go back to spanking you with my hand? Or do you want me to do something else for you, Lilah? Do you want me to do something that satisfies your current need?'

She acted with unseemly haste and before he realised what was happening, Lilah had pulled herself from the floor and straddled him. He didn't know how she managed it with her thighs still encased in the leather pants but she kicked one leg over his lap, took his erection from his trousers, and pressed it against the dewy centre of her pussy. Ordinarily he would have told her to slow down – and threatened chastisement because she hadn't asked for permission – but he could see she was beyond playing by those rules. The discipline had fired her need and he knew, if he tried to make the encounter into a battle of wills, she would either win or walk away. So saying nothing, taking his pleasure from the knowledge that he was finally fucking her, Todd allowed Lilah to guide his length into her sex.

Her cry echoed his rush of satisfaction. Her pussy was as tight as he had hoped and her inner muscles squeezed around him with brutal ferocity. Wilfully controlling the pace, allowing no measure for Todd's involvement, she rode up and down with furious abandon.

He marvelled at her for a moment, awed by her beauty and unable to believe that she was using him to sate her need. Since he first found himself working for the dark one, since the first time he glimpsed Lilah's cool and sulky beauty, Todd had longed for this opportunity. And now he was finally enjoying that yearned for pleasure, now her sex muscles were squeezing slickly around his erection, he tried to tell himself it was the fulfilling achievement he had anticipated.

Her bared breasts jostled enticingly in front of him, and beyond caring if it met with her approval, he lowered his mouth over one stiff bud. Her gasp of pleasure was enough encouragement and he caught the tip lightly between his teeth. It crossed his mind that she was used to more forceful pleasures – she was a vampire and in the habit of biting her lovers at the peak of pleasure – but he wasn't prepared to spoil this moment by trying to be someone he wasn't. Tracing his tongue against the rigid bud, smiling when he heard her deepening sighs, he made no complaint when she held his head against her breasts and began to ride him faster.

It was a struggle to stop her from wringing the climax from his cock, but he fought her efforts valiantly. Matching her determination, snatching every bitter inch of satisfaction that came from the sensation of her pussy muscles sliding up and down his erection, he grunted with fierce determination.

Lilah echoed the sounds and he couldn't decide if she was cruelly mimicking him or genuinely caught up in the thrill of sexual bliss. Her cheeks were flushed with colour, her scarlet eyes shone with malicious glee, but it was impossible to tell if she was parodying his excitement or genuinely enjoying herself.

Even when she pulled his head from her breasts, then pushed her mouth over his face to extract a deep and intimate kiss, Todd couldn't convince himself that she was really lost in the moment. The heat of her sex broiled against his shaft, the friction of her bared breasts inspired shivers as she bounced up and down, but she left him with the impression that this wasn't the same monumental experience that he was enjoying.

He glanced over her shoulder and was annoyed to see only himself in the mirror. There was something frustrating in not being able to watch the vampire riding her body against his. Lilah was painfully beautiful and the image would have been one he could have treasured fondly for years to come. But, instead of seeing himself in Lilah's enviable embrace, he could only see his own body. And although he considered his physique athletic and imposing, he thought the man in the mirror looked somewhat foolish sitting alone and aroused in the otherwise empty dressing room. Todd knew his life was solitary, realised he had no one with whom to share his successes and achievements, and he wondered if the reflection might be showing him more than he wanted to see.

Pushing the introspection aside, focusing his thoughts on the task of pleasing Lilah and achieving his own satisfaction, Todd tore his gaze from the mirror and returned her kiss with feverish passion. Matching her avaricious pace he rode in and out with renewed enthusiasm.

She gasped and embraced him more tightly. He could sense a pulse trembling through her sex and made no protest when she pulled him against her chest. Behind her breasts he could feel the unhurried pulse of her heartbeat and its sullen, inhuman beat almost curbed his arousal. But knowing they were both close to their climaxes, he willed himself not to think about that disquieting detail. He held her tight, and when Lilah released her first groan of ecstasy, Todd allowed the orgasm to erupt from his erection.

It was impossible to tell how long the pleasure continued. Lilah's sex clenched with spasmodic fury as she grimaced through her joy. She half-pulled herself away from him, then lunged more determinedly into his embrace, and finally pushed herself from Todd's trembling shaft. Writhing on the floor, angrily grumbling as she savoured the last dregs of pleasure, she glared at him with unveiled contempt.

He tested a smile and asked, 'Did that help?'

From the severity of her expression, he knew they had now gone back to their former relationship. She once again considered him inferior, and whatever had happened between them would never be thought of as anything more than an aberration. Without saying a word Lilah managed to convey every ounce of her disapproval as she pulled herself from the floor and began to straighten her clothes.

'Did that little exercise help?' Todd repeated. 'Did the spanking allow you to understand what the virtuous one has been enjoying?'

'She's a slut,' Lilah said, fastening her pants. Her tone was dismissive and rich with disgust. She started to button her waistcoat, and with obvious bad grace added, 'She's a depraved little slut who must have been wanking herself senseless after each spanking. I can't think she's been containing herself any other way.'

Todd didn't care to talk about the virtuous one. It would be an inconvenience to have to find a replacement lead for the following evening's final performance of Tosca, but he already knew that Marcia could take the role. Other than that minor consideration he no longer had any interest in Faith and the alleged threat she presented to the dark one. 'Virtuous sluts aside,' he said pointedly, 'you haven't forgotten that you now owe me, have you?'

Lilah nodded and exercised her most seductive smile. 'I haven't forgotten,' she assured him. 'And I've already decided how I can return the favour you've shown me this evening.'

Intrigued, he raised an eyebrow and encouraged her to continue. Spent, his erection had faded and he tucked it back in his trousers, but something in her tone made his arousal surge with fresh enthusiasm.

Lilah fastened the last button on her waistcoat and leaned close to him. She placed an icy hand on his arm, and while her touch was colder than marble, Todd was happy to tolerate that minor discomfort. 'Should a change of leadership come about,' Lilah whispered. 'Should the virtuous one triumph, and remove my brother from his rightful place at the head of the coven, I'll remember this favour you've done for me and I'll take special care of you.'

A prickle of unease stirred in his stomach and his arousal began to wane.

Still smiling, her glistening teeth glinting wickedly in the dressing room's brilliant light, Lilah went on, 'I'll make your death swift and painless, Toad. That's how I intend to repay you.'

It wasn't the gratitude he had hoped she would show, and once Lilah had left him alone, he decided it would be prudent to reconsider his future with the coven. Using his mobile to call Fiumicino, booking the first flight out of Rome and not caring that it only took him as far as Orly, Todd studied his reflection with a grave frown. Unless he acted quickly and wisely he knew it might be the last chance he ever had to see his face in a mirror.

Lighting a cigar, and trying to quash his fears, he reasoned that as long as the dark one remained in charge of the coven Lilah would never present a threat. He told himself that the virtuous one didn't stand any chance of succeeding against the vampires' powerful leader, and considering his own efforts to undermine her confidence, and all that Lilah had told him about her endeavours to strip the girl's virtue, he felt sadly certain that Faith was fighting a lost cause.

But, while there was still a chance that she could fulfil the gypsy's prophecy, he thought it might be circumspect to vacate the city for a few days and see how events developed from the perspective of a safe distance. Assuring himself he wasn't fleeing, telling himself he was making a tactical withdrawal, Todd didn't bother to collect any of his belongings from the Excelsior. There was no time for calls or excuses to explain why he wouldn't be appearing as Scarpia the following evening. He simply ordered a cab, tossed his cigar into the Tiber, and vowed to be out of the city before the hour was finished.

Faith

Act III, Scene III

Faith could hear the growing murmur of voices and the faraway melody of music. After spending the previous three nights standing on stage at Castel Sant' Angelo she felt confident enough to gauge the sound of a large audience without seeing them. Judging by the heady volume that came from the crypt, she knew there were a lot of vampires gathering to witness the night's entertainment, and the thought made her shiver uneasily.

Nick and Helen held her in an antechamber, away from the main body of the coven, but Faith still received enough attention to exacerbate her growing worries. With monotonous regularity individual members of the coven appeared in the doorway of her makeshift gaol, and then circled her with hungry intent.

There was something attractive in every one of them; the males seeming sinister, domineering and capable; the women looking voluptuous, wanton and lewd. Some touched – caressing her face, stroking her arms or trying to fondle her breasts – while others only stood close and inhaled. Their hands were cool – their fingers possessed the warmth of icicles – and the brush of each intimacy turned her skin to gooseflesh. Yet, although the chill should have been as unappealing as the dingy surroundings, Faith found herself revelling in the unsolicited attention.

The mulatto appeared, stood boldly in front of Faith, and then held her shoulders as she extracted a kiss. Faith tried to resist but the invitation of the mulatto's mouth and the seductive caress of her embrace was irresistible. The heat between her legs began to swell, and would have continued to rise if the mulatto hadn't snatched her mouth away and then tried to tear Faith's blouse open.

Faith slapped her hands away, only to have Nick and Helen hold her still so the vampire could take her prize. The fabric was left hanging from her shoulders and she was left bewildered and cold and feeling increasingly vulnerable. However, when the next member of the coven came, and tried to take her skirt, Faith decided not to make any protest. It was easier to let them think she was beaten rather than waste her energies in fruitless battles with the dark one's minions. The argument became less convincing when one of them stole the remnants of her blouse, and she was ready to fight furiously to retain her panties, but knowing such a fracas wouldn't really benefit her, she simply suffered the indignity of being undressed and tried not to think of the hungry approval her nudity generated.

Her cheeks blazed crimson with blushes, the heat burning furiously each time a new vampire appeared and appraised her with a wicked, knowing grin. Each of them studied her with expressions that were greedy and menacing, and she knew they all expected to have some opportunity to feed from her before the night had ended. Considering her nakedness, and the vast odds that were stacked against her, Faith could understand their obvious confidence. Counting the scores of different faces that passed before her, and sure that each one of them possessed more speed and strength than she could ever summon, Faith began to believe they might all be proved right.

'You've got a visitor,' the mulatto said, appearing briefly in the doorway.

225

Faith only glared at her. After all the visitors she'd received so far she didn't know why the mulatto would mark one out for a special introduction. The squalor of the antechamber was lit by a burning torch, and the acrid stench of smoke and flames brought the threat of tears to her eyes. Wilfully trying to maintain a show of defiance she hid her unease from the vampires and held herself with all the pride she could manage without clothes. However, when the choir mistress appeared in the antechamber, Faith knew her relief must have been obvious. Ignoring Nick and Helen she rushed to Ms Moon and gratefully embraced her. Not thinking about the gloomy surroundings, or the way her naked body rubbed against the woman's clothes, she tried to take strength from the choir mistress's arrival.

'Claire found you,' she blurted. 'Is she safe? Is she all right?'

'Claire's taking the rest of the choir to Fiumicino,' Ms Moon said quietly. 'Our performance for tomorrow night has been cancelled. I haven't been able to tell Mr Chalmers as much yet, but I thought it would be best to send the girls home on the first available flight.'

Glancing around the antechamber, Faith whispered, 'I wish I was going with them.'

Smiling bitterly, Ms Moon shook her head and extricated herself from Faith's welcoming hug. 'You've got a job to do here, Faith,' she said simply. 'And wishing you were somewhere else isn't going to get that accomplished, is it?'

Despondently, Faith shook her head.

Ms Moon turned to Nick and Helen, and her commanding presence lent her a natural authority as she said, 'Go and tell the dark one that Faith is ready.' Then turning to the doorway she pointed at the mulatto and said, 'You can go and find me a gypsy.' Turning back to Nick and Helen, looking surprised that they were both still standing there, she snapped, 'Do as I've told you. Go and tell your leader that the virtuous one is ready. Go and tell him she will face his challenge as soon as he wants.'

Helen glared at her resentfully, but Nick dragged her from the antechamber in his hurry to obey the choir mistress.

As soon as they were alone, Faith stared doubtfully at Ms Moon. She wanted to ask why the choir mistress had demanded the mulatto go and find a gypsy, but there were more important things to deal with first. 'You do know that I'm not ready for anything, don't you?' she explained. 'I don't even know what I'm supposed to do, so how can I be ready?'

Ms Moon laughed as though they were sharing a joke. 'You've been more than prepared by my lessons in discipline,' she said confidently. 'And you know exactly what to do because I've taught you that.' She took Faith's hand in her own and placed it between her breasts.

Faith stared into the woman's eyes, not allowing her gaze to drop to the modest swell of Ms Moon's chest. She remembered the last time she had touched the woman in such a way her response had been embarrassingly obvious, and to her shame this time was no different. Faith's nipples grew hard and a surge of longing simmered between her thighs. Maintaining eye contact, not looking at the choir mistress's body and hoping the woman wouldn't glance at hers, Faith almost became lost in the mesmerising beauty of Ms Moon's face.

'You remember your instruction, Faith.'

Her eyes glinted with cold meaning, and Faith easily remembered the brutal instruction the choir mistress had given for defeating the dark one. Before she had the chance to object, before she could think how to explain that the viciousness might be beyond her, Ms Moon was leading her by the hand and taking her out of the antechamber.

'...*You've been a naughty boy, telling me your lies; You've been with some other girl, and not out with the guys; You've been screwing both of us, so I'm gouging out her eyes; Then I'm coming to get you too...*'

Faith wasn't surprised to hear Charity's voice echoing around the crypt. Considering BloodLust's popularity, and believing the coven were probably a good example of their intended demograph, she knew she would have been surprised to hear anything else.

There were hundreds of vampires pressed into the crypt, and they applauded with mock enthusiasm when Faith appeared. Nerves squirmed in her stomach, and the embarrassment of her nudity made the acuteness of her shame unbearable. But she continued to walk by Ms Moon's side. The crowd pushed back to allow her and the choir mistress a path to the centre of the room, but she was painfully aware that they all remained within easy touching distance.

'...*You said I was the only one, and you told her that as well; You heard my heart's confession and you swore you'd never tell; You've hurt me bad, but I'll hurt you worse, and I'll see you both in hell; Cos' I'm coming to get you too...*'

'This is one of your sister's songs, isn't it?' Ms Moon enquired softly, and too nervous to speak, Faith could only nod. 'There seems to be a lot of aggression in the content. From what I've heard it seems to be a familiar theme.'

'Her manager says it sells,' Faith explained.

Ms Moon nodded. 'I wonder if her manager is related to Mr Chalmers?'

Faith heard herself release grudging laughter. 'Didn't you know? I thought he might have said something. Her manager *is* Mr Chalmers.'

The conversation didn't get any further because the dark one appeared and raised a hand for silence. Someone muted the volume on the BloodLust album and the coven shuffled back to the walls of the lair to make an arena. 'The virtuous one,' he cried. 'How good of you to grace us with your presence.'

Someone giggled. A neophyte applauded. The remainder of the vampires watched on with gleeful grins.

'How do you think you'll fair against my new champion?' the dark one demanded. He reached to his side and Faith was amazed to see he was holding Marcia. Looking as arrogant as ever, her beauty somehow pronounced by the vampiric pallor of her flesh, she tossed back her head and fixed Faith with a threatening glare. The last time Faith had seen Marcia, the choirgirl was dressed in a stylish designer outfit and looked like a model of manicured and well-groomed excellence. Now she stood in a torn skirt with her blouse rent and tied to conceal her breasts.

'This one has an innate gift for violent confrontation,' the dark one proclaimed, holding up Marcia's hand. 'This one has a natural ability for triumph through cruelty.'

Faith nodded. 'I know. I've seen her at boutique sales.'

'Do you think you can better her?'

Faith glanced at Marcia and then turned her defiant stare on the dark one. 'Your champion won't be any problem,' she declared confidently. 'I'm going to defeat you by the end of the night, so bettering your pet choirgirl shouldn't prove to be a great challenge.'

She saw a flicker of uncertainty in the vampire's eyes, before he laughed at her bravado. 'You show spirit,' he said approvingly. 'I always like to see that being broken. Let the tournament commence.'

He tapped Marcia on the back and Faith cast a hesitant glance in Ms Moon's direction. The choir mistress nodded approval and took a step towards the pallid faces at the edge of the makeshift arena. Faith didn't know what was expected of her but she realised, whatever it was, she would have to do it alone. Fears about her inappropriate nudity were suddenly pushed to one side and she fixed her attention on her opponent.

Marcia came at her with blinding speed.

Faith stepped to her side and saw her opponent whirl past in a vague blur. She was quietly congratulating herself on the manoeuvre when Marcia caught her from behind and tripped her to the floor. Acting reflexively, Faith kept hold of the blonde and dragged her down as she fell. Determined not to let Marcia get the better of her, trying to convince herself that she could win this fight, Faith rolled over and over as both she and the vampire struggled for the superior position.

Marcia broke the hold before it could become a deadlock, pushing Faith away so they could both climb to their feet. She glanced at the dark one and he threw her a bullwhip.

Faith glanced at her opponent's weapon doubtfully and turned to try and find Ms Moon amongst the crowd. She couldn't see the choir mistress and wondered if the vampires had taken her, or if the woman had simply deserted her and left her to the mercy of the coven. She was still pondering Ms Moon's disappearance when Marcia snapped the bullwhip. It cracked the air and the tip scored a sharp kiss against Faith's face. She put a hand over her cheek, nursing the painful sting and glaring viciously at her assailant.

Marcia seemed oblivious to the animosity because she was already raising the whip and hurling it for another blow. Faith didn't waste time wondering when Marcia had become so skilled with such a weapon, or if the choirgirl's passion for cruelty had been there before she joined the ranks of the undead. Instead, she waited for her moment and watched for the whip striking towards her. Timing her actions perfectly, she raised a hand and caught the tip before it could land. The length of leather twisted around her wrist and inspired a brief flare of pain. Not letting herself think about the discomfort, Faith took advantage of the grip and pulled hard. Marcia maintained her hold on the other end and stumbled towards Faith, who could see a clear path for defeating Marcia and knew victory was within her grasp. Marcia was clearly confused by the surprise and Faith knew she would be able to defeat her opponent if she used that to her best advantage. The feeling of triumph was rising within her breast when Marcia kicked Faith's legs from underneath her. She hit the floor squarely and the breath was knocked from her body.

Grinning maniacally, Marcia squatted over Faith's face, and it came as no great surprise to discover that she wasn't wearing panties. But it still came as something of a shock to find herself naked and pinned to the floor while the blonde squirmed her pussy against her face.

The contact was unwanted and sickening. The scent of Marcia's dark excitement filled Faith's nostrils and slipped wetly over her lips. The blonde's knees pinned Faith's arms to the floor and she used her hands to hold Faith's legs down. At the same time she writhed her buttocks in a seductive wriggle, pressing her sex more firmly over Faith's nose and mouth.

A roar of approval sounded from the coven. Someone

started to clap time and Faith could hear muffled cries of encouragement through the thighs against her ears. And as much as she struggled to get free, she could feel herself being suffocated by the wet flesh that covered her face.

'Eat my pussy, you little bitch,' Marcia demanded. 'Eat my pussy and I might just go easy on you.'

The command was obscenely tempting. It was an intimacy she had wanted to share with Claire – a secret liaison that she yearned to experience – and with Marcia's sex already pressed against her face, Faith was drawn towards the idea of surrendering completely. She tried to splutter a response but was only rewarded by the taste of the blonde's musk and the delicious frisson of her tongue gliding against wet labia.

'That's it,' Marcia growled. 'Eat me, you little bitch, eat me.'

Faith remembered that the tip of the whip was still coiled around her wrist, and pulled on it. There was little room to shift her arm but the movement was enough to make Marcia shift her weight to one side. Pushing up with all her force, denying herself the temptation of doing as the blonde demanded, Faith sent Marcia tumbling to the floor.

Marcia snatched the whip back. Her gaze was pure scarlet and her teeth were drawn back as though she was preparing to devour. The knot at the front of her torn blouse had come open and her breasts swayed in and out of view from the shadows of the clothing. She took a single step towards Faith, her leg moving through the split of her short skirt, and then she held herself rigid. Every muscle in her body was taut with tension, and when she hurled herself at Faith for a second time there was no chance to get out of the way.

Faith rolled with the blow, not surprised to find Marcia on top of her again. She struggled to win the superior position but Marcia had clearly become adept in the art of overthrowing her opponents. The blonde pressed her body against Faith's and squirmed with lewd intention. The sultry sheen of sweat that covered both their forms gave the contact a slick lubrication, and Faith was appalled to find her thoughts being filled with sexual imagery. The importance of winning this fight hadn't been lost to her and she wondered why her twisted mind kept dwelling on the sordid details. Rather than helping her to think how she might stand a chance of beating Marcia, her mind seemed more content to brood on the delicious friction of the blonde's breasts squashing against her own, or the base satisfaction of the feminine thigh that pressed against her sex.

'You're going to drink from me,' Marcia hissed. 'And then, when you've satisfied me, I'm going to drink from you.'

Faith was determined not to be intimidated. 'I think that becoming a vampire has helped to calm down your volatile temper,' she observed. 'You seem to have a better control over that nastiness that used to trouble you.'

Marcia slapped her and Faith reeled from the blow. She didn't have the chance to recover before Marcia was shifting position and sitting over her face again. The taste of her sex was more obvious this time and Faith struggled not to give in to temptation and properly taste the girl. With every breath she grew more greedy to draw her tongue against the lips that pressed at her mouth. The viscous film of the flushed labia demanded that she kiss them, and it was all Faith could do to resist the salacious impulse.

'Do you need a little encouragement?' Marcia asked, her tone low and mocking, combining cruelty and suggestiveness in the same cadence. 'Do you want me to sway your decision?'

Faith could feel something being forced against the lips of her sex, and didn't need to be able to see what was happening to know that Marcia was pressing the handle of the bullwhip against her, and she tried to squirm her thighs closed to prevent the intrusion. Marcia thwarted her attempts to foil the penetration and the rounded tip began to push its way into Faith's sex. Slowly, shocking her with every millimetre that crept inside, Faith realised the handle was going to fill the warm, greedy haven of her pussy.

Yearning to feel more, but determined that she wouldn't be beaten, Faith threw every effort into pushing Marcia away. She didn't know where the surge of strength came from but she clenched her thighs together, pushed Marcia to the floor, and rolled away from her. When she stood up she discovered she was holding the whip. The end was slick with the sheen of her arousal and her stomach folded uneasily. Trying to concentrate on the fight, she told herself that she didn't regret the missed opportunity and wouldn't really have wanted to feel the entire length impaling her sex. It was an unconvincing argument because she knew that greedy desire still pulsed feverishly between her legs. But, determined not to be distracted by arousal, she turned to face her opponent.

Marcia found her feet and glared at Faith with an unexpected look of worry, but Faith didn't allow herself to think she had already won. She had previously fallen into that trap and knew its seductive lull could prove her downfall. There was an expression of genuine fear in the blonde's eyes but Faith knew her opponent wasn't really scared of her. She could see Marcia stared reverently at the bullwhip, and realised the blonde was simply convinced that the winner of the fight would always be the one who held the weapon.

'Take it if you think you need it so badly,' Faith offered, coiling the whip and throwing the handle towards Marcia.

The blonde snatched it out of the air, but her incredulous expression said that she had never expected Faith to part with the weapon once it was in her possession. Taking advantage of the surprise, acting while Marcia was still trying to understand how the whip had come back into her hands, Faith tripped her and pushed the blonde to the floor. Marcia struggled and fought, but she was trying to maintain her hold on the whip and Faith used that handicap to her own benefit. She straddled Marcia's writhing figure and forced her sex over the girl's face. There was the brief worry that Marcia might bite her, the scarlet inflection in her eyes had not gone unnoticed, but Faith didn't think that would be one of the ways the blonde played this game.

Knowing what was expected of her, sure that there was only one way to be feted as the victor, Faith pushed her sex firmly over Marcia's face and grunted, 'Eat me.'

Marcia wriggled. The tip of her nose rubbed against Faith's clitoris and shards of delicious arousal spiralled from her sex. She wanted to remain oblivious to the pleasure, unwilling to have a coven of avaricious vampires leer at her as she provided such torrid entertainment, but her body's response wasn't something she could so easily dictate. Flurries of searing pleasure tore through her pussy and threatened to overwhelm her with every delicious sensation. 'Eat me,' she demanded, surprising herself with the ferocity of her command.

The coven was silent, but concentrating solely on the task at hand, writhing her sex forcefully over Marcia's face, she bristled against another shock of excitement and repeated her command. 'Eat me, Marcia. You know you want to.'

Marcia released a pained grunt and slammed her hand against the dirt floor. Faith ignored the vampire's unspoken plea for release and wriggled more forcefully. The tip of Marcia's retroussé nose was wedged firmly against her clitoris, and it only took the slightest movement to make her dizzy with the prospect of a climax. Then she felt the inquisitive penetration of Marcia's tongue, stroking against her sex lips and wriggling within her vagina.

Triumph and elation intermingled, and Faith knew she could have been carried away on a rush of orgasm in that moment, but she gritted her teeth to savour the pleasure and pressed harder against her opponent.

Marcia pushed her tongue as deep as she was able and then began to hammer one fist against the floor as a sign of surrender. Not wanting to prolong her opponent's torment, and unwilling to stretch out the perversity of the show she was providing for the rest of the coven, Faith pulled away. She stood over the blonde, extending a hand to help her from the floor, but Marcia ignored the conciliatory gesture.

Her lips glistened with the wetness from Faith's sex and her eyes shone with crimson malice. 'You might have beaten me, but you won't get out of here alive.'

Faith pulled her hand back, knowing Marcia wasn't going to take it. 'I'll be all right,' she said quietly. 'Unlike you, I have friends.'

Marcia snorted and spat on the floor. 'Friends,' she sniffed. 'I know all about your friends and I think you should be more careful who you trust.'

Faith shook her head, determined to savour her victory. 'Don't try undermining my confidence,' she growled. 'It hasn't worked so far and it won't work now. I know you and this coven were trying to drive a wedge between

Claire and me. And I know the dark one wanted to get me scared that the rest of the choir had been made into vampires. But I know that was just a ploy. I know who I can trust: I know I can trust myself, and Claire, and Ms Moon. And nothing you say will change that.'

Even though she was defeated, Marcia's sneer was chillingly confident. 'Do you trust Ms Moon?' she asked spitefully. 'Would you trust her if you knew her first name?'

Faith stared at the blonde with growing doubts. 'I don't understand. Why would knowing Ms Moon's first name make me trust her less?'

'Would you still trust her if you knew she was called Lilah? Would you still trust her if you knew she was the dark one's sister?'

Uneasily Faith glanced up, and when she saw Ms Moon standing beside the dark one, she thought the family resemblance was unmistakable. Ignoring Marcia's derisive laughter, stumbling away from the fallen blonde, she staggered to the centre of the arena.

Faith

Act III, Scene IV

It was the curse, Faith thought bitterly. It was the Harker family curse, and once again it had chosen her as its victim. '*A Harker's happiness was the moment just before the shit happened.*' The memory of Charity's words blurred with the sound of her vocals as the unseen CD player pounded out another BloodLust thrash ballad.

Seeing Ms Moon standing beside the dark one, and despising her own folly for trusting the woman, she didn't think her predicament could have been more bleak. The vampires surrounding the arena were cheering her triumph, but Faith detected a note of ridicule in that sound. The hands that reached out to touch her – caressing bare flesh and stealing intimate contact – seemed to mock her for her pyrrhic victory. Someone stroked her nipple, tweaking it to full erection, and another hand glided against the lips of her pussy, but Faith remained temporarily immune to the seduction of each caress. Marcia skulked into the midst of those gathered and left Faith alone and in the centre of the baying throng.

The dark one stepped from his seat at the head of the makeshift arena. His sister followed him and Faith took an instinctive step back. The woman was no longer Ms Moon. Her face remained identical but she had changed into a leather outfit that hugged her slender contours and gave her beauty a sultry, provocative air. Her eyes shone crimson in the flare of the crypt's torches and her teeth had become the razor-sharp smile of a predator. For some reason that Faith couldn't understand, Lilah held a battered wooden box. The arc of its lid made it look like a miniature treasure chest, and she held it against her front as though it was a prized possession.

'You did well, little sister,' the dark one declared.

'Thank you, sire,' Lilah purred, and while she talked to her brother her eyes remained fixed on Faith. There was a glint in her expression that tried to convey something, and Faith was shocked to realise Lilah was subtly offering reassurance. The knot of her brow, and the casual way she kept glancing at the dark one, made Faith believe that the night could still have some more surprises.

She clung to that hope, not wanting to accept that she had really made such monumental errors in judgement and trust. If she allowed her thoughts to continue on that bleak, downward spiral she knew she would have been sobbing at the idea of her easy defeat.

'She's been thoroughly stripped of her virtue,' Lilah boasted proudly. 'She's been trained to relish pain and torment. And now she's beaten your most recent champion. I think she'll make an ideal addition to the coven. Don't you, sire?'

The dark one chuckled and a handful of the more sycophantic neophytes echoed his mirth. Faith was unnerved by the attentive silence that came from the rest of the vampires, wondering what they now expected and how she would fare at their mercy. Their crimson glares glinted from every shadow and the evil glint of their smiles terrified her.

'I could have the virtuous one as my champion,' the dark one mused. 'That would be a wonderful irony, wouldn't it?'

Faith didn't bother backing any further away from them,

knowing there would be no chance for escape. She stood defiant and proud, hands by her sides, legs hip distance apart, not hiding her nakedness, and trying hard not to reveal her nerves. She tilted her jaw defiantly as she faced the brother and sister.

'Do you want to see how well trained she is, sire?' Lilah asked. She placed her wooden box on the floor at Faith's feet, and opened the lid to reveal that its velvet-lined interior was empty and barely large enough to fit a fist. 'Would you like an example of her servility?'

Faith glared at Lilah, but the vampire wasn't looking at her. Studying her brother, smiling for him with saccharin sweetness, she asked, 'Do you want me to prove her subservience, sire?'

'How do you propose to prove that?'

Lilah smiled and snapped her fingers for Faith's attention. The brisk click echoed crisply from the crypt's flat acoustics. 'Turn around and bend over, girl,' she demanded. 'My brother wants the chance to punish you the way I've been doing over these past three nights.'

Faith weighed her options and realised obedience was her only recourse. Defiance would have been futile; there were hundreds of vampires lining the lair's walls and Lilah and her brother both looked formidable and dangerous. Any attempt to flee would be easily vanquished, and if the coven started on her in a feeding frenzy, Faith doubted they would have the restraint to ever stop. Trying not to think of what she was submitting to, wanting to believe she had seen something in Lilah's eyes that could genuinely give her hope, Faith turned around and bent over.

'You've trained her like a dog,' the dark one mumbled approvingly.

'No, sire.'

Faith could hear Lilah shaking her head as she spoke.

She was also aware of the woman's fingers stroking lightly against her bottom and the delicate touch began to work its familiar, tantalising magic. She had never wondered why the choir mistress's touch was always so cold, but now she knew she had been under the hand of a vampire, Faith cursed herself for overlooking something so obvious.

'She's no dog, sire,' Lilah assured her brother. 'And there's no limit to her servility. I can prove that to you, if you'll watch.' Her frigid touch crept to the valley of Faith's sex and she brushed an icy finger against the labia.

Unable to stop herself, trying to believe that reaction was an involuntary spasm, Faith shivered. She didn't want to accept that the caress excited her and she tried to shut her mind from the reality of the unsatisfied ache in her loins. Her pussy lips continued to tremble long after Lilah had withdrawn her hand, but Faith wouldn't let herself think that the touch had fuelled the restless need of her libido.

'I've wanted her since I first saw the virtuous bitch,' the dark one confessed.

'And now I'm giving her to you, sire.'

Faith shivered as the dark one's masculine fingers touched her. His hands were as cold as his sister's, but far less subtle. He briefly caressed the swell of one buttock, his callused palm scratching the sensitive flesh, but his attention was clearly focused on her pussy. His fingertips glided against the wet length of her sex and then plunged deep inside.

She held herself still, listening to the murmur of approval that whispered from the coven, and trying to deny the surge of arousal that seared through her body. He had pushed two chilly fingers into the confines of her sex and they wriggled deliciously against the pulsing tube of muscle. Her sopping arousal had facilitated his entry and she knew the heat of her need was warming his freezing flesh.

'The little bitch is fucking desperate for it,' the dark one observed.

Faith's blushes deepened.

'Don't just finger her, sire,' Lilah murmured. 'Spank her a little first. She's a joy to watch when she's being disciplined. You've never seen anyone get as much pleasure through suffering pain.'

The fingers were snatched briskly from her sex and a bolt of frustration momentarily stung Faith. She bit her tongue to stifle a cry of complaint and clutched a tight hold on her legs. The posture was undignified, her thighs ached from being held stiff and her back protested at the prolonged chore of being bent double. But she could also feel herself being overtaken by the greedy longing for satisfaction. Above all her other desires she knew it was that urge she had to resist.

The dark one slapped her bottom. The echo of his palm clapping against her flesh rang from the walls and the coven growled approval and encouragement. Ashamed by her base appetite, Faith knew her own voice had joined those who had called for him to go harder. After the punishing disciplines Ms Moon had graced her with, Faith felt able to tolerate much more than such a casual spanking.

'You really have trained her to enjoy this,' the dark one mused, and didn't wait for a reply before smacking her again. The second blow came with more force and threatened to topple Faith from her awkward position. But she maintained her balance. She savoured the glorious sting of punished flesh and then wallowed in the marvellous after-warmth that always followed the torment. Relaxing, allowing her fears to temporarily abate, she accepted the third slap and basked in its furious impact. The heat that broiled at her cleft felt like a blazing furnace.

'May I, sire,' Lilah asked quietly, and the dark one's grunt was grudging but, from the corner of her eye, Faith noticed him step aside. She couldn't see what Lilah was doing but the woman's actions became clear when Faith felt a hand on each buttock. The cheeks of her backside were spread apart, stretching the flesh and straining the delicate skin around her anus and pussy. She grimaced with the discomfort and then held herself deathly still when a tongue touched her cleft. The embarrassment of being spanked seemed like nothing compared to the shame of having her sex tongued in full view of the vampires. The slap of the dark one's hand had been a tolerable punishment, but this was sexual intimacy and the worst part was that it felt so good.

The attendant hoard seemed to take Lilah's actions as a sign for them to forget their inhibitions. Couples embraced, kissing passionately. Legs intertwined, and above the dull pounding of blood through her temples, Faith could hear the unmistakable grunts and groans of eager arousal. She glanced up to see a woman's bare breast being suckled. A male vampire had his mouth over the nipple, and as he bit a trail of crimson dripped from her swollen orb. The woman arched into his kiss and her face was strained with the bitter triumph of ecstasy.

Faith tried to concentrate on the pair, wanting to think about anything other than the bliss being awoken between her own legs. The spanking had warmed her cheeks and sparked a need within her sex, but Lilah's tongue was heightening her arousal. The tip stroked wetly over her pussy lips, occasionally slipping inside and teasing the fetid warmth within, and Faith didn't want to succumb to the escalating excitement.

'Is this how you trained her?' the dark one asked.

Lilah ignored him, plunging her tongue deeper and wriggling the tip of her nose against Faith's anus. The puckered muscle was as responsive as her sex and she had to renew the grip on her thighs to stop herself from pushing back against the woman and begging her to take her. The twisted idea of having Lilah's tongue slip through the ring of flesh was so darkly exciting Faith felt light-headed with the threat of encroaching orgasm.

'I asked a question,' the dark one intoned solemnly. 'Is that how you trained her?'

Lilah pulled her face away and Faith sighed with frustration. The vampire's hands remained at her buttocks, stretching the skin and spiking barbs of pain where her fingers buried into the cheeks. Faith felt as if her sex was being held open for the view of Lilah and her brother, and she cringed from the thought of the view they were enjoying. 'This isn't how I trained her, sire,' Lilah said softly. 'But I thought a little extra stimulation might make her more receptive.'

The dark one seemed unimpressed. 'More receptive for what?'

Instead of answering with words, Lilah slapped something hard against Faith's rump, and it didn't take her more than a moment to realise what had struck her – the memory of that weapon's blistering impact too powerful to ever forget – but Faith didn't know where Lilah had been concealing her bamboo cane. But there was no time to dwell on the anomaly because the roar of pain silenced every other thought. A blazing barb burnt brightly across both buttocks and she almost fell to the floor.

She was chugging breath and squirming from the indignity of the punishment, when Lilah sliced a second shot across her rear.

Some of the gathered coven cheered, but the majority of the vampires were involved in their own intimacies and generally ignoring Lilah, the dark one and Faith. Not that Faith had any time to register their disinterest as she struggled to maintain balance and deal with the swelling heat branded into her bottom.

Arousal struck her with renewed force and she savoured the third slice of the cane. Not knowing where her need had come from, only aware that she had to feel every pleasure and pain being administered, Faith pushed herself into the cane's impact and savoured its crippling anguish.

'Turn her around, sire.'

Faith heard Lilah's words through a mist of euphoria, but it was impossible to work out what they meant. Her thoughts were filled with the wicked delight of being punished and she was unprepared when a hand grabbed her hair and the dark one turned her around and pushed her to her knees. She stared up at the brother and sister, uneasily watching Lilah pass the cane to him.

'What do you expect me to do with her?' he asked, but Lilah didn't get the chance to respond before he answered his own question by slashing the bamboo across Faith's breasts. His aim wasn't as sure as his sister's, and he only scored one orb, but the cane landed sharp against her nipple. Faith wanted to scream, but she contained the urge and basked in the fire that surged through her chest. Arousal held her in an enveloping thrall and she crushed her thighs together to try and pacify the demanding pulse at her sex. She knelt on eyelevel with the dark one's crotch and could see the obvious bulge concealed inside his trousers. It crossed her mind that Lilah might have engineered this position deliberately, and that she might be expected to take the dark one's erection in her mouth, but in that moment she knew it didn't matter. Whatever it took to satisfy her arousal – whatever she had to do to sate the ravenous urge of her libido – she knew she would happily endure. Her worries about the future, and her concerns about escaping from the coven, were trivialities she could easily overlook. As the dark one slapped the cane against her other breast Faith wondered if he might manage to thrash the climax from her treacherous body.

Lilah wrestled the cane from her brother's hand and snapped her fingers in front of Faith's face. 'Turn around now,' she snapped. 'Get back to the position you were in before.'

Obediently, Faith did as she was told. She glanced at those vampires that lined the walls, expecting to see them studying her with derision or amusement, but it seemed she had been all but forgotten in the atmosphere of orgiastic excess. The couple she'd noticed before were beyond the stages of vampiric foreplay and had taken their passion to a fuller extent.

Her skirt was hitched up to reveal the smooth flesh of her hips and his pants had been pulled down to release his erection. From her position in the centre of the arena, Faith could see the vampire's length plunging in and out of his lover's sex. His shaft glistened with the viscous smear of the woman's juices and her pussy lips were dewy with arousal. They bucked greedily against each other while both gnawed on the other's neck. The fury of their union was brought home to Faith as she heard their guttural cries and demands for more.

'She's ready for you now,' Lilah told the dark one. 'She'll do whatever you want.'

Faith heard the words, and bitterly she realised Lilah was speaking the truth. The danger of her predicament had not escaped her but a need had been sparked between her legs and she was prepared to do anything to satisfy that urge.

'Whatever I want?' the dark one repeated.

Faith couldn't believe the coven's leader was being so dense. Whatever he asked of her, she knew she would do. If he wanted her to get down on her knees before him and accept his penis in her mouth, she would have happily and eagerly obeyed. If he wanted to use her, slide his thickness into her sex, or even push into the forbidden confines of her anus, she knew she would have gladly surrendered to either indignity. Her need had risen to such demanding heights that he only had to give the command and Faith was ready to selflessly obey.

'Decisions, decisions,' the dark one mused. He slapped a hand against Faith's rear and kept tight hold of her buttock. The contact rekindled the ache of every punishment her backside had suffered this evening, and she moaned softly as the pain exacerbated her arousal. As he pulled himself closer Faith could feel the swell of the dark one's erection pressing through his pants and rubbing against her sex. The previous evening he had held her in a similar position and Faith yearned to feel his penetration. Now, knowing that moment was so painfully close, she squirmed urgently against him. The weave of his pants rubbed coarsely against her pussy lips and the friction was almost enough to force her climax. Faith was tempted to rub a little harder and revel in the first flush of the orgasm her body demanded.

'If you're torn between choices, perhaps I could suggest something?' Lilah whispered.

The dark one's fingers squeezed possessively against Faith's rear. 'Go on,' he said guardedly. 'What might you suggest, little sister?'

'I've been training her rigorously,' Lilah began.

The dark one chuckled. 'I'll bet you have.'

Lilah continued as though he hadn't spoken. 'And there's one thing she can do that no mortal or vampire has done for you before. Should I tell her to do it?'

Faith listened to their conversation, not sure what was going on, and only wishing one of them would satisfy the pounding need that tormented her sex. She felt giddy with the desire for release and would have touched herself if she hadn't feared such an action would earn the disapproval of her tormentors.

'There's a pleasure I haven't experienced?' The dark one sounded bemused by such a concept. 'I'm an epicurean and a hedonist,' he laughed. 'I've lived for two centuries and travelled the world in search of new and more stimulating pleasures. I can't believe there's anything I haven't experienced and I don't think this virtuous choirgirl is going to be able to teach me anything.'

'Trust me, sire,' Lilah promised. 'You haven't experienced this.' Brushing his hand away from Faith's bottom she called for her to turn around and stand up. 'I want you to do something for my brother,' Lilah demanded. 'I'd like you to show him your special trick.'

Faith glared at her, not knowing what the vampire wanted and sure she had never been taught a special trick. The dark one was studying his sister with wry amusement, and taking advantage of his distraction Faith shrugged her shoulders to show she didn't understand.

'Surely you remember your instruction, Faith?' Lilah glared as she spoke and then repeated the words with added emphasis. 'Surely you remember the instruction I gave you?'

The BloodLust CD was still playing and Faith caught Charity's lyrics over the passionate cries coming from the rest of the coven. '...*You had me day and night without any rest; You said our loving was the world's fucking best; Then you tore the heart from outta my chest…'*

The meaning came to her with a clarity that was sudden and sickening. She didn't know if it was the inflection of Lilah's words, or the lyrics from Charity's song, but Faith knew what was expected of her and she acted without hesitation. She faced the dark one, saw his foreboding smile was turning towards her, and pushed her hand against his chest.

Surprise crossed his features as her hand tore through his shirt. Not thinking about what she was doing, only aware that she had to vanquish the evil leader of the coven, Faith grasped the heart from within his breast and tore it out. As she'd been told it would be, the organ was cold and black.

The dark one fell back, his bewildered expression switching from Faith to Lilah, then back to Faith. He clutched at the hole in his breast before his lifeless body fell to the floor.

A whisper of amazement scurried through the coven.

Faith was sickened to observe that the dark one's heart continued to beat within her fist.

Lilah stepped closer and took the organ from Faith's hand. She dropped it in the box placed on the floor and pushed the lid closed.

Aghast by what she had done, and unnerved by the horror of holding the dark one's heart, Faith watched the lid tremble each time the organ inside pulsed with another beat.

'You defeated him for me,' Lilah smiled. 'Just as I knew you would. Just as I'd planned you would.'

Still shaking, Faith could only cast her glance from the pulsing box and then to the dark one's fallen body.

Lilah smiled encouragement and opened her arms into a familial embrace. 'Come here,' she coaxed softly. 'Let me thank you for usurping my ridiculous brother from his role at the head of our coven.'

Faith stepped into her arms without thinking about what she was doing, and the truth of Lilah's intentions didn't strike her until she felt the vampire's painful kiss against her throat. Even then she made no complaint as Lilah began to suck the blood from her body. As her gaze turned crimson, and she tried to work out if she was being taken or made, Faith realised the Harker family curse had struck her for the last time.

The Second Prophecy

Dank squalor hung on the air like the fetid breath of a gargoyle. A ring of blazing torches filled the sconces on the lair's wall and their spluttering flames licked orange tongues against the soot-encrusted masonry. A pair of ecstatic neophytes, still high from an early evening blood-rush and giggling hysterically, danced together in the black and amber light. The remainder of the clan lurked in the lair's furthest shadows and watched the naked gypsy kneeling at the foot of Lilah's throne.

Her hands, small and dirty, trembled as they clutched the final rune. She frowned at its position in the earth, shook her head unhappily, and then dared to glance up at her. 'Hope,' she whispered softly. 'It's the same message again. It doesn't matter how many times I read them for you. The stones keep saying the same word over and over again.'

Lilah's nostrils flared with impatience. She was naked on the throne, her legs spread over the ornate arms so it was easier to enjoy the attention of Faith's tongue as the newly made vampire lapped at her. But even though she was now the leader of the coven, and even though she had managed to make the virtuous one, and force her to submit to every torrid fantasy, Lilah still wasn't happy. The unfinished business with Todd Chalmers rankled every time her thoughts turned to the dark one's former errand boy, and the gypsy's prophecy wasn't making any sense. Reaching down to the side of the throne she strummed her fingers against the lid of the miniature treasure chest.

251

The cold black heart inside continued to throb dully, rattling the small latch that fastened it closed.

'Hope,' Lilah mused. 'Hope.' She glanced down between her legs, and grabbing a fistful of Faith's hair, lifted her face away. The virtuous one's lower jaw was glossy with Lilah's wetness and her ruby lips glistened with a viscous lustre. 'Your sister's called Hope, isn't she?'

Faith nodded. Her gaze kept flitting back to Lilah's cleft and her need to return her tongue to her mistress's sex was obvious. 'One of my sisters is called Hope,' she confirmed. 'She's living in Paris at the moment.'

Lilah released her hold on Faith's hair and allowed her to return to her chore. Enjoying the gentle kisses against her pussy, she settled back into the chair and tried to fit the fact into the puzzle of what she already knew.

'That makes sense now,' the gypsy decided.

Lilah sniffed but the gypsy was nodding enthusiastically. She pointed from one rune to the other, unable to disguise her joy at having solved the mystery. 'The runes are showing me your only obstacle,' she explained. 'If you want to retain leadership of the coven, if you want to keep this new slave as an obedient pet that licks your pussy every night, you'll have to defeat this girl called Hope.'

Lilah sat bolt upright and pushed Faith away. Stepping out of her throne, walking deliberately towards the gypsy, she curled her lips into a sneer and asked, 'What happens if I don't defeat this girl called Hope?'

Paling beneath the threat of the vampire, the gypsy scrabbled to retrieve her runes. 'If... if you don't defeat her, you... you won't remain leader of the coven,' she stammered.

Lilah dragged her from the floor and pressed her lips over the gypsy's throat. She remembered seeing her brother in a similar position, and warning him about the dangers that befell those who fed from gypsies and nuns, but that consideration was beneath her now that she ruled the coven. Pressing her teeth hard against the young girl's throat, she savoured the smell of fear that radiated from her. 'Is that the best future you can tell me?' she asked.

The gypsy trembled, her bared breasts rubbing Lilah's in a sweet, terrified friction. 'I don't write the runes,' she explained pitifully. 'I only read them.'

Lilah bit. She drank from the gypsy's throat, greedily enjoying the rush of warm blood and its rich, coppery fullness. She usually preferred her victims to be aroused, savouring the sweet flavour of sexual excitement when mingled with the spicy taste of fear, but she still found satisfaction in draining this victim.

Dropping the girl's body to the floor she turned to the rest of the coven and called for their attention. 'Someone get me another gypsy,' she demanded. 'And the rest of you should prepare to travel.'

Nick stepped out of the shadows, Helen hovering behind him. 'Prepare to travel?' he echoed. 'Where are we going?'

From her place by the throne, Faith had wanted to ask the same question.

'You heard the gypsy,' Lilah reminded him. 'She told us what needs to be done to ensure my place at the head of this coven. We're travelling to Paris to meet Faith's sister, Hope. Unless I can get a gypsy to read me a better future, we're going to Paris and we're going to *make* me a better future.'

The story continues in:

BloodLust Chronicles – Hope

More exciting titles available from Chimera

For a copy of our free catalogue please write to:

Chimera Publishing Ltd
Readers' Services
22b Picton House
Hussar Court
Waterlooville
Hants
PO7 7SQ

or email us at:
chimera@chimerabooks.co.uk

or purchase from our range of superb titles at:
www.chimerabooks.co.uk

*Titles £5.99. **£7.99. **All others £6.99**